INTO THE WALLWOOD
By: L.M. Hosley

This text was originally edited by Karen Clark Ellis, and then some technically challenged numbskull formatted, uploaded, and published the wrong draft. (It was me...) Thank you for all your hard work Karen. And I appologize to everyone for losing the much cleaner version of this story.

Special thanks to Shane Slattery for designing the cover art. For real, man! That thing rocks!

Extra special thanks to Lynn Hosley. Everytime I said I can't take the next step, You came in and took care of what I could not or would not take care of myself. Thanks Mom, I never would have completed this without your help.

For Suzy, my beautiful wife. Without your support this story would have faded away inside my head. You have always made me a better me.

I love you, My Light B.

The Woods can be dark, but their depth depends on the direction One chooses to travel.

-ANONYMOUS

INTO THE WALLWOOD

P

The Eager Watcher

Reverend Cotton watched Mary struggle against the ropes, she couldn't move much. That was good. Her hands had been tied together at the wrist, arms at her sides. The long rope tying her to the stake snaked neatly around her from shoulder to elbow. The stake itself was new, this was a first for the town of Kingston.

"Should we hear her last words?" Aldon Jones croaked beside the Reverend.

Cotton looked at the young woman. A strip of cloth was tied tightly around her mouth. It had darkened with tears. Shiny streaks fell from the corner of each large brown eye. Her hair was unnaturally red. Red like fire. Red like the Devil she had been dancing with.

"No." He turned to Aldon. "She would only use her words to tempt others to Satan." Aldon did not look at the Reverend. He only bobbed his head while looking around at the crowd that had gathered. Cotton had noticed the onlookers as well. It looked like the whole town had come to see the witch burn.

The Reverend walked forward pulling the pre-lit torch from its perch, and began to speak loud enough for everyone to hear. "Mary O'Donnell, you have been found guilty of consorting with Dark Forces." He was pacing in front of her, holding the flaming torch high above his head. "Turned in by your own husband who did see you dancing with the Devil under the full moon."

She began to sob loudly. It was muffled by the cloth, but it still seemed to carry. Reverend Cotton did not stop to listen. "For this offense against mankind you have been sentenced to death by fire. These Earthly flames will consume your body before the fires of Hell consume your soul." He paused for a moment before bending down to light the kindling at her feet. He lit the pyramid of sticks in several places before dropping the torch and taking a few steps back.

"May God have mercy on you Mary O'Donnell." Her eyes were closed, but tears continued to stream down her cheeks. It wasn't long before her eyes shot open in pain. The long black dress was aflame now, her legs must have been burning underneath. Cotton could hear people screaming all around him. He understood that it was awful, but it was important to witness God's wrath.

Just before she passed out, Cotton thought he saw her eyes try to smile. His confusion intensified when a strong hand grabbed his shoulder and pulled him backward. He spun and fell on his face. The force of hitting the ground pushed all of the air out of his lungs. He tried to take a breath but found he could not. He rolled in the dirt creating a small cloud for a few moments as he gasped for air. Struggling to catch his breath, he saw others fleeing in terror. There was no one else in the town square but the Reverend, his breath raspy as it first came back to him.

Glowing orange rain began to fall all around him. It burned where it landed on his bare skin. He scrambled to his feet trying to get away. The fiery rain continued to fall. To his horror, some of it landed on the thatched roof of the church. It started smoking immediately. He ran for the structure as quickly as he could. The building was nice, but the Bible on the altar was the most valuable item in the whole village. Cotton entered the church and was happy to see that the inside was relatively unharmed so far. A bit of smoke could be seen roiling around the rafters, nothing more. The pews lining the wooden floor of the sanctuary looked more and more like fire wood as the temperature quickly increased. The book was all that mattered.

He reached the altar as a chunk of burning thatch fell onto some pews behind him. Sparks and smoke exploded in the small room. He grabbed the Bible and turned to run out. Embers were raining down freely from the flaming roof. Thick, black smoke began to fill the sanctuary as the flames spread from thatch to the pews and flooring. He clutched the Bible to his chest and prayed as he ran through the stinging, orange rain. He burst out the doors and into a firestorm. The crackling of fire came from all around him. Almost every building around the town square was smoking or collapsing in flame.

Ropes were hanging limply from an empty wooden stake in the center of the public space. The fire below the stake was gone. All that remained were deep gouges in the ground that seemed to have thrown the flames in every direction. He did not want to find out what could have done something like that, so he ran.

Several people ran into their wooden houses, others ran straight into the woods. Cotton wasn't so foolish. All these buildings were going to burn and running into the woods would be death. There wasn't much more than a couple of farmhouses between here and Frankfort, just dense forest that appeared to be burning as well.

There was only one stone building in town and Cotton ran for it. The King's Cellar distillery sat on the banks of the Elkhorn River, it was the safest place to be. There were others who were thinking the distillery was the best place as well, but at the last minute they turned toward the distillery offices. Those buildings were only stone on the outside. Wooden floors and walls would burn even when coated in stone.

Cotton ran to the stone warehouse that was used to age the bourbon. When he closed the heavy door behind him he could no longer see. There was a bit of light coming from several small windows along the walls, but Cotton couldn't make out the dark shapes before him. The air was thick with dust and the smell of oak laced with an astringent tingle. After a few minutes, a narrow corridor began to take shape in front of him. Barrels, two high, sat in racks along both sides of the path. The hall ended in a T intersection. One direction led to a dead end, the other to a stone staircase. Judging from the low ceiling, only a few inches above Cotton's head, he thought this building must be barrels from floor to roof.

Cotton began toward the steps, every 3 to 4 feet was another barrel lined path into the darkness. He ignored these and climbed the stairs all the way to the third level of barrels. The roof was much higher up here. He could hear the pops and crackles of fire all around the building. Cotton found a window in one corner. The town was burning.

The church was a burning pile of rubble. Several other buildings were in worse shape than the church. Even the trees were burning, sending up waves of black smoke. Smoke that Cotton was beginning to smell over the scent of oak and alcohol.

A trickle of sweat ran down Cotton's cheek, flying off his chin when he began to cough. The pops and crackles kept getting louder and the warehouse appeared to be getting warmer. Cotton was not worried though. As soon as all the nearby wood had been burned the fire would move on and away from his stone edifice. He probably should move to the center of the building, but the Miller's house just collapsed sending a shower of sparks into the air. He prayed that they were not inside, and wondered which building would be next.

Cotton coughed a few more times, but did not really think anything about it until he began to feel the hot stings on his neck and head. He saw a shower of sparks falling from the wooden roof on top of the stone building. A piece of roof fell free in a blaze of horror right in front of Cotton. A huge gust of cool air rushed past him and into the warehouse. Cotton tried to run, making one single step before a concussive burst of sound flung him into the stone wall. A wave of heat and light followed turning everything else black.

WEDNESDAY
May 26th

1

The Dying Woman

Looking back on her life, Cheryl Rutledge concluded that it had been a good one. She sat in the rocking chair in the corner of her living room in darkness. There was no electricity in the cabin her great-grandfather had built. When the daylight started to fade into night, she had been too tired to get up to light the candles. Now the only thing keeping the dark at bay was a bit of moonlight shining through the windows.

She was just coming to terms with a fact she had been denying for far too long now. The Cancer that had been a part of her for seven years, was finally starting to win the battle. She had fought long and valiantly and on her own terms; not with any of the doctor bullshit. Even her closest friends had started suggesting she visit the hospital. No, her weapons of choice were a balanced diet and her own concoction of juices. Each meal and juice had been made with ingredients grown in her own garden. She had an arsenal of dried herbs and spices, also grown, dried and bottled herself. She used these medicines to combat certain symptoms such as fatigue or headache. She thought of this practice as similar to how the Native Americans handled illness, but is more closely resembling the manner of old wives and their tales.

But now it seemed she was no longer able to fight the alien cells from growing inside her stomach. If the asshole in the white coat was correct, the cancer was most likely spreading to the rest of her GI tract or farther. She rose from her chair slowly; it was painful. But everything had been painful these days. She walked with a slight hunch, which seemed to help with the hollow and painful feel of her middle area. It felt like her stomach was dead and was leaking its black poison up to her breast and down to her legs. But she was compelled to take a look around this cabin which had housed four generations of the Rutledge family. She would be the last.

She ambled past her dining room with the large rough wooden table, which had been built by her grandfather. It wasn't the thousands of meals that she had eaten with friends and family that came to mind now. But the hundreds of guided meditations and dream discussions that happened around it. A decade ago she had been teaching some class or hosting some gathering four or five times a week. That was back when there was still a trace of red in her greying hair and her cheeks were much less gaunt. After her health started to decline she had focused more on her own diet and had little time for metaphysics.

She continued onto the back porch. Each step was a jolt of pain as her rotten organs jostled around inside her. She frowned causing the wrinkles in her well-lined face to deepen. She would not be able to walk around the porch as she had hoped. Taking one last lap to circle the house as she had done with joy and vigor as a child, just was not possible. She was too tired. She was in too much pain.

She looked over the railing at her garden, which would be considered by some measurements to be a small farm. It was a bright night and she could see all 12 plots separated by a well-traveled dirt path, six on each side. In her prime she had tended all 12 plots with little help. She canned and salted and stored. She sold what she didn't eat. But, just as the illness had diminished the fire that once lit her green eyes, it had also stolen her stamina. Last year she had struggled to keep up with the two plots closest to the house. This year she had only sowed a single corner of a single plot, and had failed to maintain even that. She did get a small crop of beans, peppers, kale and tomatoes. Unfortunately, what she harvested was stunted and sickly due to lack of watering. Mother nature bore some of the blame, but in years past, dry weather would not have hurt her crop.

She carefully navigated the stairs to the yard, one jarring step at a time. Her bare feet reaching out for each wooden plank slowly and deliberately. If she fell, she did not think she would be able to get up again.

When both of her feet were on the earthen path she let go of the railing. The moon was full, or near enough that it did not matter. She was at once overwhelmed with the urge to pull her old cotton night gown over her head and toss it to the side. In her youth, she had earned the name Moonbeam for doing just that. Stripping down to nothing before dancing in the light of the moon. But that had been nearly 50 years ago. She would have thrown off the long white gown still, but there was a chilly breeze blowing. The night was warm enough but she had lost too much weight, leaving little to protect her bones from the biting wind.

Moonbeam continued her slow march down the dirt trail. A trail she had walked countless times. She thought about all the rituals and thanksgivings, the Solstice and Equinox celebrations, the harvest moons and blood moons, the parties for the hell of it. All had taken place in the sacred meadow at the end of this path.

Her mind focused on the meadow. She had to get there. When she entered the forest, moonlight filtered through the foliage laying dappled silver and black along the trail. She stared down at her feet to make sure she didn't trip on a wayward tree root or fallen branch. Eventually the black dapples became so large that the moonlight no longer helped her see the way.

She stopped for a moment to rest and tried to see the meadow at the end. Her once leathery feet had grown thin and frail. They were bloody and stinging, but that pain was nothing compared to her stomach. The woods opened before her into the familiar meadow just a hundred feet ahead. She was filled with more energy at the sight and took an excited step accidentally kicking a large stone. Her right foot tried to move up quickly to compensate for the new and unexpected position of her left foot. Her reflexes were not what they once were and she fell forward. She put her arms out in front of her but did not have the strength to catch herself. She only succeeded in abrading her hands before she smashed her face on the hard-packed earth.

She lay for a moment, taking inventory of her pain. Her feet felt raw and caked with muddy blood, her toes throbbed with every hammering heartbeat, her hands burned and felt a little wet, but all her fingers were intact. Her head felt like her brain had been shaken but she had been able to turn to the side as she fell to protect her nose. There would be quite a bruise, but that didn't really matter now. Her insides were singing in pain, but that was the new normal.

She got to her hands and knees very slowly, then realized that she could rise no further. She would have to crawl the rest of the way. She moved her right hand six inches forward, then her left, and then each leg. She continued like this for several minutes before disaster struck again. One of her hands got tangled in a stretching tree root, causing her arm to give away. This time she was not quick enough to turn her head.

Blood exploded from her nose as it struck the ground. Blinding white pain became her reality for several eternal seconds. When her vision returned, there was a blur creeping in from her periphery. Her whole face was throbbing now, just like her toes. Despite the pain, she knew she had to keep going. Unable to push herself back to her hands and knees, she was resigned to crawl on her belly.

She stretched her arms out in front of her, grasping for something, anything to help pull herself along. Her left hand found nothing, her right hand found a young tree. She didn't seem to notice that no tree should have been there, or the short wiry hair that covered it. She began to feebly pull herself forward but stopped when she felt hands grab her. They were strong but gentle, and she was lifted into the air. One last glimpse of moonlight through the trees and her vision, which had become a shrinking tunnel, turned off completely.

FRIDAY
September 17th

2

The Excited One

Albert's eyes had hardly left the map all class. He had been getting his books out before class and had inadvertently flipped open the old almanac he had found in the library. The page he was fixated on contained a detailed map of the property owned by a man named Clinton Rutledge. After a few minutes of studying the book he thought he had discovered something wonderful, The actual location of Cry Baby Lane.

"Mr. Taulbee…" The voice seemed to be coming from very far away. Albert slowly turned his head up, tilting it a bit so that his shaggy brown hair fell out of his eyes.

"Welcome back to class Mr. Taulbee." Mr. Smith was smiling broadly amid a chorus of giggles. "Care to enlighten us with your thoughts on our current topic of conversation?" His upper lip twitched a bit under his thick black stubble.

Al glanced around the classroom for a little help. Bash's big brown eyes were open wide but unhelpful. The big guy was right in front of Mr. Smith, but he only sat there biting his lip instead of offering any hint. Al turned to Jay next and found even less help there. The pale redhead sat with his head down, slowly shaking it back and forth. Judging from the way his shoulders were bouncing, Al guessed he was trying to suppress a laugh.

"The topic, of course, is the representation of Satyrs in Greek Myth." Mr. Smith appeared to be having a good time.

"Satyrs usually represent excess." Al spoke slowly, not quite sure of the answer Mr. Smith wanted. "Satyrs are agents of Dionysus and encourage people to drink to excess and..." Al paused before adding with a sly smile, "...and do other things to excess as well."

Mr. Smith's forehead furrowed bringing the thick dark brows close together. His thin lips turned downward slightly. His bright blue eyes however, were squinting in a way that would normally accompany an approving smile. He managed to convey disappointment and gentle admiration at the same time.

"Well class," he turned around and began to walk back to his desk at the front of the room. "It appears that Mr. Taulbee has given you a good start on your homework assignment for this weekend." He sat on the front of the desk facing the class. "But I was hoping he would summarize today's lesson." He winked in Albert's direction. "In recap, the satyrs were companions of the God Pan. They were nature loving and due to their affiliation with Pan, they were also connected to fertility for both humans and the land. Despite all of these good qualities," the teacher glanced over at Al again, "as Mr. Taulbee so astutely pointed out, they have a bad reputation."

At that moment the school chime sounded, signaling the end of another week. "Over the weekend read Euripides' comedy Cyclops, and the corresponding chapter of the Odyssey." The kids continued the ritual of packing all their stuff into book bags, so Mr. Smith raised his voice further. Small chords began to appear in his thin neck. "The chapter is..." He trailed off as he leafed through papers on his desk. "Uhh... it's in your study guide." More than half the class had shuffled out the door. The rest had already started conversations about the weekend and did not hear.

Al was still as his desk carefully folding the map in the old atlas back into its original shape. He had already placed his books back into his bag. Jay and Bash were waiting for him at the classroom door.

"Mr. Taulbee." Al jumped at the sound of Mr. Smith's voice. "I appreciate your knowledge on certain subjects." The dark-headed, but balding, man was behind his desk, still shuffling papers. "But I would appreciate your attention more." He didn't bother to look up at Al.

"Yes sir." Al replied feeling relieved that he had only received a minor retort instead of the normal weekend killing punishment dished out by teachers on a Friday afternoon. Al smiled at his friends as he started toward the door.

"One more thing, Mr. Taulbee." It appeared that Mr. Smith was not finished with him yet. Al felt the chilly explosion of fear in his stomach. He slowly turned around, brown eyes squinted against the upcoming detention or worse... Saturday School. Mr. Smith was no longer rifling through papers on his desk; He was looking right at Al. His mouth was stretched in a wide grin revealing the nicotine stains on his front two teeth. "Book 9."

"Excuse me. Sir?" Albert actually squeaked when he said me, like he was backtracking through puberty.

The smile never left Mr. Smith's face. "Book 9 of the Odyssey is the other half of the reading assignment." Al continued to stare at him blankly. "That is all." The teacher then returned to organizing his paperwork, flashing his bald spot to Al.

Al quickly joined his friends who had migrated into the hallway during his exchange with the teacher. "That was a close'n, Al." Bash offered once they were a safe distance away from the classroom door.

Albert reached up and pushed some hair out of his eyes. "I thought I was gonna get detention or something." His hair fell back into place as soon as he let it go.

Jay was walking on his other side. "Why do you know so much about Satyrs?" Jay's close cropped red hair was only slightly brighter than his face.

"He pulled that out his ass." Bash offered with a laugh.

One large hand clapped Al on the back ruining his first attempt to enter his locker combination. Al looked up at Eric Sebastian, the florescent lights were shining off his nearly shaved head. At 15 years old, he was over 6 feet tall. Eric had earned the nickname Bash by hitting 2 homers in a single T-ball game, a feat that had not been duplicated since in the small town of Buffalo Crossing. Albert only smiled and shook his head before turning to his combination lock again.

"I dunno," Jay was closing his locker which was just a few spots down the hall. "He is always reading some ancient book or another." He gestured to the almanac in Al's hand. "That thing looks like it is old enough to have been written in Homer's own hand" Jay's face has returned to its normal shade of pink, revealing a starburst of freckles.

Al shoved his book bag in his locker, completely forgetting about any homework assignment for the weekend, and slammed the locker shut. He looked down at the book that was still in his hand and smiled. He tapped the cover with his index finger, "This is gonna help my research."

Jay and Bash looked at each other, "Dogman." Jay said in derision what Bash said with hopeful intrigue. They made an odd harmony.

"Cry Baby Lane!" Al replied. His muddy brown eyes gleaming in the fluorescent lights of the hallway.

Jay rolled his eyes, the blue disappearing behind a pink lid. "Here we go again."

Al ignored him, "I finally found it."

Jay conjured an imaginary microphone, "I'm here with Albert Taulbee the II who has a major announcement for the world." He annunciated every syllable like a TV Reporter which helped to mask his slight southern drawl. "Have you, in fact, found the location of Cry Baby Lane in King County?" He held the invisible mic out for Al to comment.

Al only smirked while raising one eyebrow confidently. After a few seconds Jay pulled the microphone back. "How insightful. Now to Eric Sebastian for commentary."

The big guy waved away Jays' empty hand, "Whachu got Al?"

"I found a spot on this map that has matching details from three different accounts of people who heard the cries." Al began to open the Almanac to the right page.

"I'm having a flashback to Thorny Hill to see the mysterious lights." Jay added a spooky undulation to the last two words.

"Well," Bash offered, "we seen lights."

"I guess that's true," Jay agreed solemnly. "but they were headlights!" Jay and Bash both doubled over in laughter.

Al unfolded the map while ignoring his friends. It was an intricate center-fold within the almanac. He pointed to a spot on the ancient looking paper. "There is a long gravel road leading to a small gravel parking lot." He traced a dark line on the map with his finger and circled a small greyish blob. "Just like the story told by Jim Parker and Valarie Webb."

His finger jumped to a thin blue line zagging across the creased map. "And here is the small creek running through the valley just like the Mike Robinson account."

Jay wasn't impressed. "The Parker story is from the Fifties and the Robinson thing happened in the Seventies." He put air quotes around the word "happened". He then leaned in close to the map squinting his eyes. He reached up to the corner of one eye to adjust a pair of glasses that, like his microphone, did not exist. "1812."

"1913," Al corrected, then turned his gaze on Bash.

"That's only two." The big guy's cow-like brown eyes were focused on Al.

"Well…" Al lifted the left side of his mouth in a smirk that his friends knew well. "The map is difficult to read so we may have to verify the third thing for ourselves."

"Excursion?" Bash opened his mouth in a toothy grin while Albert nodded his head. They both turned to look at Jay.

After looking from Bash to Al several times he focused into the middle distance between them. "This just in," he had conjured his microphone again. "I need new friends."

3

The Ones Who Start a Journey

The wind was whipping through Al's hair and screaming past his ears. The sun was beating down hard, but Al didn't mind. Today was the day that he was going to find the location of Cry Baby lane. He could start his study of the area and find out what was making that noise. He saw a speed bump ahead so he stood on his pedals to absorb the jolt. He stopped when he reached the light at the end of the parking lot, it was red. Jay pulled up next to him. His face was already red enough to hide his freckles. He looked like the stop light.

"So, you are looking for a narrow path into the ravine?" Jay was still in disbelief. But was apparently too out of breath for his normal antics. His yellow shirt was already darkened by sweat around his collar.

Bash rode past at his normal relaxed pace. "It's green." His shirt rippled behind him like a grey sail flapping over a boat. Albert and Jay followed closely behind.

"That's right." He tried to match Jay's speed as they rode. "According to the old newspaper article I found in the library, a kid was heading down into a valley to play in a stream. But before he got the bottom of the valley, he heard a screaming sound." He had to fall behind Jay a bit when they reached the side walk, so he began to speak more loudly. "He ran back home and told his big brother what had happened. But his brother told him to quit being a crybaby." Al found that talking and riding at the same time was not easy. He began to lose his breath. "So," he huffed, "we are looking for the path down into the valley." Al continued pedaling but took a few breaths before finishing his thought. "That trail is the actual Cry Baby Lane."

Jay only shook his head and grumbled a bit under his breath. The trio rode in relative silence through town. It was only a short distance from school to the turn onto Rutledge Road, a highway that narrowed to a country lane as it passed through the Wallwood. The woods were dense and traffic was extremely light on this stretch of Rutledge Road, giving the boys the illusion of isolation. Civilization seemed a long way off after the first curve in the road. It was a feeling the boys were familiar with as this patch of highway was a frequent destination for their excursions.

The trees that lined the road seemed slightly yellowed. They normally reached proudly up and over the road forming a sort of open-topped arch. But now they seemed to sag a bit. The trees weren't the only ones who were unhappy either. Jay had started recounting (Al would have said complaining about) some of their previous treks in this area. He had already covered that time "he froze one of his balls off" looking for Wallwood Devil tracks in the snow. He got halfway through the tale of torrential rain on the trail of Dogman of the Elkhorn before Bash interrupted.

"Was that the same day you flipped over your handlebars?" The big guy had sweat running down his bald head. He was forced to wipe his brow every few minutes to keep the stinging liquid out of his eyes.

Jay's face had been red from the exertion but began to get even brighter as he blushed, and stopped talking. The dense forest lining the road provided ample shade. A thin line of sunlight shown down on the road in places, but disappeared completely in others. The boys could easily avoid the heat of the light but the shade was not much cooler.

When they came around the last curve and Al saw the

road climbing up the hill, his heart skipped a beat. Before he could tell the guys to be on the look out for a path or trail into the woods, Jay began his banter again.

"We aren't going to that old hippie's place again are we?" He was eyeing a gnarled oak with a giant knot hole. Despite his complaining, Jay kept pedaling.

"She had," heaving breathing made it difficult for Al to reply, "a run-in (huff-huff) with Dogman."

Jay laughed between heavy breaths. "She had (huff-puff) a run-in (huff) with some drugs."

Yeah that whole place smelt like weed." Bash had dismounted and was walking beside his bike. His long legs allowed him to keep pace with the other two struggling on their bikes up the steep incline. "And that awful green stuff she tried to make us drink. Yuck!" Despite the sweat running down his face, Bash showed no sign of being winded.

Jay gave up the battle and placed his feet on the pavement too. After a few deep breaths, he began walking up the hill with his bike beside him. "I believe you are referring to," Jay's voice had taken on the tone of an announcer warming up the crowd for the main event. "the assuredly healthy, the positively anti-delicious, the one, the only..." He paused and looked around before finishing loudly, "Kale Juice!" He began to imitate a cheering crowd noise.

Al had dismounted as well and was enjoying the show. "Come on down in the next five minutes," Al reached up to push his sweaty locks off his forehead, they kept getting plastered there uncomfortably. "And we guarantee that your kale juice will taste just like dirt." He couldn't get all the way through before he started laughing. He hadn't liked the thick green liquid any more than the other two, but he thought her Dogman story was genuine.

The road began to level out, so Al stepped back onto his

bike and pushed off the ground. He heard Jay and Bash do the same behind him. "According to the map there is a trail on the right side of the road. It's near an elbow curve." His heart was racing as he saw a sharp turn ahead.

The woods were dense all along the road. There were occasional trails into the Wallwood or even a few picnic areas along the road but Al couldn't see any spaces between trees until he was passing them by. He slowed to a crawl before stepping over the middle bar of his bike and to the ground. He wanted to make sure he didn't miss the spot. It was most likely overgrown. He had walked all the way through the curving road and it was straightening out again when he heard Bash yell from behind him.

"Hey Al, I think I found something." Al could tell even from this distance that the big guy was excited. He saw him bent over at the waist and waddling into the woods when he came around the bend. Jay was waiting by the road.

When Al reached the spot that had swallowed the big guy, he heard Bash again. His voice was muffled coming from within the forest. "It looks like it goes all the way through."

Al saw an opening beneath a few branches. When he bent down to take a look, he saw that it was indeed a path through the woods. It was no longer a path that teenagers could drive through to get to a secluded place. Al had to con-tort his body several times just to make it through. The path had a taller clearance after the initial few branches and turned into a completely shaded lane through the trees. The narrow trail was only around four feet wide and trees towered all around. Thin blades of light made it through the foliage and landed on the ground in front of Al as he pushed his bike through. After a few bends and whirls in the path, it opened into a meadow of grass and stone.

Bash was standing in the middle of a brown field of grass that was laced with gravel. The ground on one side of the meadow dropped away into a valley. Al wordlessly walked across the meadow, passing Bash. The grass gave way to gravel before he reached the edge of the cliff. Al kicked a few pieces of gravel over the edge as he approached. These unlucky stones rolled and bounced off stunted tree roots that clung to the severe slope, then disappeared down into the void.

Even Jay remained silent as they surveyed the scene. Each of the boys checking off items on a mental checklist. Al believed it all added up. His heart was hammering in his chest. He half expected a shuddering cry to rise out of the valley right now. When he spoke, it was no more than a whisper. "That's where the cries can be heard coming from."

"I can't see the bottom." Bash also whispered reverently. All of them peered over the edge as far as they dared. Searching for some hint of scale. The longer they looked, the louder the sounds of the forest became. Twenty different birds were singing, creating a nice background sound. The leaves were rattling in gentle gusts of wind, providing some soft percussion. And there was an accompaniment of insects too. The lead player in this symphony was a squirrel that was chewing on a nut somewhere high above them.

After a few minutes, Jay started to speak softly. "You know how I know we aren't in a horror movie?" There was a dramatic pause before he continued in his normal voice. "That was the perfect place for a jump scare, but nothing happened."

"I still think this is the right place." Al was looking around trying to find the little trail down into the valley, while trying to ignore the commentary.

Bash had bent down to tie one of his shoes, his shirt was soaked in sweat. Al could feel his own shirt sticking to his back. In the middle of this meadow there was no shade at all and the sun beat down hard and hot. The sooner they found the trail down the sooner they could find some shade.

"We could still be in a horror movie." Bash was now tying his other shoe. "Maybe there is a bad director."

Before either boy could respond to this insight, something fell out of a tree and hit a rock with a loud thunk. Bash jerked and caught one of his fingers in his shoe laces. Al's heart skipped a few beats. But he quickly saw the walnut rolling away through the yellowed grass. Jay had been facing away from the sound, and had been hit in the leg by pieces of walnut. He jumped over the kneeling Bash and kept running.

Al could only watch laughing as Jay ran though the field. The pale boy in the sunshine yellow shirt running across a drought-yellowed field. It was a funny sight until he jumped over some low growing bushes and disappeared down, and into the Wallwood.

Al's feet were beating against the ground before he even had time to think. It looked like Jay had just jumped into the ravine. He could hear Bash's heavy footfall's just behind him.

4

The Stoppable Force

The path down into the valley was barely wide enough for Albert and Jay to walk next to each other. On one side, the path was confined by a sheer wall of earth and stone. On the other side was a slope so steep, it was almost straight down. Little vegetation clung to the side of Cry Baby Lane. It was a miracle that they had found this little trail at all. The entrance was overgrown with tall grass, waist high milkweed, and a couple of thick sticker bushes. In his terror, Jay had leapt over the whole thing and continued down the hill.

The trio walked along in silence that was only occasionally broken by one of the boys muttering, "I don't believe this is actually Cry Baby Lane." Albert and Bash said it with an heir of wonder and curiosity. Jay said it with derision, like someone who would never admit to being wrong despite mounting evidence to the contrary.

The trail eventually let out onto a lightly graveled road wide enough for one vehicle. The Wallwood grew in close to the sides of the gravel and dirt path in both directions. They could see a culvert running under the road to make room for a small stream that ran out of the valley. "We should follow the creek into the valley." His voice wavered a little as he spoke, Al was starting to feel the first hints of fear now. A small heavy spot formed in the pit of his stomach and a single butterfly took flight. He wasn't sure why though.

"We can't do that!" Jay was a bit too excited and he squeaked on the word 'can't'.

"You ain't skeered is ya?" Bash asked in a playful, mocking tone. Al secretly hoped Jay could come up with a good reason. Jay's face was turning red, but was not deep enough to match his freckles, which stood out a little less each second.

"No, I'm not scared." Jay bowed his head for a second but immediately looked back at Bash. "I'm wearing my white shoes." He said with confidence. "Mom would kill me if I got them muddy."

Albert looked down at Jay's feet, white shoes with red swooshes and laces. They were slightly dusty, but Jay wiped his shoes with a cloth several times per day. A practice he started soon after he had tripped up some steps in the third grade. He had busted his lip as he fell and it swelled up to the size of golf ball. When he got home from school his mother had spanked him for scuffing his nice shoes.

"Maybe," Jay continued, regretting the words as soon as they came out of his mouth, "we can plan on doing this some other time. That way I could wear some old clothes." His face was returning to its normal shade of pink with bursts of fiery freckles on both cheeks.

Al looked at Bash who seemed indifferent. "I think the old distillery is down here a little ways." The big guy was pointing to the left. "Could be wrong, but I think Gramps used to take me out here when I was young."

"What about our bikes?" Jay seemed genuinely concerned. "We left them up by the road."

Albert shrugged. "I'm sure they will be fine." And with that he put one arm around Jay's shoulders and started down the graveled path in the direction Bash had suggested. Jay did not resist. The gravel on the dirt road all but disappeared as they came to a spot where the Wallwood fell away from the road. A small gravel drive ran out from between a stone gateway flanking a cattle gate in the ground. This road intersected the one they had been following right in front of the ruins of some ancient stone building.

Piles of rotted wood and rusted iron. Charred and barely standing stone walls and rubble that was no longer recognizable. Al knew that this was the King's Cellars distillery before Jay pointed out the old barrel still standing in what remained of a stone corner. The road that they had followed here had most likely been a major throughway in the time of Kingston. And these ruins had been the heart of a thriving community 200 years ago.

Al was slightly disappointed. He thought a spot that was so rich in history would stir something more in him than the mild intrigue he was feeling. A waist-high stone wall separated the road from the rubble. Al watched as Bash took one large step over the wall, sat and then pulled his other leg over.

The big guy looked back, "You comin?"

Al and Jay climbed up on top of the wall and were preparing to drop down on the other side when the man spoke.

"Git back 'n 'is side." The voice was high and shrill. " 'ats riiight. Niiice and slow." He seemed to spit the words out while mumbling at the same time. "Ain't got all day boys."

Al turned to find an old man wearing a dirty straw hat over thin stringy hair. The greying strands framed a gaunt face with hollow eyes and a nose red from drink. The situation kept getting more alarming as Al noticed the sunlight glinting off an object in the man's hand. He was holding a gun that looked like it belonged in the Old West. The long silver barrel was pointed toward the ground, but his deeply shadowed eyes never blinked, or left the trio.

The heavy spot in the pit of Al's stomach returned, but this time it was accompanied by millions of butterflies. He didn't know what else to do, so he started to climb back over the stone wall. He kept his eyes on the gun, but could hear that Bash and Jay were following him.

"Yup, keep a comin', niiice and slow, niiice and slow." The stranger drew out his "I"s so that "nice" sounded like he put an "N" in front of "ass". When all three boys were back on his side of the wall he said. "Don't move now. Cops a comin'," he patted a radio he had clipped to his belt. "Yuns is trespassin'." He spat a stream of brown liquid off to the side after he spoke. He reached up to wipe his lips with the back of his hand. Then his tobacco stained lips returned to their pursed sneer

None of the boys seemed to have any trouble complying with his order. Albert was hoping the police came quickly. He would feel much safer once they arrived. Jay on the other hand was white as a ghost and looked to be frozen in place. Bash was unreadable, but his big eyes were fixed on the old man.

He leaned back on a thick wooden post on the other side of the dirt road. He kept his hand on his gun and the gun pointed to the ground. His eyes were bloodshot and cloudy as they flicked nervously between the three of them. His scowl never changed.

"Sorry sir," The freezing lump of fear that had formed in Al's stomach had begun to soften as soon as he heard that the police were on their way. He spoke timidly at first, hoping to quell whatever fear the old man had of them. The fear that told him he needed a gun. "We were just excited that we found the Distillery." Al wanted to get the old man talking, he thought he might holster the gun if he got into a conversation. "I mean, this place was built over a century before Buffalo Crossing was founded." The old man gave no reaction. "Are there any signs of the town that surrounded King's Cellars here?" Al gestured to the ruins behind him.

The old man finally responded. With a 'snick' sound, a long stream of tobacco juice shot from his mouth and flew across the road. It landed with a splat about six inches from

Albert's sneakers.

Al kept steaming ahead, still hoping to start a conversation, "Maybe some clue showing what started the fire that caused this," He gestured to the ruins again. "and destroyed the town?"

The old man's eyes flicked over to Al, "Must be the loud'n." When he said the word "loud" he pulled the hammer back on the gun, but kept it aimed down.

Al sat back down on the stone wall so fast that he dislodged a stone. He had to flail his arms to maintain his balance. That was the last time anyone moved until the Sheriff's Deputy arrived. It may have taken five minutes for the deputy to get there, or it could have been an hour. That time seemed to stretch on for an eternity. The old man was gripping his gun, white knuckled, the entire time.

Eventually an engine was heard in the distance. As it drew closer, it sounded like a four-wheeler, or some other kind of ATV. The motor stopped behind the stone gate, out of view. Seconds later a man wearing a sturdy hat and big reflective sunglasses walked through the stone gateway. His light brown shirt had a shiny badge pinned over one breast. Dark brown accents lined his shoulders, sleeves, and pocket flaps. Even at this distance, Al could see the light reflecting off the black shoes marching toward him under the dark brown slacks. Al relaxed at the sight of the uniform.

The deputy walked slowly toward the unhappy foursome. He was obviously appraising the situation. The hat and glasses obscured his features, he might have been 20 or he might have been 50. Al could not tell.

"What in the Sam hill?" He stopped on the other side of the road, right next to the gun-toting hillbilly. "You boys don't think the King's County Sheriff's department has anything better to do than keep your dumbasses from breaking your neck's in that rubble?" His voice was thick with authority and strained by youth.

"Sorry sir." Bash was cut off by the fast-talking officer.

"Son, don't get me wrong. I'm glad it was me coming to get you and not some emergency helicopter from King's Daughters' hospital." He seemed to be just winding up, "If there is ever a next time I will have to take you down to the station..." He trailed off as he finally turned to look at the old man holding a cocked revolver. "If I get here in time, that is." He turned back to the boys and jerked his extended thumb down the road the way they had come. "Now get out of here before I change my mind. Trespassing is a serious crime."

All three of the boys had started running before the deputy had even finished speaking. All thought of the local legend that brought the boys to the area had been temporarily forgotten.

5

The Lost One

The instant the coffee touched his tongue, Wil knew that Sherry had made this pot. He added more creamer to the cup, he needed it to help cut the fur growing on his tongue after that first sip. Sherri's brew was more like speed than coffee. He took another sip, and then walked out of the break room.

Wil always got up to get a cup of coffee right before the first run of the newspaper came to his desk. He wanted to be wide awake while looking for spelling or grammatical errors within the print. The first story he wrote for the BC Journal had gone to print with four grammatical and one spelling error. Caffeine was needed to make sure he was wide awake and able to catch any mistakes.

In his days at the State Ledger, the Frankfort newspaper, his editor would have caught the errors. But Buffalo Crossing was a quarter of the size of the Capital City. This tiny village was lucky to be able to support a paper, but not lucky enough to have an editor.

"In a big town like Frankfort, I'm sure the local paper can afford to hire people in all kinds of luxurious positions." Beth Dixon was in her 50s and had shoulder length straw colored hair that would soon be more silver than yellow. "I've been the publisher at the Buffalo Crossing's Journal for 15 years and am positive that an editing department is outside of our current budget." This conversation happened six months ago but Wil remembered how her smile was genuine, even though she was quite serious.

"We all have to do a little editing. At a small operation like this everyone has to pick up some slack. I think some of the other staff let these go to print as some sort of hazing." Her eyes twinkled as she continued. "We may be a small paper but we can still have pride dammit." She smacked one hand on her desk as she cursed. She met Wil's eye and held his gaze. "I need you to put on your careful eyes when you are proofing the first run." He thought of that moment at least once per week, right before the paper hit his desk.

Now that his careful eyes had been thoroughly fueled, thanks to Sherry's super brew, Wil was ready to play editor. He exited the little kitchenette break room and waved down the narrow hallway to Jackie in advertising. Then he turned the opposite direction toward the pressroom.

Wil was nearing the end of the narrow hallway when he heard someone reading out loud in a high falsetto. Was that his article? He thought he heard laughter too.

"Usually people run away from a fire," Wil turned the corner confirming that the reader was the only other reporter on staff, Steve Case. "but people seem drawn to the fiery sermons at the Crossing's Baptist Church." The last words were broken by a high-pitched laugh that grated on Wil's nerves more than any other sound in the world. He was joined in laughter by a couple of freelance contributors, a reporter named Jimmy or Johnny and a cartoonist, Betty Charles. Sherry and Shauna, who made up the whole front desk and circulation department, wore good humored smiles but did not laugh.

"Why there he is, I thought it felt a little warmer in here." Steve, who had been reclining comfortably in his desk chair, let his considerable bulk crash down. "Something's flaming in here, and I don't think it's the preacher's sermons." That piercing dolphin-like laugh came again. "But I've got some bad news for you. Preachers are celibate. And I don't think he would be interested in you to begin with," His pudgy face was its normal shade of ruddy red all the way up between the horseshoe of thin brown hair on his head. His cheeks jostled a bit with every word. "you know, the whole Leviticus thing and all."

Wil was pretty sure Baptist Reverends were allowed the sacrament of marriage, but didn't bother to correct the older journalist. "I'm glad you liked the article." He sat down at his desk trying to ignore Steve.

"Like isn't the word I would use, but I'm sure the Preacher Man will love it."

Wil grabbed the newspaper on his desk and noticed for the first time that his article was on the first page, above the fold.

Steve picked up his breathy falsetto again as he picked another excerpt to read. "I'm not a Baptist myself," Shauna and Sherry made their way back to the front desk. Sherry patted Wil on the shoulder as she passed. Steve continued, "but I may go to more services just to hear the spices that Reverend Todd throws into well-known stories as he stands at the blah blablah blah" He threw the paper in disgust and it slid off the end of his desk. A sheet of notebook paper followed the newsprint, see-sawing lazily to the ground. Jimmy or Johnny and Betty stood behind Steve grinning.

Wil made a show of flipping through the paper until he found Steve's story on A4. Could it be that Steve was a little jealous? "Well, we can't all find a story as good as yours." He glanced down to read the title of the article. "Young Drug Addict Loses Kids to State; Living Conditions Deplorable" Wil looked back to Steve. The older man's ears were so red that Wil thought they might start smoking at any minute. So, he pushed harder.

"How do you find such uplifting stories to write

about?" With one sarcastic lash, the whole feeling in the room changed. Wil saw the smiles melt off Betty and Jimmy or Johnny's face as they both turned to busy themselves elsewhere.

No smoke came out of his ears, but the rest of his head purpled darker than his ears had been originally. He stood up as quickly as his jiggling belly would allow, which was not very quickly at all. His greying mustache seemed white against the plum that his face had become.

"You got a problem with the stories I write!?!" Each syllable was spit out under his mustache. "I guess I'm just not afraid of a hard truth." His fan club had disappeared to a corner of the office, Jimmy or Johnny was busying himself with an old filing cabinet while Betty began to study a copy of today's paper. Steve didn't notice, or care. His fists were balled at his sides, and his face was rapidly purpling.

Wil was a little worried he would have a heart attack right here. Otherwise he would have made a snappy retort about how many hard truths Steve may have seen in his 30-year career. Luckily, he was saved from having to come up with any reply by a commanding female voice.

"Put'em away boys. No pissing contests inside." Beth had opened her office door and was leaning against the frame. Her arms were crossed like she had been standing there watching for a few minutes. "I just had the carpets cleaned." She turned her attention to Jimmy or Johnny, "Jeffrey," He looked up, eyes wide with what might have been fear. "Do you have a story in this week's edition?"

The young man, whose name turned out to be Jeffrey, swallowed before he squeaked out an answer. "No ma'am."

"Then go write something for next week, and quit wasting my paid staff's time" She turned and looked at Betty for a few seconds while Jeffrey scurried out of the newsroom. "The rest of you," she broke her stare at Betty to focus on Steve and Wil, "Careful eyes." She enunciated each syllable and then slammed her office door.

Wil folded the paper back into its original shape, and started reading his own story. He found he couldn't concentrate. Wil kept flicking his eyes over to Steve sitting at his desk across the room. The older man appeared to be seething as well, his normally pink face was reddened and a droplet of sweat left a glistening trail down his bald head.

After a few minutes, Wil forgot all about his rival reporter. He was just enjoying the fact that his article was on the front page of the newspaper. He read through the paper three times, taking care to make sure that his own articles were free of any error. He found none in the entire paper, but he didn't look too closely at any of Steve's pieces.

When Wil got up to get more fuel for his careful eyes, Steve looked up from the paper and spoke. "You should write something about Old Moonbeam and her Dogman sighting out on Rutledge Rd." Steve's face had faded back to its original shade of ruddy pink. He leaned back in his chair, placing two leather boots on the desk. He opened the paper and buried his head into it before softly adding, "It would certainly be more interesting and factual than the crap you wrote this week."

For a few seconds Wil tried to come up with the perfect comeback, but decided against it. Instead he just turned and walked away smiling. He thought to himself that Steve could have the last word, after all, Wil had gotten the front page.

6

The Meanderer

Each of the reporters was expected to write about the normal happenings in town. They divvied up the topics evenly between them. Wil got BCHS and Steve got BCMS. Wil covered Democratic politics and Steve covered Republicans. They both covered local elections like Sheriff, Constable, and City Commission. Each reporter was also expected to write two extra stories per month. These could be about anything, and were the source of much pride and competition between the only two reporters at the small paper.

Wil was already starting to think about his next extra, but found his mind kept drifting back to Steve. He needed some amazing piece, something that would shut Steve up. He checked the wire desk before he left the newspaper office. Stories from the Associated Press were faxed to the wire desk. The BC Journal only received the biggest of nationwide news; the outbreak of war, presidential elections, or natural disasters. The heads of the tiny paper must have only paid for the cheapest package the AP offered.

His initial thought was to try and find a new angle on an AP story. Beth liked to run the original article next to the one written by one of her own reporters. She said she liked to show that her boys can go toe to toe with the national guys.

Beth also liked saving the front page for a local story. With that in mind, Wil ignored the AP inbox and went to the other inbox on the 'wire desk'. The plastic tray only contained one piece of paper, an update from the King's County Sheriff's

Department. Someone has spray painted the word 'Balls' on the sign in front of the high school again. The sign normally read, Welcome to Buffalo Crossing High, Home of the Buffalo.

Wil didn't think there was much news in the fact that this was the fourth time that has happened since he got to town. The report in the plastic tray made no mention of suspects. Either one person is very bored or a whole town full of vandals lack any creativity. Feeling a bit discouraged he left the BCJ building and walked to his car. The few specks of silver paint that remained on it shone brightly in the sun. Or at least they looked bright when surrounded by the reddish-brown that covered most of the vehicle. His little Nissan lived a hard life, but kept on rolling, and Wil planned to drive it until it stopped.

He started the car and pulled out onto Broadway with no idea where he was going. No idea what he could write about. His mind drifted back to his office nemesis. Front page or not, Steve's words had been running through Wil's mind all day. "I guess I'm not afraid of a hard truth." He could still hear the high-pitched laugh that darkened Steve's already ruddy face. A laugh that would have been annoying coming from a thirteen-year-old girl, and was maddening when emitted from that pudgy and mustachioed face.

"Ask Shepherd's Bank about how afraid I am of the truth." Wil was muttering under his breath, but alone in his car, there was no one around to hear him anyway. "That fat tomato has focused on crime and misfortune for every extra."

As he drove by the courthouse he took a second to watch how the setting sun cast sharp shadows across the flat porch and up the front of the building. The gold and red sunlight reflecting off the polished marble. It was an effect that created a depth and grandeur not often seen in towns the size of Buffalo Crossing. "A tiny town, built on Bourbon may have a way of lining some pockets along with the city coffers. And maybe it's not quite legal." Wil dropped that line of thought almost as soon as he had muttered the words aloud. Then it hit him. Steve's words had cut him so deeply because they were true.

In Frankfort ,Wil had started to uncover some interesting connections between a local banker and certain members of the City Commission. It wasn't enough to make any accusations in a court of law, but Wil found several nice sized threads to start pulling. He turned in the initial draft to his editor, and was called into the Publishers office 15 minutes later. Mr. Quire had mentioned something about how it wouldn't be smart for the State Ledger to start negative press for loyal advertisers. When Wil had argued that the story may put the paper on the map, he had been fired on the spot.

Since coming to the BC Journal, all his articles had been little more than puff pieces. The critique of the town egg hunt as seen through the eyes of Elma Harrod, a three-year-old resident. A three-week journey with the BCHS baseball team that followed them from try-outs to a record of 7-0. Though the Buffalo lost seven of their next ten games, his articles had been a favorite of the townsfolk. He was told hundreds of times that he should continue the series throughout the season, but he knew that the magic in the story was gone. Or maybe he just got bored.

One hard truth that Wil was not afraid to face concerned his latest story about the Reverend Lloyd Todd. It wasn't very good. It didn't deserve Steve's childish treatment, but the article didn't belong on the front page either. "Maybe an article about Dogman isn't such a crazy idea." Wil was racking his brain trying to remember the name that Steve had said. It wasn't a name it was a thing like sunshine, or moonlight. "Moonbeam?" he wasn't sure.

Wil pulled into a small shopping center and parked in front a health food store called the Green Grocer. He was more interested in the phone booth on the sidewalk in front of the little shop. When he entered the small booth, he saw a thick yellow book laying on a table underneath the phone. He grabbed the phonebook and found it was connected to a short chain. The directory included several surrounding counties, but Wil was only interested in the King County section.

He found around 8 pages of phone numbers in the center of the book. The Ms were less than a column. Moodey; Mooney; Mundy; Munson... There was no Moonbeam listed. It was a longshot anyway.

Wil glanced up from the tiny print and noticed a greasy handprint on the glass of the phone booth. It was glowing green as the light from the neon open sign shown through the smudge. He thought he saw chilled drinks through the giant glass windows of the Green Grocer and decided at that moment that he was done for the day. "I wonder if they have beer."

7

The One on the Trail

It was extremely dark this far out on Rutledge Road. There were no street lights. The only other light source were the three illuminated mailboxes he had passed a while ago. The sun had still been peeking over the horizon when the three boys on their bikes had rushed passed him in the other lane. They had been riding like hell.

When the sun disappeared under the tree line, the night fell quickly and completely. Wil could barely see anything outside the beams of his own headlights. He prayed there would be no more kids on bikes because he might not be able to see them in this inky black. It seemed the Wallwood welcomed the night, while at the same time, making Wil feel very uncomfortable. He began to mumble to himself again. "I should have just taken my beer and gone home." He scoffed at himself in the rearview mirror. "But no, you had to ask about Dogman."

He shook his head thinking about his interaction with the clerk. Long sandy hair was twisted neatly into two large braids that hung down to rest on his shoulders. The clerks eyes were hidden behind a pair of yellow tinted glasses with circular lenses. His thin lips were turned up in a vacant smile. Wil thought he would be funny and asked the young hippie if he knew anything about Dogman.

"Anything," Wil flashed a huge fake smile, "anything at all would be helpful." Before Wil could let him in on the joke he replied.

"You should go talk to Moonbeam." He bobbed his head up and down while maintaining the mindless grin. After a few more questions, Wil found out that Moonbeam was a nickname. Her real name was Cheryl Rutledge, and she had a Dogman sighting about 15 years ago. According the Willie Nelson look-a-like behind the cash register, she got national attention at the time. A few magazines wrote articles about her and she gave countless interviews.

The clerk also said that she didn't have a phone, but always welcomed anyone who dropped by. But it was the last thing he said that made him feel a little guilty about coming out here at all. "She has been sick lately though." His braids bounced against his shoulders softly as he shook his head. "The big C, man. Cancer."

He passed a sign proclaiming a speed limit of 55 miles per hour, which seemed like a joke. The road bent and curved around huge trees that hugged the edges of the so-called highway. At least he didn't need to take any turns off this Godforsaken stretch of concrete, in the dark, he would surely get lost. The road narrowed to a single lane as he approached a sharp curve. He slowed down a bit as he approached. He didn't see the headlights of an oncoming vehicle so he kept going.

Even at 15 miles per hour he had to slam on his breaks to avoid crashing into the beast standing in the center of the road. As soon as he could see around the bend, large black eyes met his own, glistening in the headlights. The light cast an elongated shadow with its twisting mass of horns against a massive oak behind the creature.

The breaks squealed and tires skid across the concrete. The rusty Nissan slid to a heavy bouncing stop. The giant deer was no more than three feet in front of the vehicle. Majestic and huge, the creature stared at Wil for several minutes, his heart was pounding the entire time Before the shock wore off enough for Wil to count the points on his rack, 12 or 13 at least, the creature began to slowly walk into the woods. Before it had completely left the area illuminated by the headlights, the deer turned and gave him one last look. Its eyes were impossibly black, and unnervingly knowing.

He sat in his idling car for a few minutes just staring at the Oak in the beams of his lights. "This is crazy, this is crazy, this is crazy." His voice was a horse whisper. Wil decided that it was too dark to try this unfamiliar road tonight. If he kept going, he was sure to get lost, or worse. That deer would have totaled his little car. The deer itself would probably have been fine. Walking away with only a few scrapes and bruises, and a good story to tell his deer buddies over a few deer beers.

While the deer would have walked away largely unscathed, Wil would have been left on a narrow stretch of country road with a long walk head of him in the dark. Assuming he could walk. The thought sent a shiver down Wil's spine.

He pulled his vehicle slowly around the next curve and attempted to perform a K turn on the next straight stretch of road. The road was so narrow, and the trees so close, that he was forced to turn his K into a misshapen asterisk. Eventually, he was heading back toward town. Wil drove the whole way back to town at 15 miles per hour, only adding a little bit of speed once he had passed the first street light. He would have to try again in the daylight. Besides, he thought it might be bad luck to meet a woman named Moonbeam on a night with no moon.

8

The Knower of All

"HAL-LE-LU-JAH!" Each syllable was spoken with enough force to stand as its own word. The sanctuary before him erupted into thunderous echos of his proclamation. Lloyd Todd had brought his congregation to their feet at the crescendo of his sermon. All but a few elderly members in the first pew were standing and peppering Lloyd with encouraging shouts.

"Preach On!"

"Amen!"

"Go on, Testify!" Lloyd recognized the deep voice of the County Sheriff, Andrew Hawkins.

Lloyd produced a handkerchief from his coat pocket and wiped the sweat off his forehead. He replaced the cloth into his pocket while stepping out from behind his pulpit. The congregation was still buzzing with excitement, it was time to bring them down a little. Lloyd strode down the first few steps that led from the 'stage,' as Lloyd liked to think of it, down to the 'audience.' The fact that he believed every word that he said did not make Lloyd any less of a performer.

He unbuttoned the two buttons on his suit jacket and sat right on the steps. He had transformed into just a normal guy. Someone you could just sit with, and 'chew the fat.' Holding court was probably more accurate, Lloyd still expected them to listen.

His stormy grey eyes flashed like lightning as he waited

for the group to find their seats again. His thin lips spread into a smile noting how long this ritual took in the tightly packed sanctuary. When he had first arrived at Crossing's Baptist Church, the light streaming through the eight-foot tall leaded glass windows colored mostly empty pews. The Wednesday and Friday services were attended by more vagrants than parishioners. Not anymore. This Friday, service was full to the brim. There were even a few people standing in the back.

When nearly everyone had returned to a seated position, Lloyd began to speak again. His voice took on a conversational tone. "Does anyone know who William Booth is, or what he is known for?" A confused murmur rippled through the mass of shapeable putty before him. "William, along with his wife Catherine, founded the Salvation army in 1865." He waited as another rumble made its way through the crowd, this one conveyed satisfied recognition.

"Mr. Booth reached out to vagrants and miscreants. Those who had lost their way; those that had lost their faith. Those who could not, or just simply, would not help themselves. In other words, he reached out to those that most other people would have ignored. The people who needed faith the most." Lloyd paused to admire his work. The church was silent, the people rapt in the words he spoke.

He lowered his head and raised one hand to smooth down his short sandy hair. It always became a bit askew while he was giving a good sermon. "Mr. Booth and his wife offered those lost sheep three things." Lloyd was speaking so softly now that he could see people near the back leaning forward, straining to hear every word. "Soap, Soup..." He took a deep breath before nearly whispering the last words. "...and Salvation."

Suddenly Lloyd hopped to his feet, standing on the steps and looked at the crowd. "Mr. Booth saw the fallen, the lost, he saw these men and women and children, and he said."

The reverend squeezed his eyes shut so dramatically that his normally long face, scrunched together in a pained grimace. "You must be hungry, come with me. But wait, you're filthy. I can't let you eat like that."

Lloyd's eyes shot open and he dashed up the steps to the pulpit. He began gesturing at it like it was the miscreant in question. "Let's get you cleaned up." He turned back to the congregation as if in soliloquy. "That is the soap." He turned back toward the pulpit and extended both hands. He was cradling an imaginary bowl filled with imaginary soup. "Now that you are clean, have something to eat, fill your belly, have your fill." He turned once again. "That's the soup."

Lloyd heard a few giggles after that line. That was okay. He had what he wanted, their undivided attention. He shot a quick smile in the general direction of the laughter. His eyes flashed like lightning in the bright church lights. "Now it was time for Mr. Booth to do the most important work." Lloyd turned back to the pulpit, continuing to act out the scene.

"Now that you are clean, now that you are full, now that you feel... human again," Lloyd began to slow the pace of his words. "Now sir, madam, sweet child," Lloyd paused with eyes closed, just enjoying the silence in the packed sanctuary. "Do you know why I have afforded you with these comforts? It is only because I would like to share with you another comfort. The comfort of salvation through Jesus Christ." There were a few hoots and squeals at the mention of the Savior himself. Lloyd carried on without missing a beat.

He strode back to the pulpit and looked out at the congregation. "Did we not just learn from the writings of Paul, that all works must be done in order to glorify Him. Our Lord." He had picked up his favorite cadence and tone of voice. The tone the reporter had called 'Fiery'. One syllable words were awarded a second syllable. They became they-ya, him became him-ah. And any word worthy of holy elevation was done so with undulation. Lord became Law-wad, God became Gaw-wod.

"Ephesians 1 5-6 (NIV); He predestined us for adoption to sonship through Jesus Christ in accordance with his pleasure and will, to the praise of his glorious grace which he has freely given us in the One he loves." Lloyd quit reading and stepped out from behind the wooden stand so he could gesticulate properly. "You see, the only reason we are offered salvation is so we can spread His glory and grace through the Word and Love of Jesus Christ in everything we do. Unless we do it to further the glory of God, it has no meaning. This holds true no matter what the action might be."

Lloyd was really picking up speed now. He was building to another crescendo. "That-ah popular rock band had a concert to raise money for charity?" He looked up at the crowd as if someone out there was speaking to him. "Oh, they-ya raised a million dollars for hungry children?" he sounded surprised. "But they-ya raised that money in order to glorify themselves-ah, not to glorify Gaw-wod above-ah. It amounts to nothing in the end, this is not a good work." The congregation was hanging on every word. They were just waiting for the cue to jump back into frenzied cries and hoots and hollers. He would draw this moment out a little longer. The anticipation was building like electricity in the small building.

"Your favorite actress raised hundreds of thousands of dollars to build schools in a third-world country?" He frowned gravely. "But she didn't spread the Gospel to a single soul?" He paused to smooth down his hair again. "These are not good works. Good works are like those performed by Jesus; good works are like those performed by John and Catherine Booth, good works..." He took another pause to draw in a deep breath of the gathering excitement.

"Good works are those that bring people to faith. Those works that spread the Good News of Jesus Christ. That is why you must do all things to bring glory to the Law-wad above-ah." He was standing still with one arm raised high above his head to show reverence to the heavens. "Whether you are stocking shelves with boxes of cereal, or speaking about the gospel to a large group of people..." Lloyd paused to flash a smile to the congregation before continuing. This drew even more giggles out of the crowd. "You can hold Jesus in your heart while you do it. And that is how you can honor Jesus Christ in everything you do. Making good works of every task. Making your life shine as a good work, a beacon for others to follow. That is how to be Christlike. That is how to live."

The nervous excitement overwhelmed the crowd at that moment. Cheers and hoots erupted from the congregation as they jumped to their feet again.

"Amen!"

"Hallelujah!"

And Lloyd could barely hear a yell from the back, over the other noise, "Testify!"

SATURDAY
September 18th

9

The Unsuspecting Visitor

The branches were so overgrown around the driveway that several made horrible screeching noises as they scraped against the car. He almost missed the small wooden sign that was nailed to a tree marking the address, 100 Rutledge Road. There was no way he would have seen the license plate sized board in the dark, and that was the least of the reasons Wil was glad he gave up the night before. The hair pin turn that nearly ruined his night was only the first in a series of similar curves. Each one bent around a 200-year-old maple, oak or walnut tree. The Wallwood seemed to lean over the road in some places, causing more driving hazards.

When the narrow gravel drive led him out from under the canopy, the ranch style cabin before him took his breath away. The roughhewn wooden planks that made the walls were huge, fifteen feet long and a foot wide, at least. It didn't take many of them to build a house. The whole place had an ancient feel to it, like the boards that built it were repurposed from the Mayflower. The roof overhung the porch leaning on carved and sanded branches. The railings that lined the porch were made of sticks or limbs, some straight, others twisting, but they were all beautiful. Each section of rail, each support post, each individual slat was unique in shape, size and imperfection.

Wil climbed the three steps from the ground to the porch, the second step groaned slightly under his weight. He couldn't find a doorbell so Wil knocked on one of the heavy wooden doors. He looked down the porch as he waited. His eyes were immediately drawn to a couple of chairs that appeared to be made of deerskin stretched over the same craftsmanship as the porch railing.

"No there wouldn't be a doorbell, would there." Wil knocked again, louder this time. He felt like he had bruised his knuckles on the dense door. After a few minutes, he decided that no one was home and that a quick trip around the porch wouldn't hurt anyone.

The Wallwood allowed a very small front yard, and then came very close to both sides of the house. The woods grew so close that Wil could lean over the railing on the porch and grab a few leaves, brittle and brown as they were. When he reached the back of the house he lost his breath to awe again. The forest opened into a wide meadow. There were several large defined garden plots separated by a dirt path. The hardpacked earth trail appeared to start at the bottom of the steps off the porch on the backside of the cabin. It disappeared over a little wooden bridge and into the Wallwood. Only one of the garden plots had anything growing, the rest were unkempt and empty.

In one of the unsowed plots a woman appeared to be laying on her face in the dirt. The words of the Willie Nelson clone at the Green Grocer echoed in his head as he stood stupified. "The big C man, Cancer." Wil was sure that he was looking at a dead woman. "The Big C." How long had she been out here, exposed to the heat of the day, the chill of the night, the wind and the rain. Not that there had been any rain lately. "Cancer" Why was he thinking about the drought? He was looking at a dead woman.

She was laying face down with her butt up in the air. Her knees were tucked underneath her torso. Suddenly she moved. Her back arched into a semi U shape and her legs extended behind her. She began to push herself up by extending her arms, but her hips remained attached to the ground. Wil took off running toward her as soon as he saw movement. She was trying to get up. She needed help. His heart was pounding three times for every step he took. He kept repeating in his mind, "She's still alive, still alive!" He continued to run toward her, leaping down the steps to the ground. Then he saw her smoothly move back to her previous position. It took him a few seconds to realize what was happening. She wasn't in any danger at all, she was exercising.

Wil was so confused that he continued to jog toward the woman. She was slowly climbing to her feet, eyes closed. Taking a wide stance, she bent her knees deeply. Her body lowered until her thighs were parallel to the ground, like some ancient warrior.

At this point Wil slowed to a walk, but he was so close that she must have heard his footsteps. He was about to speak when her eyes shot open and revealed two brilliant emeralds, sparkling in the sunlight.

"Welcome stranger." She was only slightly out of breath.

Wil on the other hand was breathing heavily, sweat pouring down his face, his heart was still pounding. He must have looked quite crazy to this older lady. "I don't mean to disturb you ma'am, but I'm Willard Frye with the BC Journal."

She cut him off laughing. "Ma'am?" the word was almost a squeak between her laughs and snorts. "Holey jeans, a t-shirt and manners. Are you here for a story, or my heart?" She smiled as Wil's face reddened slightly. Her bare feet had wriggled down into the soft earth, she was caked with dirt, dust and mud from elbow to finger-tip, knee to toe. Her greyish-white hair was pulled back into a loose ponytail. Wil thought he could see a few faint hints of red as well.

"I just have a few questions that I'd like to ask you. If you don't mind, I would like for you to be a primary source for a story." He hated how timid he sounded. He was caught completely off-guard by this whole encounter. He felt lucky that he hadn't started to stutter.

She closed her eyes and sank back into her warrior stance again. "I have a few more poses to go through." She stepped back with one foot and leaned her upper body forward. She looked like she was impersonating a ski slope with her body. "Do me a favor and I'll tell you about anything you want."

"Ahh. Sh… Sh…." Wil paused. "Sure." After he finally got the word out, his face grew hot as blood rushed to his cheeks. The yoga master didn't seem to notice.

"Fill a bucket up with water from the well." Her voice was strained a little, but steady. "Then go grab a couple of glasses from the kitchen." She took a long deep breath. "I'm working up quite a thirst out here." She finally looked at Wil. Her eyes seemed eerily green as they glittered in the sunlight. She gave him a slight smile before returning her head back into position.

"Yes ma'am." Wil said as he turned back to the house. He heard the old lady snort as he walked away.

"Quit making me laugh. Can't keep my concentration with all of the 'ma'aming' you're doing." After a few more steps she added. "The well pump is beside the porch steps. It's manual and it's a bitch. Sometimes you've got to give it hell."

She was right about the pump. He had to wipe the sweat off his face twice before he really got the water flowing. There was no way a sickly old woman could have lived out here alone. As he watched her doing yoga in the sun, he didn't think she was very sick at all. He sipped on a glass of the surprisingly cool well water while waiting on the porch.

He was having trouble reconciling his expectations and the reality before him. Willie at the Green Grocer had told him that this old lady was losing a battle with some form of late stage cancer. That appeared to be untrue based on the contortions and positions her body was assuming. Wil didn't think he could posture any of them for very long, if at all.

After several minutes and several more poses, she began walking toward the porch. She was only sweating slightly but took the glass that Wil held out to her and drank deeply. She emptied about half the glass, found the bucket and gave herself a refill.

"Would you like any more of this?" She held the wooden bucket that had a notch cut out on the lip to serve as a spout, out to him. Clear water sloshed around on the inside, a little spilled over the top to run down the side of the bucket. The trickle snaked its way to the older lady's thumb, which instantly changed from a dusty thumb to a muddy thumb. Her forearms up to her elbows were caked in a mixture of dirt and sweat made mud.

"No thanks." Wil held up his still nearly full glass. She sat down upon the steps and plunged her hands into the bucket. Plumes of brown turned the clear water opaque in a matter of seconds as she washed her hands.

"By the way," She turned her head to the side causing her loose ponytail to whip over her shoulder. Her eyes weren't as bright under the shadow of the porch, but they were still beautiful. She smiled, causing the wrinkles around her eyes and the corners of her mouth to deepen. "I'm Cheryl but, everyone calls me Moonbeam."

10

Meeting Moonbeam

The large wooden table, where she had asked him to wait, looked like it was built out of the same ancient shiplap as the cabin itself. The table was at least ten feet long and each plank ran the full length. The heavy wood was two inches thick. The heavy glass he carried inside with him made a deep "thunk" every time he set it down, despite his best efforts to be gentle.

Moonbeam, with the strikingly green eyes, told him to wait here while she changed out of her workout clothes. Normally he would have snooped around, but it was so dim in the room that he could barely see the other side of the table. There were no electric lights and little light made its way through the windows, big as they were. The awning over the porch blocked any direct sunlight from making it inside the room.

By the time his eyes began to adjust he could hear the floorboards creaking across the cabin. They announced her presence several seconds before she arrived. She had woven her hair into a single braid that hung over one shoulder. Her eyes were the brightest thing in the room. She had changed into a comfortable looking faded t-shirt that may have once been tie-dye. When she reached the table, he could see well enough to notice the dirt that was still packed under her fingernails.

"Sorry for the wait." She groaned a bit as she lowered herself onto the bench opposite Wil's side of the table. "It's been years since I have worked out regularly." She grimaced a little as she moved her legs into position under her. "I am slowly trying to get back on my Yoga legs. It is taking longer than I expected."

A thin sheen of sweat still clung to her forehead, and her cheeks were a little hollow. But her vibrant eyes dispelled any hint of illness.

"You seemed like a pro to me." Wil flashed a bashful smile, "But I am admittedly not an expert."

She smiled back, revealing a few crooked and stained teeth. "Judging from the way you came running toward me, it seemed like you thought I was dying." She cackled as Wil felt warmth flood his face. Her laugh seemed genuine enough though, so he joined her.

"Heh. Well, I was told that you were very ill." He raised his thick brown eyebrows and turned his head inquisitively. "It appears I was misinformed."

She reached one hand up and wiped what could have been a tear from one eye. "Until quite recently, your information was terrifyingly correct." Wil summoned a quizzical smile. But she didn't explain herself. "Would you like some juice? I make it fresh." She laughed again, much softer this time. "I usually offer kale juice to unplanned callers." Her lips curled into a sly smile and her eyes widened. "I think it's funny as hell, cause it tastes like dirt." Her face relaxed. "But, I may be able to grind up something sweeter for a nice young man such as yourself."

He followed her into a kitchen from another time. The sink was just a porcelain basin with a drain that fell into a wooden bucket. There was no faucet. The stove was wood burning, and thankfully not in use on this hot summer day. There was a deep wooden cabinet in one corner but no refrigerator in sight. There was a large pile of strawberries and apples on the wooden countertop. She loaded them into a blender with a hand crank that looked like it had been made at the Shaker Village. Despite its appearance, the antiquated device worked perfectly. She quickly had all of the fruit pureed and emptied into an appliance that looked like a French press coffee maker, with a large lever on one side and a spout on the other. Moonbeam pulled the lever and the press came down. She caught the liquid as it poured out the spout in a large glass pitcher.

The fruit had been pre-sliced and Wil began to wonder if he too would have gotten the kale treatment had he shown up some other time. She handed him a glass filled with thick reddish-pink liquid and warned him it was very sweet before walking back to the table in the other room. Wil followed her and sat back down on the bench at the table.

Moonbeam was right about the juice being sweet, but she failed to mention the sour. After the first sip his teeth clenched as the tartness stabbed the hinge of his jaw. She laughed.

"It helps if you pour a little bit in some water." She took a sip of her juice and savored it like it was a fine bourbon.

Wil however took her advice and poured some in his glass of water. Just a little bit though. Just enough to try not to offend his host. He would rather just drink the water.

"This was my saving grace." She raised her glass a bit and stared into it.

"Excuse me?"

"I told you that until recently I was very sick." Her eyes turned from the upheld glass to Wil. "My battle with cancer was fought with this right here."

"You didn't receive any medical procedures or treatments?"

"I grew all of my own food, raised chickens for eggs and meat, and drank juices." She took another sip and sat the glass down. A film of pink slime dotted with dark seeds coated the inside of the glass.

"You never went to the doctor?"

"I did," her eyes drifted over Wil's left shoulder and into a memory "When I knew something was wrong but, I only went to get diagnosed. I needed to know what I was fighting."

"Do you remember what he said?" Wil had been so intrigued by her, that he just now realized that this was the story. Moonbeam's recovery.

"Only because that asshole sent me a letter afterwards." She got up from the table. "And it was a she, Dr. Buxton, Laura or Lauren." She waved her hand dismissively. "I don't remember. Hold on a second." She walked out of sight but the creaking floorboards betrayed her position. She returned with a yellowed envelope that she tossed across the table to him. The return address was King's Daughters Hospital in Frankfort.

He pulled out the single piece of yellowed and wrinkled paper, skimming the letter.

Dear Ms. Cheryl Rutledge... Malignant mass in your stomach...

may have already metastasized... strongly suggest treatment...

The last line was the kicker to the whole thing.

With treatment you may have 1-2 more good years. Without treatment, you have less than six months to live.

Wil folded the letter and carefully placed it back in the envelope. "Did you go back to the hospital for treatment?" he raised the letter with one hand. "After receiving this?"

"Hell no!" She reached across the table for the envelope. Absently smoothing the edges of the yellowed paper with her fingers as she continued, "The asshole in the white coat wanted me to put poison in my veins." She scoffed, "I thought

I would have a better chance fighting it on my own terms, my own way.

"It looks like you were right." Wil laughed a little, but Moonbeam only gave a wan smile. Her eyes appeared to glisten in the dim light as she looked down at the envelope in her hands. "I've lasted longer than modern medicine would allow, but until quite recently I was losing the war, big time."

She was silent for a minute or two, still staring at the yellowed letter. Wisps of long white hair had come loose from her braid and hung down into her face. "I received that letter eight years ago, and the first six were great. I barely missed a step. A slight fatigue at the end of the day was my only reminder that I was ill. Then, my appetite disappeared, I started losing weight. Friends would comment all the time that I looked unwell and that I should eat a good meal. But I wasn't hungry. So, I didn't eat. I didn't have any energy, so I barely moved. When I did move, it was at a great cost of effort and pain. My cheeks were growing hollower by the day and all the light had left my eyes." She slowly raised her head. A few shining droplets ran down her cheeks, her eyes watery and overflowing. "One day I looked in the mirror, and I didn't recognize the old woman staring back."

Wil was slightly uncomfortable, but knew this was newspaper gold. He tried to get past the sick part, and into the cure part. "You seem pretty healthy now. What was your secret weapon? What did you finally find that worked?"

The impossibly bright emeralds flicked back to him. They were drying a bit, but she did nothing to wipe away the streaks, left by the tears, on her face. "I'm not really sure. A couple of months ago, I woke up in the woods near my home. I felt a little better than I did when I went to sleep. I have felt a little better every day since then."

"You just started feeling better?" He really needed this story had a better ending than that. This might have been a wasted trip after all. He hoped he sounded calmer than he felt. "You must have some idea. Did you eat or do something different? Did anything out of the ordinary happen?" He wanted to scream.

She shrugged. "I guess I do have a theory." A short burst of air came through her nose as she continued. "You know, this wouldn't be my first run in with Dogman either."

11

The Goner

In the glow of the lighter, her hair almost looked blonde. The normally auburn hair fell all around her face as she bent down over the pipe. She filled her lungs with that chemical sweet goodness that calmed her nerves and sent her mind racing. She simply watched as one greasy lock swayed over the top of the pipe. A tiny flame leaped from the lighter and began to travel up the strand of hair. A lit fuse careening toward the bomb of unkept, and very flammable, hair.

Debra reached up with one hand and casually smoothed out the flame with her thumb and forefinger. She was no stranger to catching her hair on fire. Normally she would put her hair up in a ponytail to avoid such mishaps, but she could not find a hair tie in the darkness that engulfed her trailer. Or maybe she never actually looked in the first place, Debra couldn't remember. She could only remember the need to get high, the need to taste that basic burn.

She had dropped both pipe and lighter onto the floor beside her. Her left hand found a bump on her leg and began to scratch. The only light she could see was the window, high on the trailer door, and the spot where that light landed. A glowing shape like the NBC peacock illuminated a large dust bunny and several discolored splotches on the linoleum a few inches to her left, but she could barely see her own hand in front of her face. Her other hand continued to scratch.

The first time she had smoked meth had been on her 16th birthday. A present from her 20-year-old boyfriend.

Debra couldn't quite remember his name, only a tattoo of a knife sticking into the skin on his left bicep. It was super realistic from the right angle, there was even blood running down his arm. It was super hot. At first the chemical taste was repulsive. It took her breath away, literally. She coughed for at least 10 minutes straight, unable to fill her lungs. She may have thrown up also, but like the name of her tattooed boyfriend, that detail was lost to her fuzzy memory. On top of all that, everything she put in her mouth tasted like bleach for days after.

But the ride was amazing. Smoking that chemical goodness was like the Adderall she used to steal from her cousin, if that Adderall had smoked some crack. Hell, it was as if she was smoking crack that was high on crack. Debra was 22 now and considered herself an old pro. She rarely coughed anymore, she never threw up, and she didn't mind the bleach taste anymore because she really didn't remember a time when she could taste anything different.

The feeling that she was forgetting something came over her. She looked up to think and noticed that the peacock of light had crept across the floor. It now illuminated her dirty foot instead of the dirty floor. She inched herself forward, scooting across the linoleum on her butt, until she could see the spot on her leg. There were countless red and pink lines crisscrossing her irritated skin where her finger nails had been scraping. She couldn't see anything, but the bump was still there. She began to scratch harder.

That feeling in the pit of her stomach that she was forgetting something was still there. In reality, there were several things she had forgotten. She forgot to pay the electric bill; she forgot to call her Mom on her birthday last week; she hadn't fed her children in days. Her eyes moistened at the thought of her children. No tears fell, she no longer thought she could produce them.

Last week, a government lady had stopped by and given her a list of things to do or else they would take away Emma and Cody. The very next day she came back with the Sheriff and took the infant and toddler away. The worst part, the moment that kept running through Debra's mind, Emma just looked at her mother blankly as the big man in the uniform carried her away. In fact, neither child had cried or protested in any way.

She stopped digging into her leg to wipe a tear away from her eye. Another tear rolled down her cheek as she fumbled for the pipe and lighter in the dark. Flame and chemical pushed all thought of her children out of her mind. Debra's eyes were drawn back to the peacock of light, that had passed over her leg. A leg that had become warm and slick in the dark.

She struggled to her feet and stood swaying for a few seconds. Debra waited for her mind to catch up to the new position of her body. Then she took a shambling step toward the peacock shaped window on the front door. It was the only light source in the entire trailer. Her bare feet made crunching sounds with every step. The floor was covered with crumbs, cereal, dirt, and dust bunnies. The loudest crunches were most likely bugs, dead or alive, but Debra chose not to think about that. A colony of ants made its home in the kitchen during the day, so who knew what was crawling around in the dark.

She fumbled with an unseen door latch for a few moments before the door swung out. Moonlight flooded the trailer revealing the gritty linoleum. She thought she saw something scuttle into an overturned milk carton, but she couldn't guess what it might have been. She turned away from her own squalor, and stumbled down the steps and onto the dirt lot.

"Like diamonds." She whispered into the night. After

staring at the glittering ground for a few minutes, she began to walk toward the tree line at the edge of the trailer park. Her thoughts were only of the river. She paid no mind to the broken glass and crushed aluminum cans that littered her path, as they cut into her bare feet.

Thoughts of the river brought up memories that Debra had not thought about in a long time. Memories of her forest friends. She hadn't thought of them in a decade at least, and she hadn't seen them for longer. When she told her mother about her furry forest friends, Debra had received a smack across her face. "I ain't got time to talk 'bout your make-believe bullshit." The alcohol fumes hit the five-year-old Debra almost as hard as her mother's open palm.

She had not been deterred. She only kept her adventures with her friends a secret. Much of her time was spent a half-mile walk through the Wallwood, and a short stroll down the banks of the Elkhorn River. Her mother never noticed her absence, or at least, never asked where Debra had been. Her memories of the creatures themselves were clouded by extreme youth and years of heavy drug use, which both seemed to exaggerate the details. She could remember swimming in the bathtub as a little girl, and knew that she could barely fit into the same one today. She supposed it was possible that she had found a pack of stray dogs in the woods. But at this moment, she was convinced that her memories were clear and true.

They were tall intelligent creatures. Fur covered them from head to, well, whatever was at the end of their two strange legs. Legs that appears to bend backwards. She couldn't quite remember what their heads looked like, only that it scared her the first time she saw one. Time and chemical abuse had stolen many of the memories Debra had created in childhood. But what Debra could remember, was a feeling of warmth and safety. A feeling that returned as she recalled the gentle giants. A feeling that was never connected to any memory of her mother. A feeling that the methamphetamine was failing to provide her right now.

Thoughts of her mother eventually turned into thoughts of her daughter. Debra was weaving absently between trees, wishing she had brought the pipe. She needed something, anything to send her mind racing in another direction. Instead she continued to picture the blank stare on Emma's dirty face. The child's expression didn't change at all as she was carried out of the trailer door and out of Debra's life. Cody never made a sound either way, so his silence wasn't surprising. But the tear free face of her three-year-old tore her heart into pieces.

Debra was so consumed with the horror of her own life that she paid no attention to the twigs and branches that scratched at her face and bare arms. The small part of her mind that noticed the warmth running down her face assumed it was tears. It was mostly blood. She would have continued to walk blindly into the depths of the river if the cold water had not brought her back to the here and now.

She stopped, ankle deep in the chilly waters of the Elkhorn river, and looked around for the first time since marveling at the broken glass outside the trailer she called home. The trees opened up over the river allowing half of a moon to illuminate the water. She tuned to walk down the river bank, but stayed in the moonlight.

Head down, she concentrated on the ground. It kept her mind from returning to her children. She watched as two bloody feet, clumsily stepped on and around roots and drift wood, Debra was only vaguely aware that they were her own. She only knew that the rhythmic movement kept her attention.

The first time the moon drifted behind a cloud, she was left in a black that was almost pitch, but she managed to avoid any trip hazards. When the cloud had passed, she was easily able to avoid a tangle of tree roots that dove into the river a few steps in front of her. She was not so lucky the second time. The view of her feet dimmed into total darkness the same as before but this time she began to walk into the shallows of the river. A stick under the water took her balance and she fell to her hands and knees. When the moon came back out she could see the splash her hands made as they hit the water.

She stayed in this position for a few minutes, hands and knees submerged in shallow water that looked black in the night. Slowly, she returned to her feet and remembered the feeling of warmth and safety. She remembered her forest friends.

Debra had no idea how long she had been walking and was only slightly more informed on the direction she was heading when the moon fell behind another cloud. After a few steps into darkness, she fell again. Her foot came down on a loose stone. The stone shifted under Debra's weight causing her ankle to roll. Her other foot took a short quick step forward to compensate and struck a pile of rocks, which prevented steady footing. Her arms flung out in front of her in a feeble attempt to break her fall. The sharp sting in her left wrist was soon forgotten as the rest of her crumbled to the ground. Her reality flashed as the breath was pulled out of her lungs.

A heap on the ground, shocked and in pain, Debra did not notice the snapping twigs or rattling leaves around her. She struggled to turn over into a sitting position. This process was made more difficult by the fact that her left wrist refused to bear any weight. All at once she was bathed in a circle of bright light. The light was emanating from an impossibly bright pin point in the distance. Anything behind this tiny sun was obscured by the impenetrable glare surrounding it, but the voice told her that it was human.

"Wha-doo 'ee 'ave 'ere?" The voice was high and reedy.

It only increased Debra's feeling of unease.

"Hello?" She reached up to shield her eyes from the light. The fear and confusion she felt at that moment was not fueled by the meth in her system. More footsteps were coming from behind her. She turned just in time to see a shadow turn into a man as he stepped into the little circle created by the flashlight.

Time seemed to slow down for Debra. She watched as the man walking toward her adjusted the black bandana, tied bandit style, over his face. He pulled something off his belt as he took the last couple of steps to her. The dark eyes, that peered through holes cut into his blindfold, never left hers.

Debra felt like she was dreaming. He lifted one arm high above his head and struck downward. Her teeth rattled as a thump rippled through her consciousness. The leather padded lead turned her vision off, but she could still feel herself being carried through the darkness. Her mind only swam in place for a while, unable to process these recent events through the chemicals and despair. But then her thoughts returned to her children, as they always did. She wished again that she had brought her pipe with her. She needed something to wipe the tear-free face of her daughter from her mind.

SUNDAY
September 19th

12

The Loner

The sun was just reaching mid-day height when Lafay-ette came into view, one-hundred cookie cutter houses differ-entiated by shades of paint. Jay's house was in the middle of the sprawling suburban maze that kept getting closer with every pedal. Though Albert had biked the two miles along the Connector to Jay's house countless times, he was already worn out. The heat of the day, and the strength of the sun were working against him.

Albert stood on the pedals for a few seconds to let the wind cool him a bit. The air that passed by was hot and seemed to increase his discomfort. Al sat back down on the seat wiped his face off with one hand, instantly regretting the decision. His sweat covered hand made the rubber handle-bars slick. He wiped the hand on his shirt but found the shirt soaked as well.

He couldn't help but think part of his fatigue was due to the weight of knowing he was walking into a buzz saw. Al had never seen Jay's face burning as bright as it did after the incident at the distillery. Jay's freckles, which normally dis-appeared into his reddening face anytime a sudden emotion came over him, stood out as white specks against his blood red face. His blue eyes burning with cold anger from within the caldera that was his face. And like a volcano, Jay erupted as well.

"I am sick of your bullshit!" He was standing on his toes, attempting to scream into Al's face, but was still a few inches too short to do so effectively. "No more... Nope. No more for me." Jay had conjured no microphone, talked to no invisible spectator and used no announcer voice. It was only raw anger.

Bash had been relatively quiet about everything. When Albert pushed him about it, he had simply shrugged before adding solemnly, "That wasn't cool man."

Al hadn't spoken to either of them since Friday night, right after the incident. He had kept his distance all day Saturday but now he needed them. Last night he had a revelation about Cry Baby Lane. Sure, their trip had ended badly, but it had also confirmed that they were in the right place.

Out of breath and dripping sweat, Al pulled his bike onto the Carter's street. Though there were no cars in the driveway, there were two bikes in the yard. Bash's big 10-speed, and Jay's orange mountain bike were lying on their sides in the brown grass. He dropped his bike next to theirs and walked to the door. Al ran a hand through his sweaty hair to keep it out of his eyes, then he knocked on the door. He wiped his hands on a dry spot on his pants that had somehow avoided the torrent of sweat pouring off him.

Quick footsteps were audible on the other side of the door, down the stairs and across the room. The door swung open, and Al watched Jay's smile melt into a red-faced devil.

"What do you want?"

"Wha's up Al?" Bash had walked up behind Jay. He seemed to be doing his best to ignore the tension. Thick as it was.

Al nodded to acknowledge the big guy, then turned back to Jay. "I'm sorry about what happened," Al couldn't help thinking that it was Bash's idea to check out the distillery, but wasn't going to throw him under the bus. "I didn't mean for any of that." He turned his right hand into a gun and waved it around slowly. "I was scared as hell, too."

Jay's face was slowly returning to its normal shade of pink. The freckles around his nose were getting darker by the second. Bash smiled and gave Al two giant thumbs up from behind Jay. "Come on in." Jay smiled revealing tiny white teeth. "We have cookies and Kool-Aid."

"What flavor?" Al felt a weight lift off his shoulders, he found it easier to breathe. Jay had not spoken to him for a week after the bike wreck in the rain. He was afraid this would be longer.

"I got Smurf Spit." Jay had stepped aside and began waving Al through the front door like he was an airplane coming in for a landing.

Al smiled as he stepped through the door. "Cool, cause I though about it and I know why we didn't hear anything at Cry Baby Lane."

Jay stopped waving him down the runway and placed a firm hand on Al's chest. "You better not be trying to convince us to go back." The color was beginning to return to his face. Above Jay's fiery red hair, Al could see Bash patting the air with one large open palm, but Al was too excited to stop.

"All accounts have taken place at night, but we were there in daylight." The last few words came slowly. He lost all conviction when he saw the anger blooming in Jays blue eyes.

"Absolutely not!" Jay pushed Al back through the doorway with both hands, lightly. There was no intention to hurt Al, only to remove him from the house. As Al stepped backward to avoid falling, Jay added, "None of these adventures ever turn out good." He gave air quotes to the word adventures. "I'm sitting this one out," he stopped and thought, "I'm sitting all of them out from now on. Don't drag me into them."

Jay tried to close the door, but Al used his foot to stop its progress. "Bash?" He looked to the big guy, but Bash only shrugged.

"I'm with Jay on this'en, too dangerous."

Al was vaguely aware that Mr. Carter's van had pulled into the driveway behind him. "I'm really on my own on this?" He hated the way his voice cracked, but he hated the blank stares that answered his query more. Footsteps climbed up the porch steps.

"Hey boys, you ready to go?" Mr. Carter was twirling the car keys around one finger. "Al, my man. I didn't know you were gonna be here." He smiled wanly causing a burst of wrinkles to appear in the corner of his eyes. "The movie is rated R so I would need permission from your mom to take you."

Al looked at Jay and Bash, who remained expressionless. "That's ok sir, I was just leaving. Already have plans today that I can't break."

"Then it's just Red and the big guy. C'mon boys." Mr. Carter either didn't notice, or didn't care that Jay bumped Al's arm with his shoulder as he passed.

13

Minder of the Flock

Lloyd loved watching his congregation milling around after his Sunday sermon. It was all smiles and handshakes, hugs and back pats. Some of his parishioners would surely never have met if not for Crossing's Baptist Church. And the church itself would surely have met its end if not for Lloyd Todd.

His hands were busy 'organizing' the sheet music on one of the platforms in front of the stage. Lloyd was just shuffling them back and forth, waiting. He glanced at the milling congregation often, he wanted to know when 'it' happened so he could have a little bit of time to prepare. The crowd was thinning rapidly now.

He was holding a copy of *This is my Father's World* when it happened. A woman, middle aged, with short brown curls broke away from the crowd and began walking toward him. Lloyd shuffled another paper or two before looking up and flashing his perfect plastic smile. His congregation had grown too fast, he had little hope of figuring out her name before she reached him. He had little hope of figuring it out at all, he couldn't even posit a guess.

"Reverend Todd," Her voice was matronly and when she smiled, he saw that the wrinkles on her face only existed to accompany her smile.

"Please, just call me Lloyd," she grimaced at the thought, so he quickly added., "or Mr. Todd, if you prefer." He flashed his big white teeth again, then trained his deep grey eyes on the older woman's faded greens. He took one of her hands in both of his, "Forgive me, Ma'am, but I am not sure how to address you." He darted his stormy eyes away from hers in what he hoped appeared to be humility.

"I'm Alice Logan," She gestured to the group that was still milling around and slowly filing through the church doors. "I'm also not surprised you haven't learned everyone's name yet."

"I appreciate you understanding Mrs. Logan," He lasered his eyes onto hers again and gave her hand a gentle squeeze before letting it go. "I vow to remember you from now on."

She smiled. "I just wanted to come over and thank you. I think you have quite a spark in you Mr. Todd." She pulled out a paper fan and began to fan herself lazily. "You have really set this church on fire. I have attended every Sunday since I was a little girl and have never seen the level of excitement that you have brought these last few months." Her eyes were bright with tears that threatened to spill down her cheek at any minute. "Thank you for breathing some life back into this sacred place."

Lloyds stormy grey eyes were preparing to rain, "I'm just glad I have found a church with people as wonderful as this one." He gestured over her shoulder at a group of people gathering behind Mrs. Logan.

She gave a little laugh, "I don't want to take up your time, just wanted to let you know that I'm glad you have joined us here at Crossings." She smiled again before disappearing between the waiting parishioners.

Lloyd used one hand to smooth down his hair. He couldn't have messy hair while meeting with his flock. "Hello." Lloyd had plastered his show smile back onto his face, and his greeting was met with a wave of giggles. He could see

Sheriff Hawkins, his wife and one of the young deputies and his wife in the back of the crowd. An elderly couple shuffled forward first. The man in brown slacks and a brown coat. His shirt might have been white twenty years ago, now it was dingy and threadbare. His undershirt was completely visible behind the thin brown pendulum he had hanging from his neck.

The old man extended one hand to Lloyd and cleared his throat, "I really enjoyed the sermon today young man." He clapped Lloyds upper arm as he shook the other hand. Before Lloyd had a chance to respond, he heard a higher voice next to the old man.

"Matthew has always been my favorite Gospel," Though small sounding her words were deliberate, "I have never heard someone with your insights speak on the subject."

The old man released Lloyd's hand and put one arm around the small woman in the green dress. Her eye shadow matched the dress and her blush matched her lips. Her dark grey hair was pulled back in a severe bun. Not a single strand strayed from its place. "This is my wife, Margaret Phipps."

She extended one limp hand and Lloyd accepted it with both of his, he even gave a little bow. "I'm glad that you enjoyed the service Mr. Phipps." He turned his charm up as far as he could and smiled at the old lady. "Mrs. Phipps, it is absolutely lovely to meet you. I would be happy to answer any questions you may have about the sermon."

"Oh, the pleasure is all mine," she pulled her hands back and clasped them over her chest. "I am still sifting through your wisdom right now." Lloyd was beginning to wonder if the red on her cheeks was make-up, or was she blushing. "I can't wait to hear what you have for us on Wednesday."

"We both will be here on Wednesday." Mr. Phipps deep

gravelly voice was the exact opposite of her feminine voice, small and coy.

Lloyd reached out with both arms, laying one hand on Mr. Phipps shoulder and the other on Mrs. Phipps shoulder. "Thank you so much for your support." He made sure to meet each of their eyes for at least two seconds. He found this type of eye contact helped to cement sincerity in the minds of most people.

Mr. Phipps smiled and nodded before guiding his wife back through the remaining people. Lloyd hoped all of those still waiting only wanted to tell him that he was doing a good job. It was unlikely, but he could hope. The next person to break away from the group was a young woman with long blond hair.

When she spoke, her dark eyebrows arched as if she was thinking intently. "Mr. Todd, I would like to talk to you about the sermon you gave on Wednesday." She gave an apologetic frown, which almost caused her pretty little chin to disappear. "I'd like to set up a time to discuss this with you. When would you be available?"

Lloyd thought it would be improper to invite such a pretty, young woman to speak with him privily. He had no intention of seduction, but he would be lying to himself if he claimed he had not noticed her. Her dress was form fitting black draped with silver sheer, modest enough to wear to church but racy enough to garner some attention.

Lloyd cleared his throat. "I would gladly answer any questions you may have about the service here," he looked around at the small group that remained, mostly the Sheriff's friends and family, "or we can discuss it over lunch sometime this week. My treat." He smiled, this one was genuine.

She glanced at the people behind her. The motion pulled some of her hair over her shoulder to fall down her back. "Well, I guess I can give you the gist of my thoughts."

She closed her eyes, hazel eyes, and took a deep breath as if gathering courage. "I have thought about this quite a bit since Wednesday," she paused again. Several seconds ticked by before she suddenly blurted it all out, "I don't understand how you can say that hungry children receiving food is not 'good'" She appeared to relax a little bit after getting her thoughts out in the open. "I bet those children would argue that the intentions of those providing the food don't really matter."

The sanctuary had cleared of all but this young woman, and the four parishioners behind her. They were all patiently waiting for his answer. Most people would hate being under this kind of pressure. Not Lloyd. Lloyd loved moments like this.

"Oh," he began fiddling with his breast pocket handkerchief, "I can see why you would be confused. Mrs...." he dipped his head questioningly.

"Blanton, Cindy Blanton... and single." Her face reddened which made her greenish-brown eyes even brighter. "Err, I mean, I'm not married, Ms. Blanton, or Cindy will be fine." Lloyd was starting to think that he might ask her to lunch anyway.

"Ms. Blanton," Lloyd fixed his eyes on hers. His show smile was creeping back onto his face. "feeding hungry children is a nice thing to do, but if those children are heathens..." he trailed off for a second, allowing enough time for his words to sink in, "if they do not know the way of Christ, then all you have done is delayed their punishment." He sat down on the first pew and motioned for her to join him. She did.

"They have given these unfortunate children more time to find the true path, and that is good. But the glory goes to God through the person who shows the heathens to the light, not through the one who has extended their life." Lloyd wanted her to feel like he was only speaking to her, but he knew the others were listening. "The road to Hell is paved with good intentions."

She broke away from his storming grey eyes to look at the hands she had folded in her lap. "I have never really understood that saying."

"You know all those musicians that hold charity concerts? If they held God in their heart while they were raising the money, it could be different." Lloyd ran his tongue across his top lip to calm down, he had almost started to preach. "The only thing in their hearts is themselves."

Her head shot up sharply and she met his eyes. Her own were wide. "Pride." It came out as a whisper.

"Exactly." Lloyd laughed. "One of the seven deadly sins. Pride is what drives this, so called, 'secular charity'." He looked to one of the stained-glass windows that lined the sanctuary. Abraham sacrificing the lamb. "And in that same vein," he flashed his stormy grey eyes back to her, "Good can also come disguised as evil. Look at this window. Abraham sacrificing a lamb." Lloyd made sure to note that all the others in the church were also looking at the window.

"I'm not convinced that the true story of Abraham's sacrifice is depicted here? Do you know why Ms. Blanton?" The question was rhetorical, and he only allowed a beat to pass before he continued. "In the Good Book, God does some things that some would consider evil." Lloyd raised his hands to quiet the sudden gasps he heard from several onlookers. "The Great Flood wiped out 99% of humanity, two whole cities were destroyed at Sodom and Gomorrah, and God allowed his own son to be tortured and killed by non-believers."

Her greenish eyes squinted as she appeared to be studying the picture in the window, but Lloyd believed she was thinking. After a few seconds she spoke, proving him right. "The Great Flood was the best way to wipe out those that were impure, not natural. Sodom and Gomorrah were dens of sin. Both cities only served to pull good men off the one true path."

She smiled when she came to the third point, revealing a small gap between her two front teeth. "And Jesus died to erase the sins for all mankind." She even giggled a little bit before adding. "All of your so- called evil deeds had a greater purpose.

"Yes, they did." Lloyd laughed with her for a second. He couldn't have scripted it better himself. She had set him up perfectly, even saving him some explaining. Lloyd was really beginning to like this lady. "And that greater purpose can be easily seen for those who wish to see." He turned toward the window again. "Not all of God's actions are so easily understood." He paused, giving him the appearance of contemplating how to continue. He wasn't. This was all part of the act. The act that he had been performing so long that even he believed it.

"Did you know that Abraham was elderly at the time his first son was born? In his eighties at least." She shook her head lazily. She didn't dare spend much energy on anything other than being attentive. "God originally asked Abraham to sacrifice his son, Isaac." He paused again and made sure everyone was listening. They were. "In the bible, an angel appears and tells Abraham to find another sacrifice." Lloyd noticed several bobbing heads in the crowd. Ms. Blanton's eyes never left his own.

He motioned toward the window again. "This shows the ram that Abraham sacrificed instead. There are other versions, old versions, that tell a different story." He closed his eyes and continued in a lowered voice. "In those other versions, an angel never appears, and Abraham sacrifices Isaac." Lloyd took a deep breath, "I think that the story in the Bible has been softened, I think the other story is much more likely to be true."

Her eyebrows made a 'V' above her scrunched up nose. "But, that would be awful." She blurted out, while her face completely changed as understanding began to dawn on her.

"It is only awful because we can't see the bigger picture in this case. Some actions may seem evil or wrong from a certain angle, but these same actions keep others away from damnation. Or some other reason that only God can foresee."

Ms. Blanton's hazel eyes were wide, dark eyebrows arched high on her forehead. "Then how can we know if any of our actions are truly good or truly evil?"

"Lloyd flashed a reassuring smile. "As long as you keep Christ in your heart, your action will be pure. Even if you are simply tying your own shoe, pull those strings with the intention of honoring the Lord."

"A friend of mine thinks your style of preaching will cause tension even among the faithful." A deep and breathy voice broke into the intimate moment, a voice that Lloyd recognized instantly. He turned toward the speaker, a thin woman in a blue pant suit, with hair so short both her ears and the back of her neck were exposed. "She's a Methodist."

Lloyd put a hand on Ms. Blanton's shoulder and gave it a gentle squeeze before he turned to face the crowd. The thin-lipped smirk on Mrs. Hawkins' face was nothing new to Lloyd. She stopped by every Sunday to let him know what her friends thought. Lloyd did not mind though, it allowed him the chance to talk to her husband on occasion. A Husband that just happened to be Sheriff in this little town, and in little towns, it paid to have powerful friends.

"She is not wrong, Mrs. Hawkins. There will be some that do not agree with my interpretation of Jesus' teachings." He stood straight with his hands clasped, right over left, at his waist. "But all I am asking is that you honor the Lord and Savior with everything you do. Who better to divide out of your life than those who can't keep Jesus in their heart?"

Mrs. Hawkins thought for a moment, smiled and then gave a curt nod. This released a huge guffaw from the big man standing behind her. Sheriff Andrew Hawkins pushed his way to Lloyd and offered one large hand. Lloyd had to look up to meet Mr. Hawkins dark eyes set in a square face. "I told her that you would be able to give her a satisfying answer. I just didn't think it would be so fast." He laughed again as Lloyd's hand was engulfed by both of his meaty paws. "I'm always impressed by the way you explain yourself, Mr. Todd."

Lloyd smiled broadly, he was no longer sure what was genuine and what was part of the act. "I just speak from the heart." Lloyd freed his hand and placed it over his heart. "Please excuse me for a second, Sheriff." He turned back to the seated young woman and offered a hand to help her stand. "Please call the rectory and leave a message if you would like to continue our conversation."

She took the offered hand and stood facing him. "I'd like that very much. Thank you, Mr. Todd."

"Please call me Lloyd."

She gave a shy, nervous smile, curtsied and then left. Lloyd had to fight the urge to watch her walk out of the church, that would have been improper. More improper than giving her his home number. But, when he turned back to the Sheriff, he saw it didn't matter.

The big man winked and grinned, I ought to give you a warning for being so smooth, you ole dog." His deep voice radiated throughout the church despite his efforts to speak quietly.

Lloyd checked to make sure that Ms. Blanton had made it out of the church before he humbly stated, "I am a man of God, but I am not immune to the charms of intelligent women.

They all smiled at Lloyd, the women giddily, the men knowing. Lloyd felt a big hand slap him on the back as the Sheriff repeated his earlier assessment. "You ole dog."

14

The Captured

When she woke up, her chin was resting on her chest and her neck was sore. Debra tried to raise her head, but a bolt of pain wrapped around her skull and back into a spot near her crown. She tried to lift one hand to let her fingers lead an exploration of her head, but instead learned two things at the same time. Her hands were tied together in her lap, and her left wrist was sprained quite severely.

Sticky sweat covered her body even though she was freezing. She could not see anything in the gloomy room. "I need to get my pipe." Her stomach cramped causing a burning sensation to creep up her throat. Debra's head seemed to catch on fire with every convulsive retch. Thin liquid dribbled from her mouth and onto the ropes, then onto her hands. She didn't remember the last time she ate anything. But she did remember the last time she smoked.

Debra tried to stand, anticipating the burst of pain in her head, but instead found her ankles tied to each other, and her thighs tied to the chair. Her heart began to race, or maybe it continued to race, Debra couldn't be sure. Was it panic? Debra's body burning the last of the meth? In the end it didn't matter, the results would have been the same in either case.

It was dark, her vision was blurry, she was tied to a chair and her mouth burned with the taste of vomit. On top of all of that, the only thing racing through Debra's mind was the location of her pipe, safe in her trailer.

As her vision adjusted to the dark space, she noticed lines of vertical light all around her. Tiny specks danced in the thin shafts of light that snuck into her room. She focused on the lines of light and a shadow rolled down the wall in front of her. Blocking out the light as it moved. Over the sound of her own hammering heart, she heard footsteps on gravel, although her panic would not let her identify the noise.

There was a thin tinny whine underneath all the other sounds. It rose and fell and rose and fell like some giant bee buzzing around in the distance. Debra fought down another bout of nausea and then tried to escape, kind of. She tried to wriggle her hands out of the ropes, but only succeeded in hurting her already injured wrist while rubbing her skin raw on the rough rope. Before she could even begin to think about her legs, she felt her throat clench. She puked again, this time she was able to avoid herself by leaning to the side. The blinding pain in her head throbbed along with the spasmed retches.

When she finished she allowed her chin to rest on her chest again, ignoring the protests from her already strained neck. Her new plan was to sleep until she could get out of here and get some smoke. That droning buzz kept getting louder, and she debated whether that noise was in her head or not. The louder it got, the more her head began to throb. Its volume grew until she thought her head would explode. And then, it stopped.

The noise was silenced so suddenly that Debra's ears produced a high-pitched ring to make up for its absence. Over the tinnitus she heard footsteps walking away, then her heart skipped, and her breath caught in her throat.

"Heyoo!" a deep voice, almost a growl. It was muffled and distant.

"Yip." Another voice answered, closer.

There were men outside. Debra's panic doubled along

with her heartbeat, her breath was still caught in her throat. She could hear the men talking, but was unable to make out much of what they were saying over the pounding in her chest. The little bit she did hear made little sense to her.

"I hear you may have some concerns about our mission." Gravel was crunched underfoot as the two men walked toward her.

"I guess..." The younger man paused for a moment, but the gravel continued to grind underfoot closer and closer. "This isn't what I signed up for. I thought this was supposed to be about race."

"Though it is true that we started as a branch of the KKK, at this time, race has taken a back seat." The growling voice continued. "You see, the King's Men have been called into action by a higher power. Don't be fooled by her skin color, the thing in that shack is not the same as me or you."

The pounding in her head continued, but each thud began to soften a bit as if the hammer that was punishing her had been wrapped in gauze. Debra tried to focus back on the voices and found it difficult.

"...you see. Because the King's Men have been called into action by a higher power." He laughed, "Let me tell you a story." The voices began to get further away, but no gravel crunched. Her head was not thudding at all now, and she couldn't be sure, but she thought that her vision was failing as well. Her breath was caught in her throat.

"The deep voice was less audible with every word, "We don't have to do anything until sunset, so why don't you let me testify..." The last words were lost to her as her head fell to her chest and air burst out from behind her lips, dry and cracked. As she passed out, she thought first of the terror that she would feel if she had to face the "thing in the shack", but soon she drifted into sweeter, more chemical-laced dreams.

Her eyes opened sometime later, and Debra's senses slowly returned to her along with the need to get out of there. The need to get to her pipe. The light filtering through the cracks was soft and tinted red. She retched, inducing a sharp band of pain to shoot around her skull. For all her effort she only produced a single string of spittle that was tinged with red. Blood? The light? The real question she asked herself was where the saliva came from. Her mouth was so dry that her tongue had started to burn. Of course, the burning in her mouth may have been caused by the bile, or the meth, or the lack of meth.

Debra tried to remember something she had heard. Something one of the voices had said that was important. It might be crucial to getting out of this. Getting out and getting back to her pipe. She was almost positive that there was a little bit left in there. Just enough.

Over the pounding of her heart, there was a soft rhythmic sound. She didn't notice it yet. She was busy rubbing her ankles raw in a misguided attempt to escape. Her wrist was too sore and swollen. Every little jostle sent sharp spikes up toward her hand. The steady background noise continued, getting louder with every beat. She had succeeded only in breaking the skin on her left shin, when she noticed the crunching gravel. Someone was coming, and in a hurry.

She ignored the trickle of blood that was now running down to her foot, and struggled harder. She ignored the pain in her wrist and she tried to free her hands from their bonds. But she froze when the footsteps sounded like they were right next to her. She could see the shadow rolling down the side of the wall. It seemed much taller, leaner. Like the impending night was changing it into some sort of creature. Some mockery of the human form.

She heard rattling behind her, wood against wood. Then, with a short click, her world was flooded with light. She had to shut her eyes against the bright, and when she was able to open them again she saw the wood planked wall in front of her, but only for a second.

She was pulled backward. The violence in the motion snapped her head forward and her stomach clenched, had there been anything in it, it would have been sprayed against the wall. The chair slammed down which caused the fiery pain radiating around her head to spike. Her vision had whited out due to a mixture of pain, motion, and adjusting to higher light, and she continued to heave unproductively for a few seconds.

After what felt like an eternity her vision cleared and adjusted enough to see the man standing in front of her. He wore a dark blindfold with eye holes cut out and a matching bandana around the lower part of his face. He wore all black.

"You would be thanking me, if you only understood." He tilted his head to one side. "I'm keeping you away from Satan himself." He reached one hand high above his own head.

"Wha…" He struck down and silenced her with a deep thud before Debra could even get out a single word. She had enough time to note on how bad her head was going to hurt the next time she woke up before drifting off into incoherent fever dreams. Dreams of pre-warmed pipes, mountains of meth, and her furry friends. Occasionally she would catch glimpses of tiny familiar faces, streaked with dirt. They made her think there was something she needed to do when she woke up, if she woke up.

15

The Determined One

Albert left home with around 45 minutes until day turned to night. He knew that on the curves of Rutledge road, there was very little room between the two. The timing had to be perfect, so he wasn't waiting around completely visible in the daylight. God forbid he be seen by the same cop and be arrested, or worse. The prospect of meeting a gun-toting redneck made becoming a juvenile delinquent seem like a sweet deal.

On the other hand, if night fell before he reached the rutted path to the meadow, he was afraid he would not be able to find it at all. All three of the boys had struggled to find it with the help of the midday sun. Alone in the dark, it may be an impossible task.

Though Rutledge Road twisted and turned, Al found that he was mostly facing into the area of the cloud bank that concealed the setting sun. The clouds provided little protection from the light of the sun. Until the Wallwood blocked the sun for him, he alternated holding first one hand up and then the other. He remembered to attach a flashlight to his handle bars with duct tape, but did not bring a hat. "This is all Jay's fault."

If Jay had come, he would have worn a hat. Jay turned bright red after a few minutes in the sun, then he would peel for a week. More importantly, Al would have borrowed a hat from him to avoid his current problem. But the hat was a small thing, the real offense was much deeper.

Al couldn't believe they chose now to sit out. Now, when Al was so close to a breakthrough. Granted, Al had led them on many fruitless investigations. If he wanted to be completely honest, all of them had been wild goose chases with no reward. Al could even admit that Jay may be correct about certain points; Al would never be able to confirm that the Kingston fire was started during the trial of a witch. He would never get any closer to Dogman than an interview with a pot-smoking hippie.

But this... Cry Baby Lane. It felt different than all the rest. The feeling he got while standing on the edge and listening was deeper, more mysterious. Jay felt something too, Al had been able to see it in his eyes. The way he ran when the walnut fell, he felt something. Something that put him on edge.

The grass on the sides of the road was long and browning in the end-of-summer drought. The normally lush green stalks had shriveled and browned into brittle ghosts of their former glory. He could see several patches of wildflower jutting out between the forest and the road. Each were wilted and turned down, despite their prideful height over the grass. A good rain would bring them back to life, but right now they just looked depressed and near death.

Al was so focused on the withering flowers that he did not see the car until the horn blast jarred him back to action. He swerved onto the extremely low shoulder, kicking up clouds of light brown dust. The dry conditions weren't all bad though. In the heat of summer, the humidity can make any task feel like a heroic feat, like everything must be done underwater.

But not now. The air was dry and crisp. The cloudbank, that didn't do much the block the light of the sun, did wonders in blocking out its heat. Al was able to create a nice breeze while riding to keep him cool. The heat he was feeling now was anger.

This anger served him well when he reached the hill that caused the trio to walk up on their previous trip. Before reaching the bottom of the hill, Al stood on his pedals and cranked up to sixth gear. His breath was deep and rhythmic, legs pumping, building speed to meet the giant slope before him. The sun had slipped behind the tops of the trees, and was only a matter of time before it began to kiss the horizon. He had to make it to the top of the hill before this twilight could turn to night.

Al hit the bottom of the hill mid-stride and continued to pedal as he went. As soon as he started to lose some speed, he geared down to fourth. With a lurch, the pedals loosened a bit and Al pumped his legs faster. The wind whipped through his hair as he rode, and he started to feel a trickle of sweat on his brow. The incline continued to steal his speed and he geared down even further to make it easier for his already aching legs.

By the time he reached the top, Al had sweat running down his face and dripping off the end of his nose and he hunched over the handlebars, but he made it. He made it without having to walk, and before he lost all light. Al continued a little further below he swung one leg over the bike. He thought he remembered the rutted path being near a curve in the road. Al walked slowly down the side of the road, rolling his bike along beside him.

Al flicked on the flashlight on his handlebars when he found the narrow trail. The trail was shaded during the day, but now, in the twilight, this trail might have been midnight. Al took a deep breath and then ventured into the dark. All was well until he felt thin fingers scraping along his cheeks and down his neck. Thin and wispy or dry and scratchy, fine hair and rough spun cloth, unseen in the night.

Al reached up and ran a hand down his face and wiped

it on his blue jeans. He bent down behind the handle bars, and the light, in an attempt to avoid any more groping leaves or webs. By the time he pushed his bike into the open meadow, his thighs were aching from walking hunched over, or maybe it was from the ride up the hill. In either case his legs were tight and tired.

Al walked several steps into the field before he realized that all danger from overhanging trees had been left behind. Night had fallen hard. The meadow was just as dark as the shaded path had been. If there had been any moon at all, it would have been behind the same cloud bank that had blanketed the sky all day while offering no promise of rain.

Al stood and took a deep breath, trying to calm himself. "It's just a small ravine… that just happens to be known for making spooky sounds." He whispered to himself as though it would give him some kind of strength. He had always heard that fear of the unknown was much worse than fear of a known foe, but it wasn't the unfathomable monster at the bottom of the creek valley that haunted Al's mind. When he looked into the inky night, Al imagined an old redneck in dirty jeans with a mouthful of chaw, and a handful of cold steel.

Al marked the path back to Rutledge road with a stone propped up against a fallen branch. He feared that he wouldn't be able to find it again easily in the dark, or at all if he was in a panic. He walked slowly in the direction he thought the meadow eventually fell into the valley. He was only vaguely aware that the flashlight made him an easy target for any foe hidden in the dark. He just didn't have the resolve to turn it off. In his head, the light was helping him listen.

A constant chorus of crickets chirped along with a couple of whomping bull frogs, but otherwise, there wasn't so much as a leaf rustling in the wind. Despite his careful steps, Al crushed a fallen leaf. The 'snick' sound it made, caused Al's heart to skip and his blood froze. The sound seemed to echo through his mind for several seconds. The sound of tobacco juice exiting pursed lips. It was deafening over the background noise of the forest, no doubt amplified by his own fear. Al stopped, waiting for the high-pitched voice with that distinctly Kentucky drawl. It never came.

Al's heart started beating again and he was able to steady his breath. Using all of the willpower he had left, Al trudged forward. A few steps later, he heard another noise. The hairs on the back of his neck stood at attention as the tingle running up Al's spine passed. The ice cube in the pit of his stomach blossomed into a Lovecraftian beast whose frosty tentacles snaked through Al's body.

The flashlight beam had finally found the graveled edge of the meadow, and Al was frozen. A muffled cry rose weakly from the depths of the ravine. He fought the urge to run, but could not stop the tingles from rolling down his back to weaken his legs. Al still listened. He knew that Bash would be more likely to believe him if he heard it twice, and Jay... well Jay wouldn't believe it if Al had video proof. He listened.

There was a light wind, that Al could not feel, dancing through the trees overhead. Rustling leaves and singing insects backed by the two whomping bullfrogs. A blood curdling scream, that may have been human rose over the night band. The sound cut through the darkness so clearly that it could not have been carried on the wind, or amplified by echoes in the valley. Though no words were audible, no translation was needed. The person... no, the creature that made that sound was in abject horror, spiked with pain.

Al didn't remember turning or jumping on his bike, but he found himself down Rutledge hill and pedaling furiously toward town. He didn't remember looking for the stone he placed to mark the entrance to the path. Judging by the cuts and bruises he would find later on his face and arms, Al had blazed his own path through the Wallwood.

MONDAY
September 20th

16

Another Goner

The fries had gotten cold. Fast food fries just weren't tasty after losing the magic of greasy heat. Howard reached inside the bag, pulled out the cardboard container, and threw. He saw loose fries silhouetted against the reddening sky before plopping into the Elkhorn. Some of the fries landed with a thud on the silty beach. The cardboard box floated down in the middle of the fries, before catching the wind and rolling down into the river. He watched it float downstream, occasionally twirling in an eddy.

He had only risked eating one fry in the truck on his way to his secret spot. It had been full of grease and salt. In other words, it was delicious. He dared not eat any more because Sherry would undoubtedly notice salt on the bench seat, or greasy finger prints on the steering wheel or radio. If his wife knew he was eating this crap, he might as well go home and eat it in the comfort of his leather recliner. Of course, a man as large as Howard was comfortable in any seat. He was mighty comfy on this craggy rock at his secret spot. Except for that itch on his left cheek.

The comfort of his butt was not the issue he was concerned about, it was his sanity. Sherry allowed him one unhealthy meal per month, and nagged him relentlessly if she found any evidence that he cheated. It all started after his heart attack.

The location that became his secret spot was found soon after a bit of ketchup on Howard's lip had spurred her to investigate the truck. A straw wrapper that had been tucked in the fold of the seat resulted in three weeks of 'tough love'. Sherry's version of 'tough love' involved a nightly conversation that always started the same way. "Why are you so eager to take up residence in your heavenly apartment?" And always ended with some variation of, "You'd probably be happy to die just to get away from me!" He had stopped eating in his truck immediately and found his secret spot during one of these bouts of 'tough love'.

Howard hated the summer heat that caused his blue work shirt to stick to his back. He hated the buzzing, biting insects that seemed happy to leave itchy welts on his neck and arms. He hated the way the uneven surface of this boulder was making his butt itch. He absolutely loathed the muddy, mucky smell of the river which seemed to be amplified by the drought. Howard guessed that the shriveled river usually covered some of the more odorous sources, but the drought had left them open to stink up the world. The smell was almost enough to make him lose his appetite, almost.

He looked down at the last bite of burger and studied it a moment before popping it in his mouth. He relished the tangy sauce and crunching bacon. When he was done exploring the fading flavors he crumpled the foil wrapper into a ball and tossed it inside the bag. He winked at the grinning red head on the grease stained paper bag. Her smile seemed to say, "Your secret is safe with me, Howard.". He reached one pudgy hand down into the white bag, looking for some napkins. Instead he found a crispy fry laying on a bed of salt. He ate the crunchy little piece, it was covered in salt and fried completely through.

He looked in the bag, no napkins. That was alright though, Howard was pretty sure there were some in the truck. He started to crumble the bag, then stopped. He put one hand in the bag and wiped a thick greasy finger along the bottom, then licked it clean. He was contemplating a second swipe through the salt, but an image of his wife's frowning face appeared in his mind. He smashed the bag into a tight ball and tossed that into the river too. Howard watched the paper ball bobbing up and down on the river's surface until the movement in the woods drew his attention. Some animal darting around a tree, or back into its hole.

The sun was beginning to flirt with the treetops signaling that it was time to head home. Sherry would ask too many questions if he wasn't home soon after sunset. Rocking back on his boulder and then pushing his weight forward, Howard was able to gather the needed momentum to rise from his perch. He walked over to his parked truck, ignoring the itch that was still stinging his butt. He didn't know if Sherry would notice a grease stain on his pants, but he didn't intend to find out.

The truck door creaked in protest when he yanked it open. Howard pulled a wad of napkins from the door pocket. When his hands had been wiped clean, he lifted one leg, twisted and gave a hearty scratch to his itching cheek. When he was satisfied, he bent down to check his face in the side mirror. He was going to need more napkins. His stubbly cheeks were shiny with grease and there was a bit of mayonnaise in the corner of his mouth. He reached back into the door pocket for more napkins to wipe the grease from his cheeks. The mayonnaise he cleaned with his tongue.

When he pulled the napkins out something else rattled in the pocket. Further investigation revealed a mostly empty pint of BC yellow label 90 proof bourbon. This was a habit he kept from his boss as well as his wife. Howard turned the bottle up and emptied the contents with one large gulp. He cocked his head to the side a bit grimacing as he swallowed, which caused his already doubled chin to double again. Once the warm bourbon was safely in his stomach, he screwed the top back on the bottle and flung it at his boulder chair. The bottled somersaulted through the air before bouncing and spinning and shattering on the boulder. The tinkling sound reminded Howard of rain.

Before he climbed back into his truck, he had one more step before the ritual was complete. Emptying his bladder. He waddled over to the tree line and let loose. He was midstream when he was struck in the back of the head by something hard. He felt the object thump to the ground behind him. Confused, Howard reached one hand back to check his head and found it wet. His pudgy fingers came back painted red. But the most puzzling part, was that the object that had fallen at his feet was the jagged top half of the bottle he had just thrown.

Thoroughly perplexed, Howard turned around slowly to see who had hit him. Unless they were hiding behind his truck or the boulder, there was no one there. Heavy footsteps approached him from behind, and he turned around to see who was coming. Howard was still hanging out of his pants when strong hands grabbed his head and twisted. There was a deafening crunch as Howard's line of sight returned to the empty boulder. As the ground rushed up to meet him, Howard had time for one more thought. "Were those horns?"

17

The Researcher

Even though the sun was shining brightly when Wil entered, the inside of the library was dark. He thought his eyes would eventually adjust to the gloom, but they never did. He could only make out the shape of the room by the hanging lights running down the center of the high-ceilinged space. Each hanging stained glass fixture illuminated a research table surrounded by four wooden chairs. The circles of light on the floor never quite touched, leaving a bit of darkness between them. If Wil had looked up he would have seen the colored triangles of light spinning lazily on the otherwise dark ceiling, but he did not. He was on a mission.

The room had two rows of large bookcases running the length of the building. A single line of shelves on both sides of the center aisle. A black and white sign hanging on the first shelf in each row claiming fiction on one side and non-fiction on the other. Each bookcase was labeled with its own black and white sign, illuminated by a small naked bulb. He wondered how anyone could find what they needed in here with the room so dark, and was immediately rewarded with the answer. Taking a few steps toward one of the tables he could see the long florescent lights lining the bottom of each individual shelf. Hundreds of lines of soft light illuminating the spines of thousands of books.

Wil found what he was looking for easily enough, but actually reading it was another story. He had been studying the action taking place over the table next to his. The triangle of light thrown by the hanging fixture illuminated a dusty battlefield, Motes Vs. Mites, and he found it infinitely more interesting than the medical journal on his lap. When it looked like his chosen side, the Motes, had taken a turn for the worse, Wil decided to switch tactics. His original plan had been to research modern cancer treatments, which Cheryl had claimed to have avoided, to fatten up his article. But, after thumbing through Dr. Karpin's Discourse on Cellular Deformity and an AMA journal of compiled cancer cases from 1950-1980, he had stumbled onto an undeniable truth. It was boring. He also wasn't quite sure that Beth would want to run an article that basically claimed modern medicine should be avoided when it comes to cancer.

His eyes focused on a glowing computer screen on the far wall. He left the medical journal open on the table and walked toward the slightly greenish glow thinking it was some sort of inventory. He was right, it was a searchable card catalogue. He typed 'dogman' into the search bar and got a couple of hundred highlights. The story was due this week, so he didn't have time to separate the wheat from the chaff. He leaned forward and sank his head into his hands. He was grabbing handfuls of hair when he noticed a piece of printed paper that had been taped next to the keyboard. It had DOS commands to open a couple of programs. The first one was labeled Card Catalogue, which was apparently open when he sat down. The second command read:

BCJ MICROFICHE

c:lib//BCJOUR//DIR:

Wil hit escape several times on the keyboard until the screen was completely blank with only a flashing green colon in the top left-hand corner. He typed in the command code and found it was a database of Microfiche containing what appeared to be every issue of the Buffalo Crossing Journal ever published. He tried 'dogman' in the new search bar and got

10 hits. It appeared the database only had access to headlines, but listed a date and a sheet number for each entry. He marked a filing cabinet in the corner flanked by two plastic-covered dumb computers. These computers were little more than a light to project the microfiche onto the screen.

He turned back to the Dogman headlines. One of them had a typo reading Dogman's Best Friend; Fact or Fiction, three referred to a Police dog named Man, four were referring to Halloween costumes, but two were promising. Dogman of the Elkhorn; Do You Believe? And another article titled Dogman on Moonbeam Ranch.

Wil took the plastic off one of the dumb computers and flipped the switch. The machine started with a sickly buzz that did not inspire confidence. While the reader warmed up he opened the filing cabinet and looked for the two plastic sheets matching the numbers in the database. The machine was humming healthily by the time he found them.

Each transparent sheet had a months' worth of BCJ articles printed in microscopic font. After fumbling with the controls for several minutes, Wil was able to maneuver the slick plastic properly. The October 29th issue from 1945 slid into the magnified and illuminated monitor. The piece looked more like a poem than an article.

Dogman of the Elkhorn; Do You Believe?

By: Barry Dix

While the kids are out on All Hallows Eve,

keep one eye out for a beast that is far more than make-believe.

For any child wandering without a parent in sight,

could become a meal for Dogman on Halloween night.

The poem continued to hammer home the importance of making sure your children are properly chaperoned while trick or treating. It ended with the refrain, which was repeated several times throughout the poem.

Without a doubt the town would be forlorn

Should any child meet the Dogman of the Elkhorn.

The poem was cute, but offered no helpful insight. Wil exchanged the October 1945 film for the one that covered April 1982. He read the article Dogman on Moonbeam Ranch only to find that Moonbeam had not changed her story. She encountered the beast while on a spirit quest. The author of the article made the same deduction as Wil, that this quest most likely involved a hallucinogenic substance. But her description of the creature was exactly what she had told Wil.

"He looked like Lon Chaney Jr's Wolfman, but without the ripped-up pants. This thing was naked."

The only insights offered by the article were unfair editorializing by the article's writer, Steve Case. Case mentioned body hair and body odor several times while making thinly veiled allusions that her mind had been broken by drugs. The article seemed to be about a completely different person than the quick and sassy woman he had met.

"Looks like you are finding some good stuff in the ole' BC Urinal." The voice was soft and sweet, but Wil was startled all the same. "I didn't mean to give you a start, I'm so sorry." There was a light touch on his shoulder as he turned to find a beautiful young woman with sandy blond hair and dark eyebrows over apologetic eyes.

"That's ok." Wil smiled. "I'm usually much harder to sneak up on." He smiled as he gestured one open hand toward the illuminated screen, "I actually work for the Urinal in question. Just thought I would look for some loose threads in an old story and try to run with it.

Her cheeks began to redden and combined with her big eyes she looked genuinely distraught. "I've really put my foot in my mouth, haven't I?" She dropped her eyes abashedly. "My father always referred to the BCJ that way. Once again, I'm so sorry." Her slight southern drawl was almost, but not quite belle-like.

"Don't worry about it." He lowered his voice in a way that he hoped would inspire confidence. "As a reporter representing the local paper," Wil quickly looked left, then right in an exaggerated effort to see if anyone was within earshot. It was a purely comedic move, the entire BCHS freshman class could have been hiding in shadows in this dark building. "I am well aware of the crap the good people of Buffalo Crossing have been forced to read."

She slowly raised her head again, cheeks still red, but her lips were parted in a grin that brightened her hazel eyes. One front tooth was a bit crooked leaving a pie shaped gap in her smile.

"I'm Wil, the reporter." He stood and offered her his hand.

"Cindy," she gave his hand two quick pumps and released, "the librarian." She glanced at the magnified story on the terminal and raised a quizzical eyebrow. "You have a new lead on Dogman?" She giggled a bit, but it didn't sound like derision to Wil, maybe interest?

"Well," Wil didn't really know how to explain what he was looking for, he didn't really know himself, "not much happens in a small town."

"As the local librarian," The smile left her face and she was all business now, "I feel that I am required to tell you that Buffalo Crossing has its own Dogman expert."

Wil cocked his head, eyebrows knit above his nose, "Moonbeam?"

The seriousness was drained from Cindy's face and was replaced with her pleasant smile as a laugh burst through her lips. It was a sweet sound. "Gosh no." She stopped and then gave another short laugh, "Well then, I guess this town has two Dogman experts. I was referring to a high school kid." She paused and scrunched her face. Her eyes glittered in the dim glow of the monitor. "I think his name is Talbot." Her voice rose a few notes on "Talbot" as if she really wasn't sure. "He comes in all the time to research strange occurrences."

"What do you mean strange?" Wil wasn't really interested in the high school kid but, he did need a break. He also wanted to continue the conversation with Cindy and her apologetic eyes.

"Every town has its share of local legends."

"You mean like..." Wil paused to raise one eye brow comically high, "Dogman?" She laughed again, and Wil enjoyed the magical sound.

"Sure, but that's not all." She continued to smile, revealing the endearing triangular gap. Wil kept his eyebrow cocked with the hope that her smile would remain. "Well, let's see. There have been mysterious lights on Thorny Hill."

"Mysterious Lights? Are you talking about UFO's?"

Her face dropped back into the serious expression again. "Mr. Reporter, are you putting words in my mouth? All I said was mysterious lights." That pie-shaped gap peeked through her parted lips and caused Wil's smile to broaden.

"Ok, sure. Just lights? That isn't very interesting. Growing up in Frankfort there were tales of mysterious lights over Highway 421, the East-West Connector." He raised both eye brows now, "But our mysterious lights were connected to reports of UFO's. You know, missing time, paint peeling off cars, the usual."

"If the lights over Thorny Hill aren't impressive enough, I've got more."

Wil held out one hand and bowed his head a bit, requesting that she continue.

"There have been multiple strange, unexplainable disappearances in the history of Buffalo Crossing."

A burst of air shot through Wil's nostril's, "Every small town has disappearances, most of them are extremely explainable with a little investigating."

"Have you ever heard of the Elkhorn Devil?" He shook his head. "there have been reports of hoofprints found in the Wallwood after light snowfall."

Wil laughed again, "Why is it assumed to be a devil, why not a cow, or a buffalo?" He was enjoying this game thoroughly. If she kept setting them up for him, he would keep knocking them down.

"There haven't been any buffalo here in a hundred years or so."

"What about the cow?"

She reached out and playfully smacked him on the shoulder, "Oh you're no fun at all, Mr. Reporter." She appeared to be enjoying herself as well. Her eyes drifted away from his as she struggled to think of more examples, but snapped back to him before she continued. "Mysterious sounds in a place called Cry Baby Lane."

"Lights and sounds? This IS getting interesting. What kind of sounds?" His tone was mocking, but playful.

"The kind that scare necking teenagers out of their secluded parking spot." She paused before adding, "The twist is that nobody knows where it is anymore. Its location has been lost to history." She undulated her voice spookily while speaking and then devolved into giggles. Wil only scoffed. "You don't have to believe, but you may be able to find an article or two about Cry Baby Lane." She pointed to a reader which was still displaying an eerie black and white photo of a younger version of Moonbeam staring out at him. "I know I have seen our resident Dogman expert taking notes while reading them recently."

Wil Didn't think there was a story in any of these. He was about to give up the pretense and just ask her for her phone number, but she spoke before he could. "The BCJ has never been shy about running stories about Kingston and the fire that destroyed the town."

"Oh yeah? Where is Kingston?"

Her eyes widened, and her mouth opened in an 'O' shape. "Oh, I guess you're an outsider so you wouldn't know about it. Kingston was the original county seat of King County. The town sprang up organically around the King's Cellars' distillery. The distillery had moved to the location because of its perfect environment for bourbon making. Before then it was just a river passing through a dense forest." She smiled as she continued, clearly enjoying the moment to teach someone about the history of the town. But Wil was too engrossed in her words to enjoy the pie-shaped gap in her smile. "One day a fire broke out in town and made it to the distillery, which exploded. Legend has it there were no survivors. About 100 years later, Buffalo Crossing was built on the bones of Kingston."

Wil's mind was racing, he didn't think this would work for this week's article, but it may be a well he could dip into several times. There was actually a mystery to be solved, unlike the mysterious light of Thorny Hill. There was a light touch on his shoulder which pulled him out of his own mind.

"Anyway, I was just checking to see if you were done with the books." She gestured to the medical journals he had left on the table under another dusty battlefield. "If so, I am going to put them back on the shelf."

Wil felt a little silly, but half his mind was still thinking about the destroyed town which kept him from embarrassment. "Yeah, I am finished with them." He added, "I can get them, I don't want to make any extra work for you."

"It's no problem." She turned to walk away. "By the way, the library closes in 10 minutes."

Wil questioned his original idea of asking for her phone number, and eventually decided against it. He had too much work to do, and still no lead on anything for the upcoming paper. He also knew that he would be returning to the library for more research, there would be plenty of chances to talk to Cindy with her apologetic eyes.

18

The Embattled One

Moonbeam's eyes glittered as she listened to Cathy re-tell her silly little dream. Only three people had responded to the flyer she had posted in the Green Grocer about her first Dream Catcher Night in several years. Of course, back then, she would have had no problem filling the 12-foot table in the dining room. But it wasn't about quantity, it was about quality. Based on the quick conversation Moonbeam and Donna had shared earlier, this might work out to be a great session.

Cathy continued to drone on and on about trying to hop across this busy road, but she just couldn't make it across with her little frog body. The dream wasn't important. Moonbeam had known Cathy back when everyone still called her Cheryl. She could decipher any of Cathy's dreams before she ever opened her mouth. It all amounted to the same thing. Moonbeam was much more interested in the young woman that Donna had brought with her.

Shawn Parks had dark wavy hair that was currently hanging over her face and hiding her expressive brown eyes. She must have been half Moonbeam's age. She had been chatty enough when she first arrived, but the discussion of dreams had dimmed her mood. She busied herself by tracing the deep grain on one of the great wood planks that made up the table. While Cathy explained the dangers of potholes and speeding trucks, Shawn hid behind a tangle of thick dark hair.

If the young woman's dreams were not the cause of her posture, Moonbeam suspected that the bruises on her upper arm played a part. It looked like somebody has a firm grip, and Moonbeam would have bet heavily that the gold band on the third finger of her left hand was a memento from the culprit. Moonbeam had decided that even if Shawn did not end up sharing tonight, or her dreams sound benign, she would ask her to stay back to discuss the bruises, one on one. After all, dream exploration was only a tool used to know oneself, and to better oneself.

When Cathy stopped talking, Moonbeam looked across the table to Donna and Shawn. "Does anyone have any thoughts about Cathy's dream?"

Shawn absently lifted some of her hair out of her face with one hand while she continued to explore the woodgrain with the other, her eyes never left the table. Donna's face contorted in thought for a few seconds before she spoke. "Is there a project you are working on, but you feel like you aren't getting anywhere?"

Donna's deductions weren't too far from the truth. Of course, Moonbeam already knew what was at the root of the dream, but only because she knew Cathy.

"Oh honey, there is nothing I like doing except sipping some tea and watching the boob-tube. A hobby might make me miss my stories." Cathy snorted.

Moonbeams lips curled into a smile as she spoke. "You have the right idea Donna, just the wrong subject." She turned to look at Cathy, her blue eyes had been dimmed by age. "Would you just go to Italy already?"

"Em, you know it's not that easy."

"You have been coming up with excuses for over a decade. What is holding you back now?" Moonbeam was tired of this argument. During her illness, Moonbeam had not wanted to push her oldest friend away, even for a second. With her new-found health, she had the strength to do what needed to be done.

"Well, I don't have the time saved to take off from work." Cathy had not expected this tonight.

Moonbeam cocked her head to the side causing her grey braid to flip back behind her shoulder. "The part-time job that you only got because you were bored?"

"Well…" Cathy's bottom lip puffed out and the corners of her mouth turned down. Her face was slightly pink. "Mark just moved to Lexington. What if he needs something while I am gone."

Moonbeam snorted, "Your son is 30 years old and hasn't called you in a month. He will be alright for a week or two without his mommy." She reached over and grabbed one of Cathy's hands with both of hers. She looked her in the eyes again, brilliant green on dimming blue, it was as if they were the only two people in the room. When Moonbeam spoke again, her voice was soft with care. "There is always going to be some obstacle you can put in your path. Today, Mark is the pot-hole in the road and when Jack was alive, his health was the tire forcing you to turn around."

Cathy visibly flinched at the mention of her late husband. She started to speak, but Moonbeam talked over her. "Don't get me wrong. You know that I loved Jack. But I think he would be disappointed that you haven't gone by now."

A tear finally spilled out of Cathy's left eye, both were red and watery. Her hands had crept under each opposite elbow. Her arms crossed tightly under her bosom.

"With a little care, even a small frog can cross the road, no matter how busy. With a little care she can avoid all the tires and pot-holes along the way. Most of your real-life obstacles are just as easy to overcome."

Moonbeam reached out her hand again to grab Cathy's arm, but it was jerked away violently as she stood. She was weeping freely now. Her tear shined cheeks, already rouged, began to purple with rage. "How dare you invoke Jack in your freaky little séance." She was growling more than speaking. "These kooky parties have always been a chore I have had to endure for our friendship." Her eyes sparked as she opened her mouth to continue, but she stopped, purple jowls quivering. A second later she turned and stomped out of the room, floor boards creaking in her wake.

The two women across the table sat unmoving, mouths agape. The smirk that deepened the lines in Moonbeam's face only increased Shawn's feeling of discomfort. Donna didn't notice the odd smile, she was too busy preparing for the heavy wooden door to slam shut. It never did.

Moonbeam had to break the silence herself. "Would you ladies like anything? I'm gonna shut the door. So, while I'm up…" She trailed off to allow one of them to ask for something. Shawn took up a renewed interest in the wood grain, Donna slowly shook her head. She started toward the presumably open door, grey braid swinging behind her. "She will be fine ladies." She called back with an easy confidence that came with belief. "She just needs to come to it in her own time."

Cathy may not speak to her for a while, but she would go on her vacation. Moonbeam could care less about leaving the door open, but she knew that Shawn and Donna needed some time to process the excitement.

The heavy wooden door was indeed open. Moonbeam watched the silver Mercedes bounce down the gravel drive. Dust rose up behind the tires in a sort of gravel fog. How long had it been since it had rained? When the Mercedes' tires bumped onto the paved road, Moonbeam heard several thuds as some gravel was kicked into a tree trunk. She closed the door.

Shawn and Donna were talking in hurried whispers when Moonbeam returned. "Sorry ladies, sometimes love hurts. But it also helps." She paused for a moment before adding, "In time." As Moonbeam sat she grabbed her braid and pulled it over the front of her shoulder. The wrinkles on the corner of her eyes webbed out as she smiled at the younger women across the table from her.

Shawn immediately looked down at the table where she had previously been tracing the knot in a board. When she spoke, her voice was a bit shaky and very low. "How can you see so much in a dream?" Her face was hidden behind her hair again.

Moonbeam's grin widened into an uncomfortable smile. She should have expected this. "Don't let my treatment of Cathy scare you, Shawn." She laughed a bit as she spoke. "I've known her for 50-some years and I know what it takes to get through to her." Moonbeam had already decided she would ask Shawn to stay, the rest was just ritual. "She has had some variation of that dream countless times. But the truth is, the dream is rarely what tells me what I need to know."

"Oh, go on Shawn." The young woman was started by the sound of Donna's voice. The hair in front of her face rippled a bit, but there was otherwise no other reaction. Donna reached out and grabbed Shawn's thin shoulder before continuing more softly. "Everyone has dreams where their teeth fall out, or they are falling." She gave a girlish giggle, "Hell, the other day, I was having a dream about this muscular blonde with piercing blue eyes." Her penciled-in eyebrows bounced a few times. Then she sighed, "Before it got really good, I found myself in the audience at the circus. And Mr. Muscles, well, he was nowhere to be found."

Moonbeam joined Cathy in slightly exaggerated giggles. The attempt to change the mood in the room was brilliant. This whole night had been Donna's plan. She was the one to notice the signs on the young woman. At work, Shawn often had bruises on her arms. Or she would be limping.

There was always a story about how she stubbed her toe and fell into a door knob or something, but they were never very convincing.

Shawn's hair was shaking slightly, and Moonbeam was relieved when she saw that her shoulders were also bouncing in laughter. The young woman stopped tracing the woodgrain long enough to tuck a bit of hair behind an ear, revealing a portion of her face again. Then she started talking.

"Ok, I guess I'll share." She looked up at Donna and playfully smacked at her arm. "Everything will be PG though." She slid into seriousness as she continued. "So, I'm pushing this buggy through a desert. Just sand everywhere, in all directions. I don't know which way to go, but I have some water and food and some other stuff in my buggy." She grabbed a thick strand of hair and began to twirl it unconsciously between the first two fingers of her right hand. "I see this cactus in the distance and think it's the most interesting thing around, so I start walking toward it. The wheels of my buggy immediately sink into the sand. But I continue to push and push, its really hard work, ya know? Just when I think I can't push another inch, all of the sudden, I look up and I'm like, halfway to the cactus. Then this wind blows." Shawn raised her hands off the table, palms up. "And all the sand in front of me blows aside revealing a paved road."

The young woman clapped, "Now I am just flying toward that cactus." She stopped and looked from Donna to Moonbeam. "This is where it gets really weird. Out of nowhere," Shawn clapped again, "I get hit. I lose my balance and tumble off of the paved road, turning my buggy over in the process. The sky and ground switch places, the sand sprays all around, and by the time I am able to look around, all I can see is the helmet and shoulder pads of a football player disappearing over a dune. I gather all my stuff and right my buggy again only to find that the road has turned back to sand."

Shawn leaned back in her chair, pulling her hands back to grasp the edge of the table. A few brown curls fell into her face. "That is about the gist of it."

Moonbeam cocked her head, "Do you ever reach the cactus?"

"Sometimes, but then Ill see a palm tree and head toward that instead."

The older woman feigned a laugh, "So, you have this dream often?" She was quite convincing.

A few seconds passed while Shawn bit her lower lip. "I've had it four or five times over the past couple of years. One time, a whole team of football players worked together to kick sand on top of the road I was following."

Donna laughed and put a hand on Shawn's clenched shoulder. "Honey next time you should just charm some of them athletes and before long you will have some of them carrying your cart, while others fight over the honor of carrying you." That got a laugh out of all three of the women.

The mirth was cut short though as Donna looked at her watch, "Oh shoot, I've got to run girls." She stood and started out immediately. "Sorry to run so quick, but I've got to pick Dylan up. He gets so mad when I'm late, you know teenagers."

Shawn stood as well, clearly uncomfortable with the thought of being left with the old hippie, after sharing so much. "I should be heading out too."

Moonbeam stood and turned to Donna, who was halfway to the front door. "Thanks for coming Donna, and I'll try."

A slight smile spread across Donna's lips. "Thanks," She turned to Shawn. "I'll see you at work young lady." Then she was gone, a weighty click announced her departure as the thick front door shut.

Moonbeam turned back to the younger woman still

standing on the other side of the table. "Thanks for coming out Shawn." She reached out her hand and began to walk Shawn toward the front of the house. The younger woman took her hand and went willingly. Moonbeam noted the four, round, evenly spaced, bruises on her arm again. "Is your husband a sports fan by any chance?"

Shawn turned, a little shocked at the question. "Umm, yeah. He does like the Bengals."

WEDNESDAY
September 22nd

The Equinox

19

The Finding One

The steady breeze felt great rippling through Wil's hair, an army of brown whips dancing on the edges of his vision. The sun-sparkled water was mesmerizing as it passed by with dizzying speed. This paddle boat was traveling faster than it had any right to go, but then again, Wil had never been on a paddle boat and didn't really know how fast it should be going.

The boat was moving swiftly down the muddy Mississippi and there were thick forests on this side of the boat. Despite the midday sun, those woods looked dark and uninviting. Wil turned around to lean his back against the rail and found one of the crewmen waiting. The young man had dark skin and a gap-toothed smile. "Drink," he said, "Slowly doe, tis fire dis far up de riveir" His words were peppered with French consonants, and his hands were steady. He was holding out a wooden mug.

Wil took the cup gratefully, but before he could take a sip, the crewman reached out and tapped him on the shoulder. "Willard?" The man's voice had changed. It had grown soft and high, more feminine than anything. Wil almost jerked out of his reach when the crewman reached out again and grabbed his shoulder to give it a light shake. "Wake up."

The crewman and the boat behind him disappeared and were replaced by a soft blur that was growing as Wil slowly opened his eyes. When he found his focus, Wil was greeted by a familiar smile framed by a waterfall of dirty blonde hair. "I brought you some coffee." Cindy placed a ceramic mug on the table, solid black with white lettering, BCPL. "I made it strong when I saw you grab Dr. Haley." She grabbed a few pages of the book Wil had been using as a pillow, and flicked through them with her thumb. "He is great on facts, but adds very little flavor."

She pretended not to notice his attempt to discreetly wipe the drool from his mouth. "Thanks, I obviously need it." He reached for the coffee. "Are you familiar with the exploits of," Wil paused a moment to look down at the page he had been reading as he fell asleep, "Bartholomew Cane?" He put the cup of steaming liquid up to his mouth.

"Careful, it's hot."

"Like fire?" he replied mindlessly. The coffee burned his lip, bringing him completely into consciousness. "Ssst! Ahh!" Wil sucked in air as he pulled the offending liquid away from his face. "Well, I'm awake now." Wil set the cup down on the table, while running his tongue over his tingling upper lip. "I'll just give that a minute or two to cool off."

Cindy smiled revealing the slight gap in her front teeth. "While we wait, I could save you quite a bit of time."

"How so?"

She reached out and spun the book around to face her. She pinched about an inch worth of pages and held them upright. "I could summarize about this much of the book for you."

He raised one hand toward her, asking for her to continue.

"A rich man named Bartholomew Cane discovers Bourbon while on a river boat trip. The rich man hires explorers, builders and a chemist to find the perfect spot to build a distillery. The rich man sees buffalo crossing the Elkhorn and decides that is the best spot." She dropped the pages she was holding revealing a map. "A town sprang up around the distillery that the rich man had built." She pointed at the map.

The distillery was just off of the river, about a quarter of a mile, but the town spread out around both banks of the Elkhorn River. As far as Wil knew, the Wallwood covered the entire northern half of King county. There was no part of Buffalo Crossing on the North side of the river. He leaned over the map to get a better look, "This isn't Buffalo Crossing is it?"

"It's Kingston." She paused. "But don't read Bruce Haley for that mystery. This book has got to be over a hundred years old."

Wil shot her a look of disbelief while flipping through the silky feeling pages.

"Ok." She giggled softly. "This specific copy has been recently updated with modern pictures and maps. We have a copy of the same book that was bound in the early 1900's." She got up, almost disappearing into the gloom. The morning light came in through a line of windows near the ceiling. That light was the only thing that allowed him to follow her dark dress in the gloom. Later that evening, when the light changed, she would be nearly invisible as she haunted the shelves. She pulled a book off the shelf and began to return with it.

It was a thick, dark tome that was faded with dust and disuse. She placed it on the table and before she opened it, Wil saw the red lettering; Early Elkhorn Life, Dr. Bruce Haley. She quickly but carefully flipped through the ancient text until she found the page with the map matching the one on the newer edition.

Updated didn't always mean better. The older map was hand drawn, each building had individual bricks or stones, every tree came complete with a tiny shadow. Despite the age-induced fade of the ink, the water of the Elkhorn appeared to actually be flowing through the distillery. It was a beautiful.

Wil reached for the coffee again, careful around the twin books. He sipped hesitantly, his upper lip was still a bit numb. He found it safe. "Are you some sort of King County historian?" He took another longer sip.

"No." She shrugged. "Every fifth grader in the town learns about Kingston and the King's Cellars distillery. When I was in school, there was even a song about Ole Bartholomew Cane. Her eyes drifted over Wil's head and she hummed a few notes. She stopped, cleared her throat, then hummed a few more notes, then shook her head. "Can't remember it."

Wil laughed, "Well that's unfortunate. I'd like to hear that song, if you ever do."

"Yesterday you were looking for Dogman, and today it's Kingston?" One dark eyebrow arched over a blue eye.

He looked down at the twin books. The text on both were identical, font, size, words. Other than the faded ink in the older copy, even the footnotes were identical. What was he looking for anyway? He looked back at Cindy with a smile that he hoped looked more genuine than it felt. "You never know when or where Dogman will show up."

She leaned forward placing a hand on Wil's out-stretched arm. "Then you are looking in the wrong place." She squeezed his arm and then let it go, withdrawing back to her side of the table.

Wil set the half empty mug down and learned forward. "How do you know?"

"There are plenty of rumors, and theories around the town of Kingston, but I have never heard of any that involve Dogman."

Wil was confused, "What do you mean rumors and theories? This didn't happen in the stone age. How can no one know what happened? This is a town we're talking about, right?"

She smiled wryly, and cocked her head slightly to the side. She reached up with one hand running her fingers through her wavy locks, each one fell right back into place. "A fire burnt the town to the ground. The distillery exploded and the Wallwood burned all the way to Frankfort." She took a deep breath before continuing. "Some say it was a lighting strike, or an accident at the distillery. Others claim it was just a careless camper that started the blaze."

"That is all very interesting," He held the mug up to his lips. "And I agree with you, that none of it sounds like Dogman."

"No." She smiled and shook her head a bit. The gap in her teeth peeked through her parted lips. "No Dogman in this story. But there is a theory just as farfetched." She looked around, there were a few people browsing the shelves on the fiction side of the library, but no one was really near them. Still, she leaned over the table, causing Wil to lean forward as well. They met over the twin books and she whispered, almost into his ear. "Burning witches."

"You mean like..." Wil had been whispering and realized how silly he sounded and grinned. "You mean like Salem?" He leaned back, regaining his normal voice.

"There you go." She leaned back as well and started to stand. "It's not Dogman, but its on the same level of possibility."

"I'll have to look into that. I'll let you know if I find anything interesting."

She turned to walk away, "And I'll let you know if I remember the song about Bartholomew Cane."

Wil stood dumbly, wanting more than anything to come up with a witty stinger to their conversation to match hers. What he said was, "Thanks for the coffee." He hung his head in defeat. And that is when he saw it.

King's Cellars straddled the river in the older book, but the newer map had the river running about a quarter of a mile behind the distillery.

20

The Detective

Wil had been avoiding going into the office since the "pissing contest," as Beth had so elegantly described it. That was the reason he had been spending so much time at the library. Well, it was one of the reasons he had been spending so much time at the library. But, according to Sherry at the front desk, Steve had not come into the office much lately either. He was chasing some big story about missing people.

Wil wanted to put some finishing touches on his review of this week's football game. The BCHS Buffalo faced off against the Wolverines of Western Hills in a match that went down to the wire. Unfortunately, the Wolverines were able to hold the Buffalo at bay in the end. Wil hadn't gone to the game, but he did watch a tape of it in fast forward while taking notes. He had only read one paragraph when Beth called to him from her office.

"Willard, come in here for a minute." The door remained open, but she had quickly retreated back inside. His heart picked up as his mind raced through possibilities for why she wanted to see him. When he reached the door, she was already seated behind her desk.

"Open or closed?" Wil grabbed at the door knob.

"Whichever you prefer." Newspapers were piled eight high across the surface of her desk. Her elbows rested comfortably on top of the scattered stacks of newsprint. She motioned to the chair opposite her before folding her hands and resting them on her chin. "Have a seat."

Wil took a deep breath as he pulled the door closed. This scene was far too familiar, only instead of a bald elderly man, a middle-aged woman sat calmly waiting to break him. He would have to move again if he got fired.

"I wanted to talk to you in person." Her voice was as flat as her chin length ashen hair, a greying-blond frame for her severe face. She paused long enough to cause Wil to shift uncomfortably in his chair. "Your story about cancer, I'm not sure it sends the right message."

"What do you mean?" Wil's heart slowed slightly but he thought he felt a bead of sweat forming on his brow. He was unsure where this was heading.

"Moonbeam has led a very interesting life. And I'm sure that hearing her tell these stories makes them seem even more fantastic." She leaned forward, placing her hands on the newsprint in front of her. But her eyes never left Wil's. "I'm just not sure it fits with the standards of the Buffalo Crossing Journal."

Wil let a small smile part his lips, his heart returned to normal speed, but the bead of sweat still rolled down his forehead. He would gladly defend his article, that was something he had grown accustomed to doing in his career. It was also much easier than defending his job.

"Did you get my updated draft? I included interviews with several of Cheryl's close friends. I also got a few quotes from her oncologist."

"Yes, I saw the latest draft. The doctor interview really helps with the credibility issues. You also keep referring to her as Cheryl. Half the town won't know who you're talking about."

Wil tipped his head forward slightly, grin never leaving his lips. "She introduced herself to me as Cheryl, so that is the name I used."

Beth's hands unlaced, and she started to tap the newsprint on her desk, absently, with one finger. "I always like featuring stories about local people, but I can't publish an article that tells people to ignore modern medicine."

Wil actually agreed with Beth, and that made his position difficult to argue. He began to scan the pristine book shelves that walled one side of the office, floor to ceiling; The Hound of the Baskervilles, A Study in Scarlet, and other books of short stories by Sir Arthur Conan Doyle. The next shelf held a collection of Edgar Rice Burroughs; Tarzan's Quest, Tarzan of the Apes, The Son of Tarzan. There were even of couple ancient looking books from The Princess of Mars series.

"Maybe I could put a disclaimer at the beginning of the article." Wil hoped she would go for it, this was the only idea he had. "I could say something like, 'the following is Cheryl's experience alone and the BCJ suggest you seek medical help if you find yourself in a similar situation." He gave a half smile and half cringe. It was the best he could come up with.

She clapped and stood up, but never quite smiled. "Good enough, have it to me within the hour. We are going to print tonight."

"Tonight?" Wil stood up slowly, a bit dumbfounded.

"Special Edition, Steve is on to something big. Missing townsfolk. People get ravenous for information about this kind of thing." Her face remained serious, but a strange expression shadowed her eyes. "An issue with no new information will be read by twice as many people as one printed in calmer times."

Wil then realized what was remaining unsaid, that the advertisers know about the higher readership as well. She continued after opening the office door to show him out. "Sometimes getting the right person, the right information will help break open a case like this. The increased readership will hopefully help solve the case. The family deserves that much."

It was a nice sentiment, but he noted that her eyes were still shadowed in what he now recognized as dollar signs. "I'll have the story to you in 20 minutes."

"With your piece, the special edition will be more than a single sheet. It gives some much-needed meat to the issue."

She closed the door before he could respond. He sat down at his desk and pulled up the article about Cheryl. Incredible as her story seemed to be, Wil had nearly forgotten about his encounter with the old hippie. His mind had completely moved on to the next lead. The lead which seemed insignificant when juxtaposed with the news that a member of the small community had gone missing.

The following article contains the miraculous account of the last few years in the life of one of Buffalo Crossing's own citizens. As amazing as Cheryl's journey has been, please remember that this story is hers alone. The Buffalo Crossing Journal recommends seeking help from a medical professional if any reader finds themselves in a situation similar to Cheryl's.

Wil leaned back and rubbed his eyes. Despite the seeming insignificance of the differences between the maps, Wil's thoughts kept drifting back to it. In the older book the river ran right through the distillery, but the river was at least a quarter mile from the ruins in the newer book. Upon closer inspection, it looked like the two maps showed different spots on the river, unless a giant earthquake occurred to shift the flow of the Elkhorn in the past 80 plus years.

He needed to focus. There was one more thing he had to add.

Cheryl will be resuming her monthly Dream Catching Sessions (DCS) in the near future. Please see the flyer on the bulletin board at the Green Grocer for details about the DCS or upcoming solstice/equinox celebrations.

Maybe this lack of focus was simply a manifestation of his worry that he actually had nothing at all. His stomach dropped down to his feet and he started salivating when Will noticed the maps. The feeling had preceded a couple of journalistic breakthroughs, but it has also preceded trouble. He began to question his intuition as he realized what he knew so far. An old book has a map in a different location than every other book in the library.

Compared to the tragedy of loss for the residents of the town, the misprinted map will be easily explained away. There is also an element of fear to consider. Will anyone else go missing and who is responsible? An outsider? One of our own? The thought made Wil shiver. He was probably much closer to being an outsider than one of their own. The sooner this whole thing was over, the better.

His mind snapped back to the old almanac he had found at the library. There wasn't a map of the distillery in the almanac. There was a map of an area that looked like the place all the newer maps showed as ruins. I guess that would be two misprints.

21

Practicing What One Preaches

Lloyd pretended to read the side of the milk carton for a minute before placing it in his basket. He waited a moment longer before closing the cooler door. Though it would soon be autumn, the late summer heat was relentless. While several beads of sweat trickled down Lloyd's sides, he watched a young man wearing basketball shorts and a tank top digging through the ice cream freezer in the corner of the store. After a slight pang of envy, Lloyd calmed himself with a deep breath and a small tug on his jacket. It would not be right for him to walk around dressed like some kind of athlete.

Lloyd always went about his business in a coat with slacks, if not a full suit. Today he was wearing light colored khakis with a dark blue blazer. And if anyone bothered to look closely enough, they would see blue on blue lines criss-crossing the entire jacket. He hoped no one would look that close though. If anyone did they would surely spot the spreading dark circles under his armpits. He turned into the cookie aisle and was immediately glad for his choice of attire, despite the heat.

Sheriff Hawkins was standing in the aisle examining two cans of coffee side by side. He was in full uniform, dark slacks with a shiny line running down the outer seam. His shoes were polished to a shine so fine, Lloyd noticed that he needed to smooth down his hair by looking into them.

"Sheriff Hawkins, how are you on this fine day?"

The big man turned and locked his gunmetal eyes on the reverend's stormy, grey on grey. A split second later a large smile bloomed across the Sheriff's face. "Well, if it isn't Reverend Todd." His deep jovial voice seemed to cut through all the other noise in the store. "Only the essentials today Rev?"

Lloyd flicked his grey eyes down to his basket; milk, eggs, lunchmeat, and bread. The way the Sheriff's voice carried, Lloyd felt like a performance was warranted. "I have heard it said that only the penitent man shall pass into the Kingdom of Heaven." Lloyd moved his basket over to his right hand to give his left arm a rest. "A penitent man is humble, and a humble man needs very little." Lloyd gave a quick wink while turning the basket a bit to give the Sheriff a better view of its contents.

Sheriff Hawkins steely eyes shot down to the coffee in his own hands. "I hope the kingdom above will forgive a man in need." He laughed a bit. "I have to find some way to stay awake on days as warm as today." The big man leaned down close, and whispered loud enough to be heard two aisles over. "It's probably a sin but half the time I drink this stuff cold."

Lloyd laughed this time, "I've yet to find any mention of the sin of cold coffee." Lloyd paused, bringing one finger up to his lips as if in thought before adding. "It has been a while since I've read Numbers. I'll let you know what I find."

They both laughed heartily at that. Lloyd was thrilled. This performance couldn't have gone better if Sheriff Hawkins had been in on it. Before the laughed faded away into an awkward silence, Lloyd continued still laughing. "Don't feel too bad Sheriff. I can't get to the checkout without passing by all of those cookies." Lloyd gestured toward the other end of the store. "I bet several of those boxes make it into my basket before…"

A loud crackle of static startled Lloyd before he could finish his thought. He flinched at the burst that was followed by voices. The big man pulled a large handheld radio off his belt. "I'm sorry Rev." He lifted the blocky tech to his mouth and hit a button with one gripping finger. "Sheriff." The tone of his voice had completely changed. It was still deep, but had become flat, emotionless, dictatorial.

Lloyd supposed the Sheriff needed to exert a certain type of authority in his position. The response that came back was preceded by another burst of static. The distorted voice said something about a truck and a reporter, but it was mostly unintelligible. The big man seemed to catch more than Lloyd, because his face had hardened.

"I'm sorry to rush out Rev, but duty calls." His voice had softened a bit, but didn't return to its original jocularity.

"I understand. I hope everyone is alright." Lloyd gave a slight frown of concern. "Will you be making it to church tonight?" The last question was more of a reflex than anything else. He said it to let anyone still listening to this performance know about the service.

"I imagine I will be." He turned and started down the aisle. "This shouldn't take too long, but you never know."

Lloyd watched him walk briskly down the aisle for a second then followed the big man toward the front of the store. Before the Sheriff turned the corner, Lloyd saw him raise the radio again. "I'm heading that way, just sit tight." His authoritative tone carried well. It was clearly audible from the back of the store where Lloyd stood.

He switched the basket back to his left hand and continued toward the checkout lanes. He caught the eye of a young woman pushing a half-full buggy. They shared a smile, and Lloyd wondered if she went to church? He didn't think she was a member of his own congregation. The reverend grabbed a package of chocolate chips as he passed the cookie section.

The cashier was reading the newspaper when he entered the line. Her stringy hair was limply touching her shoulders. Her face scrunched in concentration, which pushed her coke bottle glasses higher up her face. Lloyd emptied his basket and placed it at the end of the conveyor belt, behind his items. He had just enough time to read the headline.

Buffalo Crossing Journal

Extra Edition

TWO GO MISSING

That's when the cashier noticed him standing there, and began to fold the paper back, placing it to the side. "I'm sorry sir," Her glasses magnified her eyes, doubling their size. "I got caught up in my reading."

Lloyd recognized her from his congregation, but could not place her name. Luckily for Lloyd, God created name tags. "Mary," She stopped typing on her keyboard and looked up at the sound of her name, "Does this store have copies of that paper for sale?"

"Yeah. Let me grab one for you, Reverend." She walked to the end of another checkout lane and returned with a fresh copy of the extra edition. "I think you will be very interested in this." She handed the paper over to him.

He smiled at her, grimly. "It appears that there may be someone nearby in need of support." He looked over the front page again. Perhaps Crossing's Baptist Church can offer support to the families of the missing. And eventually become a new family for the grieving.

Mary cocked her head sideways and gave a funny look. Her already large eyes, bulged in confusion. "It is terrible what happened with the missing people." Her voice was flat, but gained confidence when she added. "But, I meant the other story on the inside. She's gonna start her Devil Church again." Lloyd opened the paper, the other article was headlined, Miracle on Rutledge Road. "She's pretending to be part of some miracle to draw people into her devil worship."

Lloyd was stunned. He felt more trickles of sweat running down his sides, and his shirt was beginning to stick a bit on his back. "Devil Worship? Surely she doesn't actually worship the devil." He did not believe that anyone could be that crass.

"Some of the stories I've heard..." She trailed off shaking her head, while trying to whistle. "I'm more afraid of Moonbeam than I am of any missing people."

Lloyd thought she might actually be paling at the thought. She was very shaken by the story. Lloyd always thought of himself as a man who practiced what he preached. "Do me a favor, Mary. All of the energy you would have spent worrying about this," He shook the paper a bit causing a light rustle. "I want you to take that energy and use it to bake a pie. Give that pie to the family members of the missing people." He gave her a quick show smile and winked one of his stormy grey eyes at her. She blushed and turned away. "If you can do that for me, I will talk to this Moonbeam person. Do we have a deal?"

She smiled and nodded. "Will you be joining us for the midweek sermon tonight?" He handed her a ten-dollar bill and two singles, he could see the total on the screen. Mary was apparently not going to tell him.

She took the cash and quickly turned to her opening cash drawer. Lloyd thought the light blush on her cheeks was reddening further. "Unfortunately, I will be working during the service. I normally never miss a sermon, but a coworker went on vacation suddenly." She counted out some change and dropped it into his open palm. "Can you believe she called from the airport to say she would be gone for two whole weeks."

Lloyds eyes widened in exaggerated surprise. "Oh.

Where did she go?"

"Italy." She tore off the receipt and gave it to him.

"If only we could all be so lucky." He grabbed the paper bag, carefully folding down the top. "I'm sorry that you have to miss tonight's sermon on the beatitudes, but I'm sure your sacrifice will reap your friend quite a bit of happiness." He picked up his bag and nodded toward the cashier with a huge show smile. "Have a nice day, Mary."

As he passed through the automatic sliding glass door at the front of the store, Lloyd's mind remained with Mary and her fears. Could there really be a devil worshiper in this small town? Lloyd didn't think so, but he supposed anything was possible. The heat outside was so oppressive that Lloyd thought the devil himself would be comfortable in it, whether or not the beast had any servants in town. His white t-shirt was sticking to his back and stomach, and he could no longer distinguish any individual trickle of sweat.

Lloyd resolved to go home and put on a pair of shorts and a clean shirt. He was going to sit in a chair directly in front of his window AC unit, and he was going to read the whole paper. And when he finally felt cool again, he would decide what to do about everything he had just read. The missing locals and the alleged devil worshiper.

Lloyd was about to climb into his car when he saw the sheriff driving his service jeep through the parking lot. The reverend raised a hand to wave when, unexpectedly, one of his deputies flagged him down, running up to the vehicle. After a short exchange the Sheriff roared, "Get in before somebody does something stupid." The deputy quickly hopped in the vehicle and in a flash of blue and wail of a siren, the Jeep was speeding out of the lot.

Lloyd hoped that everyone would be ok, but he felt confident that whatever the problem may be, Sheriff Hawkins could handle it. He was a good and godly man. Lloyd really didn't have time to worry about the Sheriff right now though, he had his own issues to handle. But, if Mary kept her end of the deal, one of his problems would be building a strong foundation for a solution. It was important that he practiced what he preached, and with all his actions, he hoped to bring others to the light of Jesus.

22

The Explorer

A white and purple splotch suddenly appeared on Wil's windshield accompanied by a soft splat. He turned the windshield wipers on, mumbling under his breath. "Someone has been eating berries." The paved road became a gravel road as the wipers first smeared and then cleared the glass. Wil slowed his rust bucket down a bit to accommodate the new surface. He supposed he was going to the right place based on Sherry's directions. But many paved roads eventually turned to gravel if you follow them long enough.

The mighty Elkhorn flowed next to the road on its path to meet up with the Kentucky River near Frankfort. The road, for lack of a better term, followed the curves of the river. It was hard to say whether Old Elkhorn road would even be passable during a summer with even a little bit of rain. The river itself, was normally not much more than a creek, but the recent drought had diminished it to a trickle. In its current state, the Elkhorn still nearly flowed over the edges of the road on a few curves.

At least the sun was shining brightly. Wil found the heat bearable compared to the unease he had felt the last time he drove down a winding country road on the advice of a local. It had been pitch-black then, the only light coming from his headlights. And the directions had been from a much less reliable source.

Wil had been at the office, typing out the obituaries and adding a little flare to the football game coverage. All the mundane stuff that had to be accomplished in order for him to chase down a good story. The extra edition had been popular, but the regular paper was still scheduled. Sherry was hanging up the phone as Wil walked passed the front desk to leave.

Sherry's hair bounced, a short grey bob. "Steve said he found a car, thinks it might be Howard's. He has been missing for days now." She puckered her lips in a pout. "But, Steve gets excited pretty easily, probably just some teenager's truck. When I was younger, that area was where couples who were going steady would park and neck."

"Where is he? Or the truck?" Wil leaned on the counter in front of Sherry.

"Down on the east branch of the Old Elkhorn Drive." After a few seconds of a blank stare, she gave him better directions. "Just head down Main Street toward the distillery, and take the last left before you drive into BC distillery."

The lightly graveled drive eventually became a rutted path of slightly tamped down grass. Before he could wonder how many gravel roads turned into nothing, Wil saw the blue lights dancing on the lowest leaves of a tree ahead. He pulled off the rutted trail next to Steve's mini pick-up.

"I'm the guy who called you!" Even if he had not been screaming, Wil would have known how angry Steve was by the color of his face. Usually a bit ruddy, Steve's pudgy cheeks were almost purple and they were getting darker with every word. "I find Howard's truck, run down to the distillery, call the police, and now you won't let me look around? This is a big ole pile of crap!"

"I'm sorry sir." The new deputy couldn't have been more than 20 years old. The hat and reflective glasses failed to hide his youth. "This is a crime scene." He tried, and failed, to suppress a smile. Deputy Youth was enjoying this.

Wil thought he could have some fun too. Steve and the deputy continued arguing in front of the meadow next to the rutted path. The police car was parked parallel to the road in a hasty attempt to block off the area. Wil slipped easily between the back of the car and a large maple, into the meadow.

Trees surrounded the meadow on two sides, and the river blocked off the third side. The Wallwood on the other side of the river bed was thick. Wide and gnarled trunks sent branches arching over the shallow waters to vie for light. It appeared nearly impenetrable. There was a large, flat-topped boulder near the center of the meadow. It had a great view of the Elkhorn. Sunlight was glinting off something at the base of the giant rock, or to be more accurate, sun light was glinting off thousands of somethings. Broken glass? The truck was parked several yards behind the boulder. That was when Officer Youth noticed Wil.

"Sir!" He managed all the authority of an entitled teenager. "This is a crime scene and you need to stay behind the police line." He left Steve and began to march toward Wil.

The other officer on the scene, who had been investigating the ground on the far side of the meadow, by the treeline, stood up and turned around. He was grabbing for something on his belt. After a burst of static the older officer said, "Sheriff Hawkins, over."

Wil quickly walked around to try to get a look in the truck. The bed was empty, and he didn't make it far enough to see much of the interior before the deputy caught him. A burst of static echoed through both deputies' radio, startling Wil. "Sheriff." The voice was distorted and unrecognizable, the word was garbled and difficult to understand. The older officer responded, but Wil didn't catch the conversation because Deputy Youth appeared in front of him.

"Sir!" He managed to maintain his previous 'air' of authority as he pointed toward the police car. "You need to stay behind the police line."

"Oh?" Wil feigned ignorance. "I'm sorry officer, I didn't see any yellow tape."

The young man did not move an inch. His arm stayed outstretched as if pointing the way, while blocking any other path. The embroidering above the brown lapel of his chest pocket named him, B. Mosely. "This way sir."

Wil followed the order and began walking toward the front of the police car. The radios burst to life again with a voice that was deep and garbled. "...heading (Skree!) ...at way. (Skree!) sit tight."

Steve had wandered closer to the older officer, who had placed the radio back on his belt and resumed his work by the treeline. He made sure to stay reasonably close to the imaginary police line, his face had cooled to a ruddy hue that was only slightly darker than normal. Right on cue, Officer Mosely corralled Steve back to the squad car. As the older reporter approached the car, he gave Wil a quizzical look. His round face tilted forward a bit. His eyebrows, that stood out as white shadows on his pink forehead, raised toward his bald spot. His lips pursed tight. A look that seemed to say, 'What the hell are you doing here?'

"If either one of you crosses this line again I WILL arrest you" His words were emphasized with spit as he spoke. He then drew a line with his finger pointing from the car to the treeline on the other side of the meadow.

"Officer Mosely." The older officer was calling from the opposite side of the meadow. "Give me a hand with this."

Mosely looked at Steve, and then at Wil before turning to go help his partner. Looking into those highly reflective lenses might have been intimidating. They seemed to scream out, "I can see you, but you can't see me." Unfortunately for Officer Youth, the baby face below the sunglasses ruined the effect.

In Mosley's absence, Steve turned on Wil. "What the hell are you doin' here?" He almost growled as he spoke, his face began to darken again.

"I was standing at the front desk when you called Sherry. I thought you might need some help."

Steve's growl seemed to deepen, "You trying to scoop me boy?" One pudgy hand grabbed at Wil's shoulder.

Wil used his other arm to grab Steve's other shoulder and looked into the shorter man's bloodshot eyes. "There was a bunch of broken glass by that boulder and the truck bed was empty," Steve's grip loosened a bit as Wil spoke, "I couldn't really see much inside the truck's cab, but what I did see looked spotless." Wil checked to see if Deputy Mosely was returning. He wasn't, but Wil lowered his voice anyway. "My first thought was robbery gone wrong, I wish I could have seen if the radio was missing."

Steve's hand fell limply back to his side, "You're trying to help me?"

Officer Mosely was heading back over, his pompous smirk had been replaced by a scowl. He ignored the two reporters and opened the passenger door to the cruiser.

Wil moved his hand and clapped Steve on the back. He started to guide him away from the meadow and the two began to walk down the rutted path a bit. When they were a safe distance from deputized ears, Wil began to speak again. "Two people have gone missing in town. Do you really think that these guys," Wil jerked a thumb over his shoulder, "have any chance of solving these crimes?" Wil's words were quiet but passionate.

Steve squinted and curled his lip, like he smelled something distasteful, "You aren't one of those King's Men conspiracy theorists, are you?"

"A what?"

"Never mind." Steve looked over his shoulder toward the crime scene. "Looks like playtime is over." Officer Mosely was stringing neon yellow police tape across the meadow. One side was tied around the tree that Wil slipped by, and he was blocking the entire meadow. "I'm gonna get out of here and see what I can find out from Howard's wife." Steve shot out a meaty hand and Wil grabbed it tentatively. "Thanks for coming down here, I'll take all the info I can get."

Wil smiled, "I didn't see much."

"Well," Steve reached down to hitch up his pants. They were constantly being pushed down by his protruding belly. "You saw more than I did." White teeth appeared in the middle of his otherwise reddish pink face. "All I saw was Ingle picking something up with tweezers and placing it in an evidence bag, didn't even see what it was." He began walking toward his car.

"Hey!" Wil called to him after several steps, "Are the ruins to the old distillery up this way?" He pointed further down the dirt and grass rutted path running beside the meadow.

"Yeah, I wouldn't try to drive to it though. Steve shrugged, "It might be a ten-minute walk." With a wave he ducked into the little red truck.

Wil gave one last look to the officers, both of whom were watching him from behind the newly strung police tape. He shot them a quick sarcastic smile and then began down the rutted path. He heard Steve's truck start and back up. He also heard a loud burst of static from the radio behind him before the song of the forest drowned every other noise out. Wind rustling leaves, birds singing, his own steps swishing through grass and crunching on dried leaves that had fallen too soon due to the drought.

The trees grew very close to the path here. Steve was right, it would have been impossible to drive even Wil's little rust bucket through here. It ran mostly straight, with a few bends and curves that kept Wil from seeing any chance that the forest would open up again. The emerald canopy was lit like stained glass in the afternoon sun. Wil could see little bits of brown glowing in the sunlight as well. Even the trees were not immune to the effects of the drought.

The farther down this trail he walked, the larger the trees became. The forest was becoming denser. With every step, less sunlight made it through the growing depths of the limbs arching out above him. The ground on the left side of the path began to rise. It started as a slight slope, but quickly grew into an impassibly steep grade. He was beginning to feel trapped, there would be no escape should he come across some fierce wild animal on the trail.

As the light faded, Wil's sense of dread increased. He turned a small curve in the path and could finally see a literal light at the end of the dark emerald tunnel. At the exact moment that he saw the light, something thin and airy brushed against his cheek. One hand quickly rose to wipe it away. A few steps farther and the feeling returned, but this time the light touch was felt over the left half of his face, tickling his lips, and sticking in his eyelashes. A word sprang into his mind causing his heart to skip. Spiderweb.

Both hands frantically rubbed at his face. He vigorously grabbed and pulled at the invisible silk clinging to his nose and chin. He thought he had freed himself from the bug trap several times, only to have another strand blow across his face. He would need to shower before he felt clean again. He knew that there was another string just waiting to surprise him when he least suspected it, or worse, an angry arachnid looking for revenge.

He wasn't afraid of spiders, but the thought of one

crawling around on him in stealth was still creepy. Wil saw that he was only about 20 yards from the place where the forest opened up around the trail again. He took a deep breath, put his arms in front of his face and ran toward the light.

23

On The Right Trail

Wil kept pinching at his nose with the fingers of his right hand, over and over again, but he could not find the invisible strand tickling him. His left hand was grabbing awkwardly at the back of his neck, elbow high above his head. There were several wisps brushing at his bare arms but, that could wait, his face needed to be cleared of the eight-legged demons.

Using both hands, Wil wiped his face from brow to chin, but the offending irritant remained in place. After several more passes, he was able to remove the resilient webbing that clung to his face. Wil began jumping and scratching every itch, every tickle, every spot his clothes touched his skin. To him, these all felt like eight little legs scurrying across his body. When he caught his breath, and his composure, he found his fingers were sticky with spider silk.

The covered trail opened into a small grass meadow, cut by a little stream. It appeared to be dry at the moment. The waist-high grass made it difficult to see, brown and sickly as it was. The steep hillside on the left of the path receded back into a valley of sorts. The little brook appeared to originate from the valley and ran under the narrow path, through a culvert. But there were no ruins, so he continued. The path was lightly graveled again on this side of the 'tunnel.'

Wil was about to turn back when the trees began to crowd the road again, but he saw an old stone wall just off the side of the path. It was about a foot tall and was made with flat smooth stones that had been pulled out of a shallow river or creek bed. Some of these stones had toppled over and now lay on both sides of the wall. Wil saw at least one tree that had fought the wall for space and won. There was something old out here, the stone wall proved it.

Wil's eyes were drawn away from the wall when the trees closing in on the trail disappeared revealing a meadow strewn with stone and wood and iron. The road split in front of the ruins. One path continued to weave its way through the Wallwood, the other ran over a cattle gate flanked by tall stone walls. Wil was much more interested in the ruins. They were all that was left of the short-lived town of Kingston. Rough cut stone blocks, were haphazardly stacked into vague wall-like lines. Stones and wood of all shapes and sizes littered the ground but he thought he could make out the general outline of the foundation of a large building. Broken and rotting wood had been discarded into chaotic stacks in several places through the ruins.

Leaning against one of the tallest of the remaining stone walls was a substantial iron sign. Time had allowed the rust to eat away at the slightly oval iron ring. Red chunks were missing from the flat brownish letters spanning the center of the melting hoop. One of the rust eaten holes, in particular, appeared to be bite shaped. The muddy red stains that ran down the stone wall behind the sign, along with the reddish shade of the earth underneath, created a pretty gruesome picture. But the letters were still legible, KCD, for Kings' Cellars Distillery.

Wil hopped over the now waist-high rock wall to get a better look at the rubble. Thickets of crab grass grew tall around some of the structures and toppled stones. There was a single barrel sitting in a still-standing corner of wall on the far side of the field. Carefully stepping over some stones and onto others, Wil crossed the debris littered ground. He heard a few scuffles behind him along the way; a stone shifting back into place after he dislodged it, a leaf or loose piece of wood moving in the wind, rats maybe. With all the rotting wood for nests and stone blocks offering protection from some weather, this was probably a breeding ground for snakes and rats and spiders, oh my. The thought caused a chill to run tingling down his spine.

The barrel was weather worn and fading. It was bleached white by the sun and greyed with age. The wood was still surprisingly solid considering it was almost 200 years old. The iron that held the barrel staves together, however, had completely rusted away, leaving only brownish stains running down the wood as evidence that they ever existed. The fact that the barrel remained together despite the lack of support was its own sort of miracle.

The ground around the barrel was carpeted with rotting wood staves and rings of rust. This must have been an aging room or the place that they assembled the casks, it appeared to be the only area that Wil could see any evidence of barrels. Wil kicked over one of the staves on the ground. It wasn't even charred on the concave side. Wil knew that bourbon barrels were burned on the inside, it had something to do with the flavor of the finished liquor. But these staves had no char at all. Wasn't there a town destroying fire around here?

He supposed it was possible that burning the inside of the barrels was not common in the late 18th century. He supposed it was possible that this area did not burn for one reason or another. As soon as the thought crossed his mind, he knew that it was wrong. The wall behind the still standing barrel had scorch marks. He bent down to examine one of the blackened stones. The smooth surface had been completely burned at some time and had faded to a smokey grey. A light wipe with his shirt tail did nothing to clean the rock.

In contrast, the stone underneath was a creamy white-beige with no sign of fire at all. Wil leaned back to take a wider look at the half-tumbled wall in front of him. There was a white stone, surrounded on three sides by stones that were completely scorched and another section looked like a checker board.

The scuffling came again. This time it was much closer, too close. It also came with the accompaniment of a shadow that fell over the reporter. Wil was bent over at the waist, and before he had time to react, a strong arm wrapped around his neck. Another crossed around his middle, pinning his right arm to his chest. The assailant was taking advantage of Wil's position by leaning heavily on his back and squeezing.

Wil instinctively stood, but that only made the pressure on his neck worse. His attacker's breaths were excited and quick, but ragged. He could feel the warm puffs of air against the back of his neck. With his free hand, Wil reached back and grabbed the first thing he found. The dirty straw hat ripped free easily. When Wil dropped it, the wind carried it away. Greasy grey locks of hair framed his vision. Something else was creeping into his periphery as well. Darkness?

Wil bent his knees and pushed as hard as he could. The assailant took a small step backward, but did not lessen his grip. The black continued to squeeze at the edges of Wil's vision. He bent his legs to attempt one more escape, but his legs just crumpled underneath him. The pin prick of light that had become his vision closed, but the wheezing breath behind him continued.

24

Starting the Conversation

Moonbeam was sitting in her rocking chair contemplating everything that needed to be done before the equinox. Or more accurately, she was listening to the rhythmic creak of the chair rocking back and forth. Suddenly, a man's voice cut through her thoughts.

"Hello?" There were three knocks following the word. The heavy double doors in front of the house and the back door in the kitchen were open to allow a breeze through the house. Moonbeam was wondering if that had been a mistake. Luckily, Shawn was out on a walk.

She grabbed the arms of the rocker and stood up while the chair was swinging forward. "Coming." She called. A man with sandy blond hair, wearing a light blue suit was standing and sweating in the doorway. "How may I help you sir?" The professional smile that was plastered on his face made her feel slightly uneasy. He was some sort of salesman, she could tell.

"I'm here to speak with Ms. Rutledge."

She laughed a little, "Well, I guess that would be me. Though, most people just call me Moonbeam. Call me whatever you wish."

The smile seemed to widen a little, which was impressive. She didn't think it could get any closer to his ears. "I am Reverend Lloyd Todd." He reached one hand out, and Moonbeam shook it cautiously.

"Pleasure to meet you Reverend Todd."

"Oh, the pleasure is all mine, Ms. Rutledge. Please call me Lloyd." The smile on his face dimmed a bit for the first time since she had laid eyes on him. "I would love to sit and talk with you, but I understand if you are busy." He held up both of his hands palms toward her, and bowed his head slightly. "I would have called before I came out here, but I was told that would not be possible." His dark eyes met hers again. "Do you think we could carve out some time this week to discuss some things?"

"No need for that." She waved him in invitingly. "Come on in, Lloyd. I'm free for a few hours." She was curious why this reverend would come all this was just to see her. Salesman indeed. She walked him into the dining room and gestured to the bench next to the long wooden table.

Lloyd didn't notice. He was too busy gawking at everything. His eyes went from the rocking chair, to the narrow hall table, and finally rested on the large dining room table. All were meticulously crafted by hand.

"My grandfather built it." She ran her fingers lightly over the surface of the table. Granddaddy built most of the furniture in the house."

He rapped lightly on the table with one knuckle, it was solid wood, thick and heavy. "This is incredible. Your grandfather was quite the carpenter." He looked around again from the rocker, to the narrow hall table, and back to the dinning room table. "You can tell he really loved his work." That plastic, professional smile returned to his lips in a flash. "Did he build the cabin as well?"

Moonbeam could spot the professional smile by the way it often left his eyes while remaining firmly entrenched on his lips. "No, that was my great-grandfather"

You have a very talented family, Moon…" He paused,

allowing a slight frown to creep over his otherwise still up-turned mouth. "May I call you Cheryl?"

She laughed, "Whatever you wish." For some reason, transplants to Buffalo Crossing had the hardest time with her name. "And you are correct. I have always found pride in the talents of my Grandy and Grandaddy. They left me very wealthy in family heirlooms." She glanced around the room until her eyes landed on the Reverend again. His Sandy hair was matted, and darkened by sweat. There was a trickle running down his cheek, it fell off his jaw and was absorbed by the rapidly darkening suit coat. "Talented as he was, my Grandy was limited by the technology of his time. A light breeze is all that I can offer you in the way of air conditioning, and I bet that nice coat blocks what little breeze Mother Nature is offering today." She glanced down at her own attire; dirty tennis shoes with a hole in the right toe, dusty sweat pants that hung off her thin legs, and a threadbare t-shirt that hung loosely from her small frame. Complete with a loose ponytail, she was ready to go on a hike, not have a meeting with a man wearing a suit.

The Reverend removed his coat, folded it carefully and placed it on the table, he even began to roll up the sleeves of the sweat soaked shirt underneath. "Thank you, I do apologize for appearing so formal," he may actually have been blushing, "but I do have a very serious matter to discuss with you today." His voice took on a grave tone.

"Please sit, this sounds important." She seated herself on the bench across the table from him.

"First of all, I want to congratulate you on your new-found vitality." His smile broadened a bit and almost appeared genuine for a second, but only a second. "If the article I read is to be believed, it is some kind of miracle. A gift from God."

She bowed her head slightly, "Thank you."

His perpetual plastic smile faded into a seriousness just short of a scowl. "But, one of my congregation has expressed some concern with what you are planning to do with the gift you have been given."

She figured that the rumors would start up again once the article had been published. Small towns with small minds were always gathering their pitchforks, but they had never actually confronted her about anything. She actually gained some respect for Reverend Todd for having the balls to come and talk to her like an adult. She smiled, blowing a short burst of air through her nostrils as she suppressed a laugh. "Was the phrase Devil Worshipper used?"

"I see, this appears to be an old complaint." It was his turn to humbly bow his head, Moonbeam thought she saw a little shame in that expression as well. "I don't mean to offend you." He raised his head and met her eyes with his own, as dark and grey as the sky before a summer storm. "I'm sure this is all just some misunderstanding. But I do have an obligation to address the concerns of my congregation." The professional smile returned, flashing a bit of big white teeth, before his lips closed again, still smiling.

"I completely understand your obligations Reverend, and I appreciate you coming up here to talk to me about it. There have been rumors about me floating around for nearly four decades." She leaned in over the table, placing her arms on the cool wood. When she spoke again it was soft enough that the Reverend leaned in close to hear her. "The truth is, people just don't trust anything that is new or different. Something they don't understand. And, I have been known to have meetings or gatherings," parties was probably more accurate, but she decided to keep that to herself, "where we discuss some of the things that others do not understand."

His eyes never left hers, a storm on the brink. "What kind of gatherings?"

She leaned back and began to absently fiddle with the hair hanging over her left shoulder. "The only thing I have planned so far are the Dreamcatcher nights. Whoever shows up shares a dream they have had recently." Moonbeam laughed a little as she thought about some of these nights before her illness. They were almost always rowdy affairs. "We always welcome a new face with open arms, but it was mostly some combination of the same six women. It was a sisterhood more than anything else. No different than a bridge club or a poker night."

The Reverend was still leaning over the table, his forearms were leaving moist streaks on the hardwood. "Sounds like you are a close group of friends. Dreams are intimate things to share."

"You know, I have often found that the only way to fully understand my own dreams is to listen to other people's interpretation of them." Her eyes had drifted off to Reverend Todd's left, not really focusing on anything as she thought of the best way to explain. Her head cocked to the side causing a short strand of hair to fall across her face. It had come loose from her pony tail to brush against her cheek. "I can then keep my personal revelations a secret and continue in the mirth of the evening with a greater understanding of myself and my purpose." She laughed again and turned her eyes back to him. "I always hoped the others were doing the same. Getting to know themselves by sharing with us."

"Thats actually quite beautiful, Cheryl. I can't believe such a gathering of friends could stir up the type of rumors that I was told." His tone was kind, but the expression on his face emphasized the words can't and believe.

"No." She agreed. "I don't suppose the dream catcher meetings inspire much fear. But for some reason, the practice of meditation and reiki don't sit well with people."

One eyebrow flicked up inquisitively on the Reverend's

head. "Now I think I understand meditation, and I actually think there is value in it. The best way to accept God is to know oneself. But I am not familiar with reiki."

"Reiki is the practice of readjusting the energy in a body back into a balanced state, in theory." Moonbeam knew what this man needed to hear. She was not a 'Devil Worshipper', but she knew if she was completely honest with the reverend, the villagers would be gathering their pitchforks by dawn. So, she fibbed a little. "In reality, it is a massage with a fancy name. Those who truly believe in the healing power of reiki, seem to find more relief than those that don't." She shrugged and continued to play with the pony tail hanging over her shoulder.

"Sounds like the placebo effect."

"You know," she paused, feigning thought, "I've never thought about it like that." She had. "You may be right." She wasn't sure that he was. She has spent many years questioning whether her actions had helped people, or had they just given the perception of help. She came to the conclusion that believers seemed to find much more relief in her treatments. Much like the Reverend's own faith, those who truly believe find the most support.

Light footsteps were falling in the kitchen and coming toward the dining room. Shawn walked into the gathering hall from the kitchen. "Oh?" Her face was slightly blushed from the exertion of her walk. Her hair was tangled and frizzed from the heat and humidity. The light gleam of sweat on her face had pasted a curly brown lock of hair to her forehead, but that only seemed to accentuate her natural beauty. "I'm sorry Em, I didn't know you had company."

"It's ok. Shawn, this is the Reverend Lloyd Todd. Reverend this is Shawn Parks, she is a good friend of mine who is staying with me for a little while."

Shawn reached out and the reverend took her hand

and shook while rising from his bench seat. Moonbeam noticed a sudden blush that took his cheeks, and wondered if that was because he was meeting a pretty young woman, or if he would have had the same reaction no matter who walked through the door. A man who would wear a suit on a day as hot as today, probably didn't like to be seen in a sweat soaked dress shirt with rolled up sleeves by anyone, let alone a young looker like Shawn.

"It is a pleasure to meet you." She smiled. "I was about to go grab a glass of water. Should I get enough for everyone?"

"Oh, I'm sorry. Of course bring three glasses and as much water as your can." She turned back to Lloyd and thought she felt her own cheeks getting a little warm. She had been preparing to launch into a religious argument and had neglected to offer water to the man in need right in front of her. "It's well water but it is still pretty good."

"You still have well water after this drought?" He asked in disbelief.

"It hasn't gone dry yet." One hand turned into a fist and knocked on the hard wood producing three muffled thunks. "Knock on wood. I guess that is another marvel you can chalk up to Grandy. He knew where to dig his well."

Shawn returned with a glass pitcher full of crystal clear water. She sat the glassware on the table and it immediately started to sweat in the heat. Little droplets of water ran down the side to wet the wood below. Shawn then went into the kitchen and brought three heavy glasses, and poured each one about half full.

"It was nice to meet you Reverend, but I think I am going to take a little nap. I had an early morning."

"The pleasure was all mine, Ms. Parks." He rose to his feet like a gentleman should when a lady leaves a room.

Shawn turned toward Moonbeam, "Are we still clearing

out the grove tonight?"

Moonbeam smiled. Shawn was so young, so enthusiastic. "Even if it is just the two of us, that is the plan."

Shawn nodded and then turned toward the hall leading to the staircase. Light footsteps could be heard going up the steps and creaking across the ceiling.

Lloyd, who had watched Shawn leave, turned back toward the older woman, "Thank you for your hospitality, but I should really be heading out as well." He began reaching for his coat.

"There is one more thing we should discuss before you go." This was going to be the hard part. She would have to thread a needle. And the size and location of this particular needle depended greatly on what type of man Reverend Lloyd Todd was in reality. But it must be done. She did not want him to think her dishonest when he hears about the celebration. "I do celebrate the Solstices and Equinox'."

25

The Other Side

Lloyd stared deep into the brilliant emeralds that were her eyes. He could not read the strange expression on her face, and that made it even more difficult to maintain his show smile. "Aren't those holidays on the Wiccan calendar?" He completely failed to keep the disdain out of his voice. Was Mary right? Could devil worship in Buffalo Crossing be a reality? He slowly sat back down on the wooden bench. His eyes never left hers, green as the medieval devil himself.

"I don't know much about Wiccan practices, so I can't say how they celebrate. Around here, a few people come over, we build a bon-fire," She reached up to tuck a loose strand of grey behind her ear, "we have a few drinks," she gave a small shrug, "maybe some smoke. But, the most important part is that we commune with nature."

Her speech did nothing to calm Lloyd's concern. Only one question mattered now. "Cheryl, are you a Christian?" The question seemed to surprise her. Lloyd had cooled off quickly once he removed his coat. She had been correct, the breeze through the house was nice, but in the few seconds before she answered his question, He began to sweat again.

"I don't believe in the old man in the clouds version of God that is so readily accepted these days."

He leaned back, folding his hands together, "I guess that means the answer is no?"

She turned her head and frowned. "Not exactly. I'd say

that I am a Christian, indirectly. Or at least, at the end of the day we worship the same God."

Lloyd felt what was left of his smile curdle, but regained control of his face before his eyes rolled involuntarily. This ought to be good, he thought, but remained silent.

She remained slouched over the table, arms folded in front of her. Her voice remained steady, but her eyes sparked with a new vigor as she spoke. "There is so much beauty in nature." She turned, looking out the window behind her.

There was a bird feeder, that had been carved to look like a little cabin, hanging from the roof. A bluejay was perched on the post casually pecking at the seed as the tiny cabin rotated slowly on the wind. The little bird was almost glowing, his blue feathers were striking, the white ones blinding, and his whole body was outlined in the golden glare of the afternoon sun. Before this beautiful bird twisted into the shadow cast by the roof, Lloyd looked into its eyes. He had always though that a bird's eye was completely black, and maybe it was, but this creature had eyes that were alive with light and life.

Lloyd was overcome with the need to speak, so he tried to do so softly. "On the fifth day, God said let the birds fly." He wasn't mumbling under his breath, but he didn't know if she heard him all the same. After a few seconds more watching the bird swing in and out of the shadow cast by the roof, she turned back to him.

"And on what day did God create the Earth? What day were the plants and animals created?" She lifted one hand in his direction.

Lloyd cleared his throat, he did not trust his own voice all of the sudden, that was odd. "The heavens and the Earth on the first day." Despite his worry that he was talking with a card- carrying devil worshipper, Lloyd was curious. This was not going the way he had anticipated, and the twists keep coming. Where was she heading with all of this? Or, is there actually no point at all? "Dry land and plant life on the third day."

"All of these beautiful things were created before man." The strand of grey was free again, floating next to her cheek. She paid it no attention.

"Yes." He agreed, "All of these things were created for the benefit of mankind. Genesis 1:28 God blessed them and said, "Be fruitful and multiply. Fill the Earth and govern it. Reign over the fish in the sea, the birds in the sky, and all the animals that scurry along the ground."."

The web of wrinkles that lined her face deepened as she smiled. "God gave all of these things to mankind. It was a gift. It's all a very special kind of gift. I always try to enjoy and care for a gift that was given to me by a friend." She raised her hands off the table and turned both palms toward him, fingers splayed. "And a gift from God surely deserves proper homage."

Lloyd leaned forward, "So you worship God's creation instead of God Himself?" He kept his voice flat.

She looked away from him for the first time in a while, and placed her hands back on the deep grain of the table. Her eyes drifted into the middle distance behind him, toward the front of the home. He was about to ask if she was alright when she finally spoke.

"There used to be places in the world where the King was not referred to directly." The old woman's eyes slowly drifted back to lock on his own. "Commoners and noblemen alike could only speak to 'his grace' or 'his majesty'. They were too lowly to address the King directly. I imagine the same could be said for your Lord above."

"You worship the natural world because you feel that you are inadequate to worship God directly? I thought you said you did not believe in the 'man in the clouds'." Lloyd stopped pulling on his fingers long enough to add air quotes to the phrase.

She gently nodded her head, eyes still burning bright. "Belief is a hard thing to nail down. But I can tell you, when I am out there," she pointed over her shoulder to the window again, the bird was gone, "the symphony of the forest ringing in my ears, the faint smell of honeysuckle blowing on a light cool breeze that pulls at my hair, the fresh air, the warmth of the sun on my bare skin, loose soft earth softly scratching my toes... In the solitude of the Wallwood... The feeling I get..." Her eyes closed as she tried to explain something unexplainable. "When the conditions are just right," she took a deep breath and slowly let it out. "I feel like God and nature are one and the same."

She paused, but her eyes remained closed. When she resumed speaking, it was much softer, just above a whisper. "I bet that feeling is similar to the one you get when you find a piece of scripture that speaks directly to you." Her lids fluttered a bit, but deep crows feet remained radiating out from the corners of her now squinting eyes. "The reverent joy exploding from within. It's almost as if you are being touched by something of unfathomable magnitude. You're exhilarated and humbled, you feel special and insignificant all at the same time."

Lloyd found himself looking at his hands as he absently cracked his knuckles one at a time. He understood the feeling, he knew it well. The first time he felt it was when he was 10 years old. His mother took him to church every Sunday. One Sunday every month, a small group would gather in the rectory for coffee and gossip after the service. Lloyd didn't care for the coffee or the gossip and often found himself wandering around in the church. On one of these Sundays, Lloyd was up on the stage, inspecting the altar, when it hit him. He looked out over the empty sanctuary, colored light streaming into the pews from the leaded windows and the tower bell ringing noon. Butterflies in his stomach erupted into something much more, he almost felt sick, he almost felt as if God had chosen him.

Could all of this be a semantical misunderstanding? What I call God, she calls nature? No. It couldn't be that simple. "Where does Jesus fit into all of this?" He continued to squeeze and pull on his fingers while he waited for a response. One could not be a Christian without Christ.

Her shoulders slumped forward a little as though she dreaded the question. "I like Jesus, I think his teachings are great to follow."

Lloyd took advantage of a pause in her speech. "But?"

She straightened back up, "Admittedly, I have never heard your own beliefs. I also realize that I have not heard the teachings of all, or even most modern Christians. But, I am familiar with some of the teachings from some Christian Churches. None of them appear to resemble Jesus' teachings in the slightest. They twist his words to fit their own agenda." Her brilliant green eyes were shining with what might have been tears. "Jesus never taught to discriminate against those who look different or speak a different language. He never advised any of his followers to go to war with those who grew up learning a different way to worship God. No!" Her voice was reaching a crescendo.

It took Lloyd a second to realize it, but she was preaching to him. "Jesus said love thy neighbor and turn the other cheek. Jesus ministered to the poor and the sick. He even befriended the dregs of society like tax collectors and women." She rolled her eyes as the word 'women' left her lips. "He was a good man."

Lloyd was enraptured by her words and cadence. She may have been mocking the very style of preaching that he employed, but she was good, she was mesmerizing. He tried to break free of her spell, but a large part of him wanted to keep listening. He wanted to know where she was going.

She took a deep breath and when she spoke again her voice was back to a conversational tone. "Once again, I must say that I know nothing of your own beliefs, so this is not directed at you personally. I have found that modern Christianity is often used as a cover for outright bigotry."

Lloyd flashed his big show smile, and easily deflected the attack. "The KKK represent a small fraction of those who claim to be Christian. Any group as large as Christianity is bound to have a few bad apples."

She sighed. "If only that were all. Christianity is also professed by Neo-Nazis to defend their beliefs."

He flapped one of his hands at her. "A small group." He was beginning to think this might be a waste of time.

"You're right. Those are the extreme examples. What about Islamophobia, homophobia and xenophobia of all shapes and sizes?" She wasn't smiling, the wrinkles that etched her face did not deepen. But Lloyd knew she was feeling very strong. It was nothing he couldn't handle.

"Cheryl," he began to speak in what he thought of as his salesman voice. He thought there was little chance of winning her over, but it was his Christian duty to try. "I'm sorry that you have had a bad experience with Christianity, but I would love to help you to a new beginning in faith." She did smile at that, her lips thinned but did not part. "What was the first one?" He paused for a second as he pretended to think. "Islam, right? There are Christians dying everyday at the hands of Islamists. They attack Christians because their faith is warlike and violent. They are commanded to kill infidels by their religious leaders."

The smile broadened exposing smoke browned teeth under her burning green eyes. "Some might claim that only a small fraction of Muslims believe in and teach hatred. Any group as large as Islam is sure to have a few bad apples."

He started to speak again, but stuttered to a stop as his own words were used against him. She began to speak again, saving him the trouble of having to argue against himself.

"What did Jesus teach about confronting violence?" Her tone was conversational, like she really wanted to know. But he knew better. She was playing with him. He had no recourse but to answer her question honestly.

"Matthew 5:39 But I say unto you, do not resist an evil person; but whoever slaps you on your right cheek, turn to him the other side also."

Now she did appear smug.

"Jesus was talking about being slapped. The Islamist want to wipe Christianity off the face of the planet." He started pulling on his fingers again. "They are two entirely different situations." He wanted to end this conversation so he quickly added, "What was the next thing?" This time his ignorance was not feigned.

"Homophobia. Why does 'God hate fags' as so many signs on sticks have proclaimed?"

He felt his confidence growing again, but he was cautious. "I don't have a problem with any man's personal choices unless they affect me directly. Everyone deserves a bit of privacy in their lives. But I also have the right to keep my church free of such sinners."

She nodded, then she spoke. "Why does it matter if they get married? That doesn't affect you personally."

"Have you ever heard the story of Sodom and Gomorrah?"

"Yes. They were destroyed in the Old Testament."

"That's correct. They were destroyed by the wrath of God for being immoral dens of sin. I would be crazy not to speak against my home becoming a modern day Sodom."

She was still nodding. "I see. And what did Jesus say about homosexuality.?"

Lloyd had been in this argument many times before so he allowed himself to slip into his preaching voice. "He did not comment on the subject. But, Leviticus states that the act of a man lying with another man is detestable. In Matthew 5:17, Jesus claims that he was not sent to abolish the laws of the Prophets before him. He was sent to fulfill them."

Lloyd felt a tinge of fear as he saw her smile growing again. "I don't suppose any of your congregation ever eats shellfish? Do any of them have a tattoo?"

"I don't know..."

She cut him off. "Have you ever refused to let a woman into your church because she was menstruating?"

"Now that is just preposterous." He had raised his voice a little more than he had intended. Calmly he added. "I see the point you are trying to make, but it just isn't valid. Leviticus has some strange passages. There is even a line advising how to beat your slaves according to the law. Some of Leviticus just doesn't apply to the world today."

She tapped the table a few times but never broke eye contact. "How do you decide?"

"I'm sorry?" He really didn't understand the question.

"How do you decide which laws are ok to break, and which ones are not?"

"I would say common sense."

"So it is just that simple?" Her eyes were still shining with moisture.

"Yes it is. Body modification and violations of dietary restrictions are not on the same level as sins of the flesh. Leviticus actually calls for gays to be stoned to death. But I would never do that. I just don't want to encourage the behavior." He cleared his throat. "That is another gift from Christianity. The words of the Prophets combined with the teachings of Christ create a set of morals that cannot be rivaled." There was no doubt in his mind. His words were a matter of fact.

One of her eyebrows raised, which created an interesting knot of wrinkles on her forehead. "I beg to differ with you on that point. I believe that empathy is the key to personal morality."

He shook his head. "But empathy without Christ is meaningless. Only through Christ can we achieve everlasting life in paradise."

"Well," She cocked her head and grimaced. "I would argue…" She stopped again and her face hardened a bit as she seemed to come to some decision. "That Heaven and Hell, as a built-in reward and punishment system actually diminishes the strength of Christian morality."

Lloyd had never heard that one before. "How so?"

She looked up to meet his eyes again. "Who is more morally sound; a woman who helps others and is honest because she feels in her heart that it is the right thing to do, or the woman who takes the same actions out of fear of punishment, or with the expectation of a reward?"

Lloyd pulled away from the burning emeralds and looked at the table. He was popping his knuckles again. Had he ever stopped?

She continued. "Don't get me wrong. I appreciate that Christianity helps those who need the fear of the stick to go toward the carrot. But, one should not be ridiculed or outcast because they don't need either."

Lloyd spoke softly, but firmly. "I guess we just don't agree on what the right thing actually is. To me, the right thing is trying to save the souls of as many people as possible. Helping the body of someone without guiding them to Jesus is not actually good."

She gave a short laugh. "We may have to agree to disagree on that. I find that the relief of suffering is good in most cases and I don't believe in the afterlife."

"Then what do you believe?"

"I believe there is no way to know what will happen after death. I just try to live the best life I can with the time I have been given."

"Seems like a dangerous way to live. Have you ever heard of Pascal's wager?"

"No I have not." She shook her head once.

He smiled, knowing this would end the argument. "Pascal was a French philosopher." Lloyd stopped tugging at his fingers and folded his hands in front of himself as if in prayer. "He argued that humans bet with their lives as to whether God exists or not. If you believe and are wrong, the downside is that there is no paradise. But if you don't believe and are wrong, you will be condemned to burn in eternal Hellfire." He opened his hands to her, exposing his palms. "The risk, in my opinion, is too great."

She glanced down at his empty hands, a wry smile on her lips. If Lloyd didn't know any better, he would say that she found his words as empty as his hands. "That would be a good argument if the bet you were making had only two choices. There are thousands of active religions on this planet right now. And there are countless others that have been lost to history. Any number of these might condemn belief in Christ to its own version of Hell, while only Christianity rewards it. How can you be sure that Christianity is the safe bet?"

"I just know." And he did too. He could feel it with every fiber of his body. Much of his sweat had dried, his voice felt steady, and he had no desire to nervously pull on his fingers. Whatever spell she had cast on him had been broken. She looked at him for a long time, but Lloyd's spirit had returned to him as strong as ever. Though her eyes burned like green fire, his remained the calm before the storm.

After what seemed like several minutes, she finally spoke, but continued to hold his gaze. "I can respect that. And I hope you can respect others who go about their worship in different ways. Is it so hard to believe that there could be more than one way to please God?"

Lloyd looked down at his hands. As far as he knew, she had never hurt anybody. If she spoke the truth… if she really was worshipping God through His creation… Can God be honored without Christ? Lloyd laid his palms on the table and noticed his watch, 4:15. He needed to get to the church and prepare for tonights service.

"Cheryl, I'm afraid that is a question that may require a whole conversation unto itself." He flashed his show smile again. "I will pray on it. Perhaps I could come back for further discussion sometime soon." He stood and grabbed his jacket, tossing it over one arm. "I need to be getting to the church. I hate to end this early but the Wednesday service must go on. Of course, you are welcome to stop by tonight, or Friday, or Sunday. I would love to see you there."

"Thanks for the offer." She followed him down the hall and through the open double doors to the porch. After he had finished putting on his jacket, she reached out her hand, and he took it to shake. "You are always welcome here as well, Reverend. I would love to continue our conversation, its nice to discuss these things with civility." Her eyes were even brighter on the shaded porch than they had been inside the house.

"I'll take you up on that." He walked down the three steps to the hard packed earth below. He had only taken a few steps toward his car when he was struck with a thought. "Oh Cheryl." He turned to see her still standing on the porch. One loose strand of grey hair blowing in a light breeze. "One last question. What does the equinox have to do with God's creation?"

She smiled and answered while chuckling. "On the forth day, God created the stars and heavenly bodies, the movement of these will help man keep track of time."

Lloyd laughed and nodded. "You seem to know the scripture pretty well for a nonbeliever."

The wind had picked a few more grey strands from her hair, in the sunlight he thought he could see a bit of a reddish tint. "I've studied many religions." After a short pause, she added. "But never Devil worship. I do feel like I should tell you, the equinox is tonight. You are welcome to observe the festivities." She smiled slyly. "You could even take part."

"I would love to Cheryl, but I've heard this drought may finally end. The festivities may be rained out tonight, but the water is needed." He looked around at the trees surrounding the little cabin. Most of the leaves were turning a sickly brown and curling around the edges.

She winked at him. "A little rain has never stopped a group of witches from dancing in the woods."

26

The Captured One

The voices were distant mumbles that could only be heard deep within himself. Or was it Wil that had withdrawn inside? "Dammit Chuck! You could have killed him." The deep roar of emotion pulled Wil back near consciousness. He was slumped forward, but still seated. A thin band of pressure running across his chest was the only thing stopping him from tumbling into the darkness and onto his face. His arms were pinned to his sides and his hands were tied together on his lap. His eyes were beginning to adjust.

"Ehh, so wut if I did?" The 'snick' of spitted tobacco punctuated the phrase.

The room was dark. The only light came from bright slits of evenly spaced lines all around him. He was in a small shack. Maybe, ten by ten and completely empty. Except for him on his chair.

"Remember number 6? Thou shall not murder." The deeper voice had calmed a bit.

"Wut should I have did?" The heavy accent did little to mask the defiance.

"Call for an officer! They could have figured something out."

"Tampering with evidence at a crime scene, maybe?" This new third voice sounded familiar. Wil heard footsteps on the gravel and he could see shapes moving in the light between boards. But he could not tell how many of them were out there. At least three.

The familiar voice spoke again. "What do we do now Sir?"

"Jess leave'm by the road. Won't know nuthin' when 'e wakes up."

The sound of footsteps on gravel stopped. "Even if he hasn't already woken up," The man with the deep voice appeared to be in charge. "He would come back here with more people and search the area. We can't risk that."

"And if he is awake?" Silence followed the young man's query. The 'snick' of spit was the only sound for what seemed like several minutes.

When the deep growl started it was so low that Wil could not make it out. "...either way, we have to take him to the hole for judgement."

"I thought killing wuz bad" 'snick'

"We aren't killing by doing this, We are allowing God to make a judgement." The deep voice took on a reassuring tone. It had the opposite effect on Wil. His heart leapt around erratically inside his chest.

"If he just disappears," The familiar voice began, "people will come looking for him. He was out here earlier with that other reporter, you know, 'Big Red'" Was that the young officer from the meadow with Howard's truck?

"It's a risk we'll have to take." The deep voice answered. "Maybe we can make it look like an accident. Like he fell into the river."

'Snick' The spitting sound was followed by a strong Kentucky drawl. "Sheet. River's down. Wouldn't worsh 'way a dead dog."

There was another long pause, Wil's heart continued to race, his fingers tingled. They were going to kill him. He struggled with the ropes for a minute. Trying to get free without making a sound, but all he managed to accomplish was rubbing the skin off his wrists. His toes were numb, hell, his feet were asleep. The ropes tying his ankles to the chair were so tight that his blood flow had been cut off. He wouldn't be able to run even if he was able to free himself.

The deep authoritative voice finally broke the silence. "Go get him, the sun is about to set." One set of footsteps twisted in and then began crunching gravel. Wil's breath caught in his chest, and his rapidly beating heart seemed to stop. The outline of a man began to grow as it moved across the light filtering through the wooden slats. Time seemed to slow down, but still, the crunching gravel drew closer.

CRUNCH

Wil planned to fight with all of his strength, but between the sweat pouring down his face, the butterflies in his stomach and his sleeping feet, he was unsure how much fight he had left.

CRUNCH

He thought about the corruption in Frankfort. He should have taken that to Beth, she would have loved that kind of story. Either that or he would have been fired because she didn't want to get involved. He would have had to move again, but where? Georgetown? None of that really mattered anymore.

CRUNCH

He couldn't fight like this. Dehydrated, tied up, sweat soaked shirt... He thought about the pretty librarian. Her sandy blond hair curling as it tumbled over her shoulders. The gap between her teeth that only showed when she laughed. He should have asked her out. When he got out of here, that is what he intended to do. If he got out of here.

CRUNCH

Both of his feet were asleep. If they had needed to breathe, they would have been snoring loudly. They were completely numb, like his legs ended at his ankle. He hoped that they wouldn't need to be amputated. Another thought popped into his head, 'I am about to become a missing person, and I am worried about my feet.' Wil found no solace in the fact that he had solved the mystery of the missing people. His solid investigative skills led him directly into the culprit's hands. And now, no one would ever know, because he was about to become a missing person with sleeping feet.

CRUNCH

'Act like you are asleep.' The second the thought popped into his head, Wil slumped forward as if unconscious. 'Like my feet.' He thought. In this position, he gained control of his breathing, and time returned to a normal speed again.

CRUNCH CRUNCH CRUNCH

The footsteps walked around the shack, behind Wil. A heavy lock rattled for a few seconds, then suddenly, light flooded the room. He could see the brightness through his closed eyes. The cool air that followed the light was the only welcome change. His heart continued to race, but he managed to keep his breath steady and even.

The footsteps now fell on the wooden floor directly behind him. Slumped forward and facing away was an extremely vulnerable position. But being tied to a chair left some level of vulnerability as the only option.

"Are you still sleeping?" It was the young man's voice, possibly Officer Mosely.

Wil remained perfectly still. The steps stopped, then. he found himself falling backwards. The legs of the chair screamed as they were dragged across the floor of the shack and toward the open door. Simple reflex caused Wil to jerk in response. He could no longer feign sleep.

The sunlight outside was reddish in tint but still over-powering after the darkness of the shack. Wil's eyes watered through his squinting lids. And the air outside the shack was almost shockingly cool on his sweat-slicked skin.

"He's awake now"

Wil tried to look at his captors, but could only see dark shapes with blurry features through the glare and tears. He had to close his eyes against the light. More footsteps approached as he worked his way up to attempting another squint.

"Yup, he gon' fo' judgment." 'Snick'.

Wil could see two dark figures on either side on him. Then a third much larger figure stepped between them. The large figure was standing, leaning over him. Wil's eyes were adjusting slowly. The green blurs became bushes and trees, the brown blurs became trunks, branches and a shack. But the people remained dark featureless blurs, back-lit by the sink-ing sun.

"What were you doing by the distillery?" The deep voice did not ask, it demanded an answer.

"I was out at the scene of the abandoned truck." Wil's voice was weak and harsh, he barely recognized it himself. He needed a drink, anything wet. "I work for the BC Journal. "His heart was beating so hard he was afraid it was visible through his shirt, sweat soaked and plastered to his chest as it was.

The deep voice growled back. "You didn't answer the question." The big man in front of him was wearing a grey bandana so low that it reached to the middle of his nose. Dark eyes blazed from holes cut in the cloth. A square jaw shaded by thick stubble was framed by the loose ends of the bandana. These strands hung down to rest on his broad shoulders.

He raised one hand toward one of the other masked men. Wil's world began to spin violently, he gasped audibly.

In an instant his vision had changed to the purpling sky with browning greenery reaching toward the fading day. His head sank into the gravel as he hit the ground. It didn't tickle, but it was a soft landing compared to his back and tailbone against the unyielding wood of the chair. Sharp pain shot from Wil's butt to his shoulders with the impact. His feet throbbed numbly.

"Ya betta' answa' for true now, ya hear?" Greasy grey hair spilled out from under the bandana as the old man leaned down over Wil. Dark tobacco stains glistened on his bottom lip. "Cuz I got sum mo' for ya." The old man grabbed the strap across Wil's chest and quickly pulled him back upright. The sensation was only slightly less pleasant than falling backward.

When his head stopped spinning, Wil found the big man right there waiting. His grey robes matched the bandana mask, but had been thrown on hastily. The robe was closed with a cloth belt, while decorative silver buttons drooped unused.

"I'll ask you one more time. Why were you at the distillery?" The large man leaned in close to Wil's face. "I need to know if I should be on the look out for any of your friends."

Wil was too terrified to think of a lie, so the truth would have to do. "I just moved to town a few months ago. I recently found out about the tragedy of Kingston a few days ago." Wil tried to swallow, but was unsuccessful. "I though it would be neat to visit a place so rich in history." Or at least most of the truth would have to do.

The big man gestured to the third masked man. A bright flash of pain leapt from the young man's hand to the right side of Wil's face. "He asked you if anyone would be following you out here." Wil felt a new trickle running down the side of his face, he didn't think this one was sweat. Wil looked at the third man, his youthful nose, lips and chin were unmistakeable. Last time he had obscured his face with a hat and sunglasses.

"The other reporter," the way his heart was pounding made it difficult to catch his breath, and even harder to think. "Steve, he is writing a story about Howard's disappearance, and several others around town. That's why we were at the abandoned truck..." huff huff "Just to write a little article to say, this is what we know so let's let the police solve the case and give us the details." He let out a nervous giggle before adding. "I did tell him I was going to check out the ruins, but he..."

"That's all I needed." The deep voice cut him off. "Get him off that chair."

Before Wil could even comprehend the words, he felt that sickening swirl again as his vision spun to the rapidly darkening sky. The jolt that traveled up his back lingered this time.

The old man reached down and released the strap across Wil's chest and Officer Mosely untied his feet. A warmish, coolish, sensation started to blossom below his ankles but he was distracted by an engine starting nearby. The engine slowly began to approach as gravel crunched under tires.

They pulled him up roughly by his arms, and Wil found that his legs had been hastily tied together again. The big man appeared on a 4-wheeler, coming around the side of the shack. There was a rack on the back for carrying supplies and carcasses. Mostly for deer and turkey, but today...

The big man got off the vehicle and helped the young man lift him into place. Hands tied together, feet tied together and strapped to the metal mesh rack by bungie cords, Wil was unable to stop any of it. Anger and fear mixed in his mind as he watched the big man get back onto the ATV. The youth approached Wil, with a strip of cloth stretched between his hands.

"Oh a blindfold?" Wil's anger erupted in a scream. "Afraid I'll remember where your clubhouse is, Officer Mosely!?!"

The fist hit the side of his head, and the other side of his head hit the metal mesh breaking the skin in several places. Wil's vision blurred and all thought was forced out of his mind, only the pain remained.

Cloth was shoved into his gaping mouth and another was tied around his head to keep the first in place. "This is to keep you from screaming like the little bitch that you are."

The cloth soaked up every drop of moisture that remained in his mouth. His whole head was ringing, and when the young man spoke, he sounded like it was coming from very far away.

"We have other ways to keep you from seeing anything." Wil's vision had cleared enough to see the long thin object in his hand. It was about a foot long, with a flat end. "Besides, after facing judgment, I doubt your memory will do you any good."

The young man raised his weapon and it wiggled a bit against the purple sky. 'Is that a Black Jack?' Was Wil's last thought before the leather wrapped lead met his skull and turned off his consciousness. He dreamed he was in a tall building. Everything was shaking so violently, but every stairway only went up. He could not find a way down to escape the building. There must have been a plane flying around the building because the engine sounded very close.

27

The Lonely One

Al saw Jay and Bash sitting at the end of one of the long tables on his way to the cafeteria, lunch trays half empty. They used to wait for him in the large foyer outside the cafeteria, but all week long they had ditched him. Eating lunch and leaving before Al could even get through the line.

Al stared out the long line of windows that ran down the length of the lunchroom. It gave a spectacular view of the teachers' parking lot. Mrs. Sell was retrieving something out of her car; nothing too interesting. He just needed something to focus on, something to keep him from looking to see if they were still at the table.

Al was concentrating so hard on not looking back that he didn't even look at his pizza until he paid at the end of the line. He didn't need to look though, every Wednesday it was the same. Rectangular slice with cubed pepperoni covered in yellow cheese browned in a polka-dot pattern. The whole thing was shiny as if with grease, but was mysteriously dry to the touch. Of course, one of the cups in the styrofoam tray was filled with watery corn.

Al's spirits lifted a little when he saw that Jay and Bash were still seated. He began toward the other end of the dining area, afraid they would get up before he reached them. They didn't. Jay waited until Al sat down before abruptly standing and leaving without a word.

He was too hurt to speak to the back of Jay's head, so

he turned to Bash. His hair was getting long, well, long for Bash. A dark stubble coated his normally shaved head. His big brown eyes were the same as they always were, vacant while somehow knowing.

"I dunno Al," he shook his head, "Jays really shook up about everything. The way he tells it, he was dodging bullets while running away." He clapped Al on the back. "What are you doing after school today?"

Al had planned on riding out to Cry Baby lane to listen for more sounds, but he wasn't sure he should tell Bash. "I... Ummm..." He felt warmth flooding his face.

The big guy smirked, "Still on the trail of a mystery, I see. Cry Baby Lane?"

"I don't expect anyone to go with me." Al swallowed. "It might even be easier if I go alone."

"Hey man, you don't gotta convince me." He laughed. "I wouldn't mind going with you but," he whistled, "Jay would be really mad." He placed both hands on the table and pushed himself up. "I'm starting not to care."

Before he could walk away Al blurted, "I heard something, Bash"

"What?" The big guy stood by the table, towering over Al.

"I went by myself at sunset on Sunday and I heard something. I got scared and ran away."

"What did you hear?"

"A scream..." Al shook his head. "A moan... No that's not it either." He pushed a few brown strands off his forehead. "I can't really describe it. It was just terrifying."

Bash stood for a few seconds, staring down at Al, but not really seeing him. "You going again tonight?"

"Yes." This time, Al didn't hesitate, but his honesty was

met with silence. The big guy simply stood there thinking for a few minutes. One large hand patted Al's shoulder before Bash walked away into the foyer without another word.

Al was once again alone in a crowded room. It had been like this all week, and he didn't think he could take much more. He cradled his hanging head in both hands. He shouldn't have been honest with Bash. He should have told him that he had a family thing, or that he didn't have any plans, anything but the truth. Maybe then Bash would have sat down with him.

Al realized that he had been sitting with his head in his hands for a while and was probably drawing some attention. Slowly, he began to rub his forehead and then pulled his hands away. No one was pointing or staring. To finish off his act of nonchalance, he picked up his pizza and took a bite. It tasted as plastic as it looked. He dropped the rectangular slice back onto the styrofoam causing the corn to splash. He did not intend to pick it back up.

Al couldn't lie to Bash either, the big guy could always tell. He would tell Jay, and they would both be mad all over again. He wiped his hands on his sole napkin. Al was overcome with a desire to bury his head in his hands again. Instead he just ran a hand through his shaggy hair to push it off his forehead, where it immediately fell again. He had no appetite, no friends, and no reason to be in the cafeteria. He grabbed the tray and walked over to throw everything away before leaving.

The back foyer was a large open area with four evenly spaced support pillars. Each pillar was surrounded by benches that were never empty. It was the hub of the school. The foyer connected the student parking lot, the gymnasium, the cafeteria, the theatre, and a bathroom. It was a great place to hang out if you finish lunch early or just wanted to skip class. There were several groups of people here, but Jay and Bash were nowhere to be found. He probably wouldn't see them again until Mr. Smith's class, last period.

Al was starting to get mad. He felt like he was so close to solving the Cry Baby Lane mystery. They had stuck by him through some pretty stupid and entirely fruitless adventures. Now he was shaking a branch with some fruit on it, and they refused to look.

There was some commotion over by the double doors to the student parking lot. A large group of students had gathered and more were heading that way. But Al was too deep in his own thoughts to care about whoever was fighting in the parking lot. He turned in the opposite direction and began down the long hallway from the back foyer to the classrooms in the front of the building. He was walking against a pretty steady flow of students, which was surprising this late in the lunch hour. He thought that these people should be heading back to class now, but he just kept his head down brooding his feelings of abandonment.

"Hey Al." The voice pulled him out of his thoughts and he looked up. "What's going on back there?" It was Taylor Eastman.

"Uhh…" Al turned back to watch as the last few students passed him and Taylor heading toward the now huge group of students. "I'm not sure." There were even a few teachers joining the crowd as well. "If you find out, tell me about it in PE tomorrow."

"Michelle Mill's uncle has gone missing." The new voice was low but feminine. "Him and some junky." She had shoe polish black hair, thick black eyeliner and a tight black choker around her neck. She lifted one fingerless gloved hand and took a drag off a cigarette. She turned her body a little and blew the smoke into the girls bathroom. "I think they ran off together." She looked down the hallway and shrugged. "Got to go boys." And with that she disappeared into the bathroom.

Taylor looked at Al blankly for a moment before mouthing a single word. 'Weirdo'. He then added out loud, "That sounds pretty awesome though. Like, it might be the craziest thing to ever happen in this boring town."

Before Al could respond he heard coach Marshall's bark. "Taulbee!" He was sniffing the air suspiciously. "You smell smoke?" The whistle he wore around his neck bounced with every step.

"This hallway always smells like that, coach." Al's eyes flicked toward the door to the teachers' lounge, which was across the hall from the bathrooms. He shrugged at Taylor before turning around toward the classrooms again. Coach Marshall continued to sniff.

Now there were missing people? That complicated things. He could imagine what Jay's reaction would have been. "I have seen enough horror films to know that nothing good happens to the guy who goes out to investigate a strange noise in the dark." The mere thought of Jay's words made him mad all over again, even though he wasn't going to be there to say it. He was more resolved than ever to go out now. He must get to the bottom of this.

28

The Ones Who Prepare

Moonbeam stepped into the clearing and dropped the sticks onto the pile. She pulled a red handkerchief out of the pocket of her sweat pants and wiped the sweat from her wrinkled brow. She could see dark clouds gathering in the West and the humidity had been rising all day. She was almost swimming through the air.

Despite the heat and humidity she was able to clear the sacred grove with Shawn and her friends help. All sticks and leaves were piled next to the fire pit. Any trash that had been found was collected and would be disposed of tomorrow. She never understood how so much of it ended up this far into the Wallwood. Maybe it floated down the Elkhorn, which ran around the edge of the property about 500 yards to the south. Then it would take a windblown journey past the stone ruins and up to her home. She supposed they could come from the sparse traffic that passed this way. Or maybe some of it was carried here by an animal. She guessed she would never know. It just needed to be cleared before the ritual.

They found candy wrappers and a few cans inside the grove, but more was discovered as they expanded their search into the surrounding woods. They were looking for firewood but found paper plates, paper wrappers, paper bags, plastic bags, plastic cases, plastic sheets, styrofoam cups and packing. And of course, bottles and cans and cans and cans. Mostly beer cans, but a few were soda.

Moonbeam normally found some bits of trash during

these ritual clean-ups, but this was ridiculous. It had been a long time since she had been healthy enough for this type of ritual. When her illness progressed she let the property go, it must have built up over time.

It was tiring work, but it gave the old woman time to work out some pent-up frustration. She kept running her conversation with the Reverend through her mind. She had wanted to scream at him that he didn't follow Christ anymore than she did. He seemed to follow the Old Testament, but only the parts that his "gut" told him were still relevant.

She had held her tongue for several reasons. She didn't want the town folk to show up with torches and pitch forks on a mission to get the witch. The thought sent chills down her spine. Her family had been here, tending this land for four generations. Her Grandy set up in the Wallwood before BC distillery had even been built. She didn't want to risk her well-being, not after being given a new vitality. The other reason was that Lloyd seemed like a nice man. Misguided, but well-meaning.

The hard work and the sun combined to relieve Moonbeam of her anger. Her heart felt a little lighter about the situation with every bead of sweat that fell into the hard-packed earth under her feet.

Jenna dragged a large branch into the clearing, it was at least 10 feet long with a tangle of smaller limbs and twigs still attached. The young woman had come at Shawn's invitation. Which worked out great because she showed up ready to get her hands dirty. Moonbeam thought she would be more comfortable to have one of her friends here tonight.

"Good find, Jenna." Moonbeam called to her. "You can leave it there. We can break that down and carry it much easier." She glanced at the pile of sticks that was waist high, and then at the pile of branches, nearly waist high. She thought that this would be plenty for tonight. "Let's wait for Shawn and then go to the cabin for some water." She wiped her face with her handkerchief again. "This heat is awful."

Jenna raised one arm, using her short sleeve to wipe her heat reddened face. "The heat wouldn't be so bad," she was still breathing heavily from dragging the tree limb and took a moment to catch her breath, "if it wasn't so humid." She wiped her face again with her other sleeve.

Moonbeam gestured to the darkening western sky "We may finally see some rain." Jenna turned to look while Moonbeam finished. "If we are lucky it will wash all this moisture out of the air."

Shawn stepped into the clearing with both hands full. She joined the other two and dropped her sticks onto the pile. Sweat ran down her brightly rouged cheeks and her curls were thick in the humidity. She was breathing harder than Jenna. She pushed a tight curl off her forehead before speaking. "I thought you said Donna was coming."

The old woman gave her a knowing look. "Donna will be here." About five minutes after the hard work is done, she added silently. "I promise you that. She had been coming to these things for at least five years before I got sick." She waved her hands over the piles of wood. "I think this will be enough. Would you girls like to join me in the cabin for some water and a toke?"

The trio took off down the tree shaded path leading from the meadow to the house. Donna wasn't who Moonbeam was worried about. She had not spoken to Cathy since the Dreamcatcher session. She didn't expect tonight to be their reunion.

Donna walked in about 30 seconds after Moonbeam lit the joint. She had a large tote bag hanging on one forearm. A bottle of Buffalo Crossing Black label in one hand and a six pack of Ale 8 One in the other. "Who's ready to Equinox!?!" It was an announcement more than a question.

Shawn and Jenna responded in perfect unison, "Whoooo!" Shawn even shot one fist into the air. Moonbeam only lifted the corners of her mouth. The group may be a little different but, it felt good to get back to the old traditions.

"Alright ladies," Her eyes glittered. "Only one drink before the bonfire."

Donna stuck her bottom lip out and lifted her eyebrows in exaggerated sadness.

"I'd rather you help me get the fire started before your breath is flammable." Even Donna got a good laugh out of that.

When the light started to retreat from the room with the large table, Moonbeam called a halt to the festivities. "Did everyone bring their robe? I believe it's time."

29

The One who Visits

By the time the fire started to catch, the reddening sky had turned purple. Dancing shadows shot out into the meadow around them as the fire grew. Moonbeam had to step back as the heat intensified, as the day was hot enough already.

"Please stand around the fire." Moonbeam took her spot on the south side of the fire, and Donna on the north. The old woman removed her robe and tossed it behind her. The night crept over her bared skin creating gooseflesh despite the heat of the night and flame. The was no moonlight tonight, but she could see some lightning flashes in the distance.

Donna had removed her robe and was waiting for the ceremony to begin. Moonbeam watched Shawn's shadow disrobe in the orange light cast by the fire. It sprang out behind her, long and slim and reaching into the treeline. The woods themselves seemed to be alive with moving shadows in the flickering light of the fire.

Jenna giggle as her robe dropped in the grass. Her giggles quickly turned into a scream. All Moonbeam could see over the flames was the girl running down the path to the cabin, white robe fluttering behind her.

"Hey Emm?" Donna sounded urgent, not at all like herself. Then she heard the grunt. She turned toward the noise afraid of what she might see. The creature was standing near the tree-line. Thin legs, shaggy and brown. They bent backwards at the knee and then turned into a rounded femur. It reminded her of a dog's leg. The fur on the legs thinned a little at its waist. He was carrying something in his muscular arms, which looked almost human. Its head, however, was anything but human.

It dropped what it had been holding and Moonbeam recognized the unmistakable rustle of paper and plastic, the thunk of a bottle and tinkle of glass. It was trash. The thing bent down, bringing its head into better light. Its long snout was covered in short brown hair, except for the tip. There, two long slanted nostril pointed toward the long stringy beard that hung from its chin.

Limp ears hung down from high on his head to frame the animal-like face. The eyes were two large black pools, one on each side of the snout. They seemed intelligent and knowing. It grabbed a bottle from the refuse on the ground and held it out to the women.

A low rumble of thunder cascaded across the sky. Rolling toward the meadow behind the cabin. It was enough to shock Moonbeam back to reality, which seemed pretty dreamlike at the moment. Shawn was frozen in place and Donna was slowly walking backward.

"It's ok girls." Her voice sounded much steadier than she felt, but she forced herself to continue. "Don't run away." She never took her eyes off Dogman. She took a few steps toward him, slowly at first. A cool wind blew around her, reminding her of her nakedness. She picked up a little speed after deciding that clothing was only paper armor anyway.

"Be careful Em." Donna called out in a harsh whisper. Shawn only squeaked. The creature was nearly seven feet tall and was towering over the old woman well before she reached him. Another gust of wind blew her own hair around her face and a chill down her spine. She reached out one trembling hand and took the glass bottle from the beast. Its hand only had one cloven finger and a thumb like claw. She reached out with her other hand and grabbed the creature's 'hand.' Moonbeam began to lead him toward the fire.

30

The One Returned

His stomach rumbled again as he rummaged through his backpack. He knew there was an apple and three granola bars in here somewhere. He had purposely grabbed them in his short trip home after school. A sweatshirt, two bottles of water, a book, a ball of twine, a flashlight, some duct-tape, a pair of scissors and a hammer. Al had pretty much just packed the entire everything drawer from kitchen into his backpack. He pushed the sweatshirt to the side revealing the apple. It was slightly bruised when he pulled it out and took a bite. He continued to dig as he chewed.

Plunging his hand all the way to the bottom, he found the granola bars. He pulled one out, grabbed a bottle of water and set the backpack aside. He was wearing dark jeans and a green shirt, making him almost invisible where he sat. Only his faded Cincinnati Reds hat could be seen through the foliage, and even that would be easily missed.

He found a spot about 10 feet beyond the treeline where he could see the path from Rutledge Road and the overgrown trail leading down into the valley. He hoped with all of his heart that no one entered the little clearing from either direction. Determined as he was to solve the mystery, he did not have a death wish. Between the news of the missing people and the knowledge of at least one gun-toting hillbilly, Al was scared. He wanted to make sure that if anyone showed up, he would see them first.

He finished the apple and placed the core back in his

bag. He took a few sips of water and removed his hat. As he wiped his face with one hand, it came away dripping with sweat. Even in the shade of the Wallwood, the heat was unbearable. The humidity was worse. The air was thick and still.

Al didn't think he would need the sweatshirt, so he used it as a towel. He ate the granola bar in three bites, then placed the wrapper next to the apple core. He had some time to kill before sunset, so he pulled out the book. The author's name was King, which was the only reason he had checked it out from the library. It had turned out to be extremely dark and scary. Al would have already returned the book, except he really liked the little boy in the book. He only kept reading to make sure Danny stayed safe.

Al was so engrossed in the book that he didn't hear the rustling leaves at first. A wasp had just come out of the nest in Danny's room, and that had taken all of Al's focus. Al did eventually see movement over the top of his book.

His breath caught in his throat as he tried to remain still. He had to move his head back and forth to get a look at the intruder through the branches. Whoever it was had a bald head and they were very tall.

"Bash!?!" Al called in a hoarse whisper.

The big guy dropped his bike and the clatter caused Al to jerk. The only sounds he had heard for the past few hours were bird songs with insect backing. Bash was looking right at him, but apparently could not see him.

"Al? Is that you?"

Al climbed to his feet and pushed into the open meadow. He felt so relieved that the intruder was friendly that he completely forgot about the oppressive heat for a moment.

"What are you doing here?"

Bash shook his nearly bald head softly, but his grin remained. A drop of sweat was flung from his chin by the movement, but was immediately replaced with another. His grey shirt had large black rings under each arm and a dark V shape from collar to navel.

"Even though people have gone missin', and we know a crazy guy lives out here." He bent down and grabbed the water bottle that was in the holder on his bike. "Here you are." He only stopped shaking his head to take a long drink.

Al became indignant. Was he going to try to convince Al to leave? "I have a chance to solve a mystery that has been around since the 50s." He was keeping his voice down. It was a struggle. "I have never been this close to solving anything before."

Bash's grin widened. "Well, we did find out them lights on Thorny Hill were just headlights." He took a few steps toward Al. "Besides, I want to be with ya when you find out that noise is nothin' but the wind."

The big guy held up one large palm, and with great relief, Al slapped him five. The smack was loud and satisfying, a sound he had been afraid he would never hear again.

They stashed Bash's bike next to Al's and retreated back into the Wallwood to Al's hiding spot. They talked in hushed whispers as the shadows lengthened. Al continued to be vigilant, but this time he was actually hoping for one more person to come crashing through the trees. But no one came.

"It's getting pretty dark." Bash said. "Should we head out?" They crept back into the meadow, which was devoid of direct sunlight. The eastern sky was purpling while an ominous dark cloud hung against a red backdrop to the west.

Al dug in his backpack and pulled out the flashlights. He handed one to Bash. "I wish Jay was here."

Bash laughed while taking the flashlight. "Can you imagine the one-man show he would be putting on? Just trying to get us to leave."

A steady high-pitched whine began in the distance, quiet, but growing louder. The boys did not notice. Al was busy trying to channel his best Jay. He leaned to one side, putting his arm around an imaginary person. "Can you believe these guys?" He pointed at Bash, but then turned back to the invisible man. "He wants me out in a storm when he knows I melt when wet."

Both boys laughed over top of the unnatural whine that continued to grow louder until it just stopped. Neither of them noticed. Bash, still laughing, imitated Jay as well. "As you can see on this weather map behind me, " He circled a huge area of imaginary map, "this giant storm is heading right for you. It's time to go home."

It was completely dark now, but neither boy turned on a flashlight. Not yet. The fun they were having slowly turned to angst as they remembered where they were and what they were doing. They slowly walked over to the ravines edge. Al's heart raced. He was expecting the bone-chilling cry to hit him at any second. He actually started to get lightheaded before realizing that he had been holding his breath. The Wallwood was alive with the usual musicians; frogs, insects, owls, a droning whine that sounded like it was receding into the distance.

"Do you hear that?" Al Whispered.

Bash listened for a second before responding with a shrug. His eyebrows raised and his lips dropped as if to say 'I hear a bunch of stuff'. Al tried to find the sound again, but it was either too quiet or gone completely, so he only shook his head.

They stood perfectly still for several minutes, letting the symphony of the night wash over them. Nothing out of the ordinary.

"How long did you wait before you heard it?" Bash's whisper was so soft, Al barely heard it over the night.

Al hesitated before responding. "Not this long..."

"How much longer do you think we should wait?"

The sound rose out of the valley softly at first, like the intake of air that precedes an explosion. Then it burst out with fear and pain.

"mmmmmmmAARROOOOOOO!"

Despite the heat, Al found himself chilled from the inside. Each trickle of sweat left an icy trail in its wake. Al flicked the light on and pointed it down the ravine, the beam was shaking. Al turned to look at Bash, his eyes were huge and mouth agape. He was desperately seeking the source of the noise.

"What was that..." Before Bash could finish another sound came rising up, spectral with echo.

"Kuh." "Kuh." "Kuh." "aaAARrg." Each sound was separate and distinct.

Al was waiting for his terror to break so he could muster his courage. His limbs were frozen as each muscle coiled in preparation for flight. His senses enhanced to the point that he could distinguish between individual crickets around him, his eyes dilated making the flashlight almost too bright. He was looking for anything that might even think about becoming a threat to him. When he realized that the terror would not go away on its own, he tried to speak. Bash was staring at him blankly, like he was waiting for some kind of a response.

"We have to see what it is." His fear fattened tongue caused the words to come out slow and wooden. But after speaking, his muscles began to relax, his senses returned to normal, but the ice in his stomach remained.

"Did you hear me?" The big guy's brown eyes were

wide. "It's probably just that old redneck having some fun with a buffalo. Lets get out of here." He was whispering but he was very insistent. Al was determined though.

"You don't have to come with me. But, I'm going." He could still feel the fear, a frosty spot deep in the pit of his stomach, but it no longer held him. He started to walk to the hidden path down into the valley.

After a dozen or so deliberate steps, he heard Bash call after him. "Wait." Al turned to see the big guy walking toward him. "I'd hate myself if somethin' happened to ya 'cause I didn't go." He put one large hand on Al's shoulder. "Besides, I still wanna see your face when you find out that noise is just a squirrel fart."

31

Another Captured One

Wil woke with a start. He immediately screamed in pain, but the rag was still stuffed in his mouth, so the sound was dampened. He began to cough but could not inhale enough to get a strong burst of air. Each spasm sent a jolt from crown to temple and back again. Tears were running down his face when he was finally able to take control of his lungs again.

He was pretty sure his eyes were open, but there was little difference with them closed. It was nearly pitch black either way. Only a few specks and thin lines of pale white broke up the inky dark in front of his face. Wil's head was throbbing, his throat dry, his hands tied behind his back and legs were tied together at his feet. His feet, however, were not asleep, and only a light feeling of pins and needles remained.

He tried to push the rag out of his mouth with his tongue, to no avail. With nothing else to do, he simply tried to yell for help around the gag. He began coughing again. The rag had absorbed any moisture that had once been in his mouth. His tongue felt like sandpaper on the roof of his mouth and his throat was on fire. He couldn't even swallow. Yelling, or even whispering, for help seemed more likely to cause painful fits of coughing than actually alerting anyone of his predicament.

His vision began to adjust as he lay on the ground taking inventory of himself. The tiny specks began to thicken and solidify into sand and smooth stones. He was laying in some sort of dry creek bed.

He tried to roll into a sitting position but his head swam with the effort. He fell the few inches back onto his shoulder and laid his head down among some stones. He closed his eyes for a few seconds.

When he opened them again, he felt like more than a few minutes had passed. The chorus of the night was still there, but it appeared to be farther away. He threw himself into a sitting position, ignoring the pain in his head and the wave of dizziness that followed. He could not afford to pass out again.

This time he made it. Dizzy and swaying, but he was able to stay upright. When the spins in his head subsided he tried to look around. From his new vantage point he could see that the creek bed was only a few feet wide, and it ran into some sort of cave in front of him. The forrest crowded the dry little stream and made it impossible to see very far even after his eyes adjusted. Even so, he was grateful for what little light he had.

He heard a stone topple over somewhere in front of him. None of the stones he could see were moving. He held his breath to listen and heard the noise again. It was coming from the cave. The entrance to the underground was several shades darker than the surrounding pitch, but otherwise invisible. Another stone flipped over. This one sounded closer.

Wil never took his eyes off the void, but began to scoot backwards. Inch by inch, he used his feet to push himself along. He heard another stone flip over and roll for a few seconds before coming to rest. Wil grabbed a stone and held it behind his back. He didn't know what good it would do him with his hands tied together, but the weight of it felt good in his hand.

A stone rocked noisily in he distance behind him. He turned as much as he could toward the sound, but the dark and his position did not allow him to see much. His heart was racing. How could he fend off two things coming from different directions?

A stone crashed around inside the cave, drawing Wil's attention back to the first threat. His dry throat clenched and fear bloomed in his stomach. Quick movement drew his eyes, a rounded creek stone tumbling out of the mouth of the cave. It clattered to a stop a few yards in front of his feet.

More rocks rattled behind him as another stone flew out of the darkness in front of him. This one stopped inches from his feet. Wil found himself unable to break free, he could only stare in the cave as the sweat covering his body iced over in terror.He could now see something else moving inside the cave.

The sounds behind him came to a stop, but there was no relief in that. A third stone was flung out of the cave, tumbling down the dried creek bed. It struck the bottom of his left foot with enough force to send a jolt through the rest of his body. It rang his head particularly hard. Something was definitely coming out of the cave.

A bright light surrounded Wil, sending his own shadow knifing into the cave entrance.

"Oh Shit!" The voice sounded almost alien to Wil. After confirming that there was nothing in the cave he turned his head as much as he could toward the light.

"Are you alright?" This was a different voice, but all Wil could see was a tiny sun that was so bright he had to close his eyes.

"He's gagged. He cant answer." The silhouette of a man entered the light and bent down over him. Hands pushed the rag down around his neck, and Wil began to push the cloth out of his mouth with his tongue. The young man grabbed it and pulled it out for him.

"Wa...ahhhhh" Wil fought the urge to cough. "Wa..ahhh" He could only manage a harsh whisper. "Watahhhh" He lost control and his throat began to spasm. When the coughing fit had passed, the young man pressed a bottle to Wil's cracked lips. He had never tasted anything so sweet in his life. Though warm, bordering on hot, it was rain on the desert that his mouth had become.

Wil found that he was unable to swallow much of the first drink. Some of it was absorbed by his tongue, quenching the fire, but most of it rolled down his chin to dampen his shirt. A few more drinks and a few deep breaths later, Wil was able to talk.

"Thank you." He still couldn't see anything against the flashlight shining right at him. For all he knew, these two were part of the King's Men who were sent out to prolong his suffering. But he had to try. "Would you mind uniting me?" He gave an uneasy look toward the cave, still empty.

The young man who had removed his gag bent down into the light, revealing that he was just a child with shaggy brown hair. He was digging in a backpack. The figure holding the light bent down and began to saw at the ropes around his wrists. The first kid produced a pair of scissors from the bag, and began to work on the ropes around Wil's feet.

"I'm Willard."

The kid with the scissors responded but did not look up from his work. "I'm Al." It seemed like the scissors were no match for the ropes.

"I'm Eric." The second voice was deep, but still youthful. With a snap his hands were free. "But most people call me Bash."

Wil pulled his hands up to his chest. The wrists were raw and a little slick with blood. His shoulders were aching from being pulled into the awkward position for so long. "I can't tell you how fantastic it is to meet you two at this moment."

Bash came around and took over for Al, the pocket knife seemed to work much better than the scissors. When the rope had been cut free, both boys reached out a hand to help Wil to his feet. The sudden change in position sent a fresh wave of dizziness through his head. It gave the pain there some company for a few minutes. He swayed forward and put most of his weight on one of the boys, the big one.

"Whoa." Bash said as he tried to steady him. "Can you walk?"

"Yeah, I think so." He took an unsteady step backward, causing some rocks to clink together. Wil snapped his head up and looked to the cave. His world began to spin again with the quick movement of his head. He couldn't even see the cave anymore. Everything outside the beam of the flashlight disappeared behind a black curtain.

"Are you ok?" Al asked.

Wil continued to stare into the darkness for several seconds. "Let's get out of here." He tried to keep his voice steady, but was unsure of how successful he had been. The boys let him lean on them for support, which was ludicrous. Al was at least six inches shorter than Wil, and Bash was several inches taller.

Limping through the darkness and leaning on David and Goliath, Wil began to fear the cave less, and the King's Men more. Are these boys just toying with him. Are they leading him to his death? He didn't really think that was the case. But he didn't think he would get caught up on the wrong side of a secret militia either. In the end he decided he was more worried that there would be guards set up watching for him, than that the boys were spies of some kind.

"Would you mind turning off the flashlight?"

The boys stopped and looked at each other for a second. The flashlight clicked off. "It's not a bad idea." Said Bash.

"What happened to you?" Al asked from Wil's other side.

Wil glanced around into the surrounding woods. He had to move his head slowly to avoid the waves of vertigo. He didn't know what he expected to see in the pitched black. His eyes had not yet adjusted to the flashlight-less night. "When we get back to town, I'll tell you anything you want to know." He whispered.

In the dark he saw the boys look at each other, a small whisper to his right said, "Gun toting rednecks?" The boy's silhouettes nodded in agreement.

The trio walked along the creek bed in the dark without a word. Wil was listening for anything that could be threatening. The clatter of stones underfoot, the singing insects, and his own ragged breath was all he could hear despite his straining. The valley eventually opened a bit. A little farther into the meadow, the creek ran through a culvert and under a lightly graveled road. The road itself, mostly dirt, ran perpendicular to the little creek, out of sight in both directions.

"Where are we?" Wil asked while taking Bash's hand. The big guy pulled Wil out of the shallow creak bed and onto the surrounding grass with ease.

Al turned around and pointed into the darkness and up at a 45-degree angle, in the direction they had just come from. "Our bikes are up this trail. We have them stashed on Rutledge Rd."

Bash pointed to the left. "The ruins of the old distillery are down this road."

Wil's stomach clenched as a million butterflies were born there. He was still very much in enemy territory. He needed to get out of here, now. "My car is parked down this way." He tried to stay calm. The last thing he wanted to do was to freak out his help. He thought his voice sounded steady, but his arm was visibly shaking, even in the dark.

32

The Ones Who Got Away

The rusty Nissan was not where he had left it. It was in the middle of the Elkhorn. The path of ripped up earth and grass that started where he had parked painted a vivid picture. His car had been pushed, while still in park, into the water.

The trickle running around its tires was not enough to wash the car away, but it was enough to make the vehicle completely useless. The way the car had been position made it look like there was water in the engine. The drivers side door was left open. A quick shine of the light inside, revealed a half empty bottle of bourbon perched safely in the passenger seat.

Wil's anger flared, dampening his fear. If these boys had not found him, it would have been assumed that he had drowned after a drunk driving accident.

A large hand fell on Wil's shoulder, provoking a slight flinch. "Wachu wanna do now?"

Wil turned to look up at Bash. I want to expose these assholes, is what he wanted to say. "I don't know boys." He was exploring the back of his head with his fingers. His hair wasn't stiff with dried blood, only sweat, but a baseball sized lump had formed. "If we keep walking down this road it takes us to BC Distillery. From there it's just a couple of miles to my apartment." Wil started walking under his own power, his rage seemed to give him more strength. "We can call a cab from there, I'll pay to get you back home."

They continued down the road in relative silence. The crunching of gravel couldn't really be avoided. After several minutes, Wil decided that their footsteps were announcing their presence just as loudly as his voice would.

"I was attacked at the ruins of the old distillery." He kept his voice low, just in case. "I was knocked out before I could see who it was." He didn't know how much he wanted to tell these kids, no need to scare them unnecessarily.

A small voice to Wil's right spoke. "How long were you tied up in that ravine?"

"I don't really know." He reached up to check the gash near his temple. The whole side of his face was firm with dried blood. The cut didn't seem to be bleeding anymore. "I woke up a few minutes before you found me."

"So, you haven't been down there for several days?"

Wil was a little hungry, but did not feel weak. He was terribly parched, he continued to take small sips from the water bottle he had been given. There is no way it could have been days, maybe a few hours at the most. "I was abducted on Wednesday September 22nd."

"That's today." Bash said, then he added. "Al heard something on Sunday. That wasn't you?"

"No. Not me." Wil replied.

They walked in silence until they could see the lights of the distillery. Two orange orbs, glowing against a sea of dark, marking the entrance to the distillery. Wil was beginning to feel dizzy again, and was leaning heavily on Bash.

When they turned onto Main Street, a single car drove toward them. It's headlights were all that was visible at this distance. Wil had enough time to hope it was not the Sheriff before the unmarked compact car drove past them.

Before Wil could even breathe a sigh of relief, the car

did a U-turn and pulled up beside the unlikely trio.

"Willard?" It was a woman's voice. "Are you ok?"

33

The Ones on the Run

The inside of the car smelled like pumpkin spice. A tiny orange candle hung from the rearview mirror. It bobbed and danced with every bump and vibration in the road. The pretty woman driving the car was half watching the road and half fussing over Wil's condition.

Wil couldn't blame her. When the headlights hit them, he saw Al's jaw drop. Both of the boys eyes widened when they looked at him. He could see himself in the mirror on the underside of the visor in front of him. One side of his face was rusty with blood. That side of his shirt was stained down to his chest. The other side of his face was almost entirely purple. There were also several disconnected grid-like cuts on his cheek and forehead.

"Please don't take me to the hospital, Cindy." Wil was firm, but managed to keep any anger out of his voice despite this being the third time he had repeated himself. "I'm fine. I just need to clean up and get some rest."

"Then where do you want to go?" Her voice was low, displeased.

Wil thought for a moment. "I don't think I should go to my apartment." He turned to look at Al and Bash. He had really only heard their voices until they got in the car. Now, in the relative brightness of the passing street lights, he could see how young they actually were.

"They already planted evidence in my car. They may

do the same in my apartment." He turned back around and shrugged. "I guess I could rent a room somewhere."

"I think I know a good place." She turned to look at the road, and moved her hands back to 10 and 2. "But, you have to tell me what happened to you."

Wil nodded, and tried to laugh, but it came out as more of a cough. "Where should I start?" He decided to start with the missing people, and by the time he had reached his flooded car they were pulling into the library parking lot.

Cindy led them in through a locked side door and into a dark hallway. Wil simply followed the sound of the keys jingling in Cindy's hand. The hallway ended with another locked door that lead into the main part of the library.

The boys helped Wil to one of the tables while Cindy fumbled around under the service desk. A low hum sprang to life and the hanging lights over each of the tables began to glow. It took several minutes for them to warm up to their full brightness, but even then, the library remained gloomy.

Cindy returned with a wet wash rag and a first aid kit. She began to wipe at Wil's face with the rag.

"Do you think the King's Men are behind the missing people?" Al asked, breaking the silence in the dim room.

"If you all hadn't found me, they would have been responsible for me going missing." Wil suddenly pulled away from Cindy's rag. "Ssss Ouch!"

"I'm sorry." Her tone suggested otherwise. "But this is going to get infected if you don't let me clean it." She grabbed his chin and firmly rotated his head to face her. "You need to go to the hospital and get stitches."

He only grunted in response.

Luckily, Bash saved him from having to answer further. "They set your car up in the river, but the cops ain't got no clues 'bout the other missin' people."

"Maybe the cops just haven't found the staged scene yet." Al guessed.

"Maybe." Wil wasn't so sure, but didn't know what to make of that either way. Was Deputy Mosely the only one? Was it the whole Sheriff's department?

"When did the other two go missin'?" Bash had a pained look on his face.

"Debra's last known contact was Sunday, I think." Wil reached up and began to feel around, gingerly, on the back of his head. The knot was still the size of a baseball, at least it had stopped growing. "Steve had more information on Howard. His wife said he never made it home from work on Monday night."

Cindy stopped wiping and grabbed a brown bottle with a white cap. "Hold still, this is going to sting." She tilted the bottle over the gash above Wil's temple. She positioned the wash cloth to catch the liquid as it poured down his face. Wil flenched, but otherwise stayed still as the cool liquid hit him setting his wounds on fire. His eyes squeezed shut and his lips puckered. He could hear the sizzling peroxide. It sounded like bacon. That probably was not a good sign, but Wil couldn't worry about that right now.

Bash seemed to be in his own thoughts. He was staring into the gloom of the library and began to speak slowly. "So… Al prolly heard one of them out on Cry Baby Lane on Sunday night. That was the same day that Debra went missin'."

Wil straightened in his chair. Cindy had only half taped some gauze over his freshly cleaned wound. She sighed, "Cry Baby Lane? That old ghost story?" She eyed Wil suspiciously. "How hard did you get hit in the head?"

"No, it's true." Bash leaned forward to pat Al on the back. "Al, over here, found it. He also found what makes the noises."

She turned her greenish grey eyes on the shaggy headed boy. "So, what makes all those scary noises?"

Al's cheeks were white, like he had seen a ghost. He raised one finger and pointed at Wil.

"Yeah, tonight it was me." Wil said matter of factly.

Cindy sat down with a far-off look in her eyes. "Cry Baby Lane is real? And the King's Men are still active." She shook her head. "It all sounds so crazy."

"What do you know about the King's Men?" Wil asked.

"The local branch of the KKK called themselves the King's Men." She knit her dark eyebrows over her nose before adding, "But, they were all killed in a massacre in the early 1900's"

"1912." Al said, "It was right before the first report of strange noises at Cry Baby Lane."

"I wonder if any other people ended up goin' missin' there?" Bash was speaking slowly and to no one in particular, but the unfocused thought set up a flurry of connections in Wil's mind.

Several minutes later, Wil was on the microfiche data-base while the reader warmed up. 'Missing' was typed into the search function, there were over 500 results.

Wil turned to look at Bash. "Any idea about how to narrow this down?"

The big guy only turned his large brown eyes away from the question. Al however had an idea. "April 18th, 1954 was the date of the Valarie Webb account and May 4th, 1976 is the Robinson tale. Those are the best known Cry Baby Lane stories."

Wil narrowed his search to those dates, and after a few minutes, he had made note of the needed files. He looked like an old pro as he quickly retrieved the desired transparencies from the corner cabinet. Despite his injuries, he nimbly moved the film under the light to find the right spot displayed on the screen.

"Nancy Graham was reported missing on April 20th, 1954." He shot a quick glance at Al. "according to this article she liked to hike along the Elkhorn with her dog." After a quick scan of the article for further details but finding nothing of interest, Wil switched the film in the reader. "Oliver May went missing on May 4th," He turned around to face the boys. "You may be onto something."

Al thought for a moment. "They seem to be patrolling the ruins of the old distillery. You were attacked there." He pointed at Wil. "We were held at gunpoint there, and Howard's truck was found in the same area. What are they guarding?"

"More like hiding." Wil said.

"What do you mean?" Cindy looked bewildered.

"Before I was attacked," Wil closed his eyes to visualize the scene. "I noticed that the ruins looked funny." He shook his head before opening his eyes again. "The char marks on the stones were not consistent."

"What are you saying?" Cindy's voice was soft, barely audible.

"One block would be completely burnt, while the block right next to it showed no sign of a fire." Everyone just stared at Wil as he spoke. "It is almost as if the whole thing had been torn down and rebuilt but the stones were put back together in a different order."

Without a word, Cindy rose from the table, walked to a shelf, and pulled two books. She laid down both editions of Dr. Haley's tome on the table. "Could that explain what you found the other day?"

Wil leaned forward and flipped the newer book to the page with the map of the distillery. Cindy carefully flipped through the older book to reveal the same page.

Al immediately recognized the map in the newer book. "This is Cry Baby Lane!" He pointed to a spot near the edge of the page. "This is where we found you."

Bash leaned over the other book. "This maps different. The Elkhorn runs right by the distillery in this'en," he pointed at the older book, "but can't be seen at all on the other."

Al ran over to the same shelf Cindy had just visited and pulled a book that looked even older than Dr. Haley's first edition. He placed the delicate book on the table and opened to a middle page. Then he began to carefully fold out a map. The terrain matched the newer book, but there was no distillery depicted at the bottom of Cry Baby Lane.

"This doesn't make any sense..." Cindy shook her head. "Why put so much effort into moving the location of the ruins?"

Bash slapped the table with one meaty palm so suddenly that Wil jumped, startled. "They are hiding somethin'. Whatever it is, it ain't at Cry Baby Lane. It's where the distillery used to be."

34

The One Getting Deeper

Another Wednesday service and another success. The pews weren't as full as they could have been. Lloyd assumed the threat of the oncoming storm kept some people at home. Cindy, the pretty young woman he spoke with last week was in attendance, which was good. But she did not stay after the service to talk with him again, which was not as good. In fact, not a single person was waiting to speak with him. The storm had not yet broken, but the sound of rolling thunder could be heard in the distance, which helped to clear out the sanctuary after the service.

Lloyd spotted Mary, the cashier he had met this afternoon, near the back of the exiting parishioners. "Ms. Mary." He called out to her. An older couple turned around with the young woman. Mary was carrying a toddler with big blue eyes and blond hair.

"Looks like you were able to get out of your shift, and looks like this guy is ready for bed." Lloyd reached a hand out and ruffled some of the fine blond hair. The child only buried his face further into his mother's chest.

"Yeah, we were slow so my manager let me leave early." She looked down at the child. "And we get to stay up a little late on church nights." She smiled at him, and adjusted the grip she had on the toddler.

"Please take a seat, he looks pretty heavy."

Mary sat on one of the pews and the older couple

remained standing beside her. Lloyd noticed that the older woman and Mary had the exact same eyes behind the exact same glasses. These must be her parents. The child stuck his thumb in his mouth and looked at Lloyd cautiously.

The older man shot out one of his hands. "Phillip Starcher, I'm Mary's father. It's a pleasure to meet you Reverend."

Lloyd grabbed the man's hand and found himself being shaken with vigor. "Please just call me Lloyd."

Mr. Starcher put one hand behind the older woman, who looked very much like Mary, and gently pushed her forward. "This is my wife, Rosie."

Lloyd took her outstretched hand and bowed as if he meant to kiss her fingers.

"It is a pleasure to meet you Reverend Todd." She squeezed his hand gently, then took hers back from him.

Mr. Starcher jumped right back in front of his spouse. "Lloyd, my daughter told me about the conversation you all had this afternoon. Normally, I would just chalk up her concern to being a silly little girl,"

"Daddy!?!" Mary's protest was quiet, but exasperated, and easy for Phillip to ignore.

He continued, "But I want you to know that she is not alone in her unease about this Moonbeam situation."

Lloyd turned his show smile, which was always on inside the church, up to its full brightness. "Actually, that is what I was going to speak with Mary about. I had a chance to talk with Ms. Rutledge, or Moonbeam, this afternoon."

"That was fast." Mary was whispering. The child on her lap's big blue eyes were closed lightly, his thumb hanging limply in his mouth.

"I found myself with a bit of free time this afternoon."

Lloyd had lowered his voice as well, "So, I paid Ms. Rutledge a visit."

Philip Starcher laughed a little. "I would have paid good money to see you talk some sense into her. A man with your fire just laying into that old hippie."

Mrs. Starcher playfully slapped her husband on the shoulder. "Phillip!"

Lloyd gave a small chuckle. "The conversation was quite calm, in fact." The double doors at the front of the church opened and the Sheriff walked into the sanctuary followed by one of his deputies. Lloyd acknowledged the large man with his eyes, then continued speaking to the Starchers. "I plan on returning to speak with her again. I feel that we have a lot to teach each other."

Mary and her Mother both gasped. "But she's a devil worshiper." Mary only mouthed the last two words as the child on her chest whined a little and rearranged himself. Sheriff Hawkins took a seat a few pews back from the Starchers.

Lloyd laughed again. "She isn't a devil worshiper. She doesn't identify herself as a Christian either." Lloyd allowed his face to grow a bit serious. "But, after speaking with her, I can tell you she respects the wisdom of Jesus."

Though he was speaking softly for the sake of the sleeping child, Lloyd still wanted the Sheriff to hear. He loved an audience. And as far as audiences were concerned, Lloyd always preferred quality over quantity.

Lloyd continued, "She even understands some of his teachings with a different interpretation than my own."

"What do you mean different?" Mr. Starcher seemed suspicious.

"That is one of the reasons I want to return to speak with her." Lloyd was trying to choose his words carefully. Mr.

Starcher didn't strike Lloyd as the type of man who understood nuance. "Different is not always bad."

Mr. Starcher replied quickly, "It's usually not good, especially when it comes to religion."

Mary spoke up almost absently. "If she believes in Jesus' teachings', why isn't she a Christian?"

Lloyd was relieved to change the subject. "She gave a couple of reasons, but what it boils down to, she just doesn't have faith." Lloyd took a deep breath before adding. "She claims some atrocities committed in Christ's name as her reason, but that is clearly a justification. She simply lacks the faith required to commit her life to Christ."

"Then why would you want to continue to speak with her?" Mr. Starcher was genuinely confused, and appeared on the verge of anger. Lloyd felt a little safer with the Sheriff present. Despite his age, Mr. Starcher was still an imposing figure.

"She is an intelligent woman with a good heart who is entering the third act of her life; Any man of God would want to inspire faith in her. It can only make the kingdom of God stronger."

"You ain't worried that her rituals will draw people away from the Lord?" Mary was speaking almost normally now, but the child was sleeping soundly.

"It doesn't seem like her rituals are much of an issue at this time. She actually invited me to something she was doing tonight." Lloyd reached up and smoothed his short dirty blond hair down. "It sounded like a few of her friends were coming over to have some drinks." Lloyd flashed his smile briefly. "It didn't really sound like my idea of a good time. But, I will keep my eye on her for any funny business."

Mary was shuffling around on the pew trying to stand up. "Thank you for speaking with her. I feel a little better hearing you say there is no devil worship going on in town."

Lloyd reached out and grabbed Mary's hand to help her to her feet. The child jostled a little but fell comfortably back down on her shoulder. "Ms. Rutledge is a little misunderstood and very misguided, but she is not a devil worshiper." He grabbed Mr. Starcher's shoulder and gave a little squeeze. "Now get this baby to bed. The poor guy is all tuckered out."

Mr. Starcher gave Lloyd a curt nod. Lloyd was unable to read the meaning behind the gesture. As the family filed out of the sanctuary Lloyd called after them. "It was great to meet you folks." Lloyd turned and made eye contact with the Sheriff.

"I missed you tonight Sheriff, but I realize that you are always on the job."

The big man stood, hat in hand, and walked over to Lloyd. "Well," His deep voice echoed in the sanctuary. "I would much rather have been here with you Rev. But sometimes, duty calls." His gunmetal grey eyes drifted off to look at the stained glass. He seemed to be studying one of them.

"Sounds like some unpleasant work." Lloyd followed the Sheriff's gaze to Abraham.

"I can't talk too much about an ongoing investigation," His eyes snapped back to Lloyd. "But, it's not looking good for our missing twosome."

Lloyd pulled both hands behind his back and held them together to keep himself from popping his knuckles. "Oh my! I'll pray that no one else goes missing. These are dangerous times."

The Sheriff's eyes drifted off toward the window again. "Dangerous times indeed." The big man turned to face Lloyd again. "I'm sorry Rev, I didn't mean to eavesdrop but, I couldn't help but to hear your conversation with the Starchers." Sheriff Hawkins was more serious than Lloyd had ever seen him before. "Now I know that you say you believe that Moonbeam is not evil, but I am not a trusting person. As a man of the law, trust is just not in my nature."

Lloyd turned his head, squinting his eyes a bit; maybe there was something he had missed about her. Ms. Rutledge certainly held the ire of the town. "What do you think should be done?" He wasn't sure he like where this was going.

The big man wrapped a heavy arm around Lloyd's shoulders. "You said Moonbeam invited you to a party tonight." Sheriff Hawkins smiled broadly. "I think we should all attend." He turned to the deputy who had entered with him and was now leaning against the back wall. "Don't you, Officer Mosely?"

The young man snapped to attention. "Yes sir!"

The big man continued to walk Lloyd toward the double doors at the entrance of the church. "You know, make sure there is no funny business going on out there. There are a couple of people missing, we must check out every lead."

Lloyd didn't want anyone to go to jail. But he was new to town, and everyone else seemed suspicious of Ms. Rutledge. Lloyd found himself saying. "I guess it wouldn't hurt to check it out, I was invited after all."

35

When it Rains it Pours

The thunder echoed down from the heavens ominously, it was getting closer with every rolling crash. Wil had started to think this was a bad idea. At the same time though, the King's Men would probably seek cover from the storm. Besides, Wil would have surprise on his side tonight. They would not expect him, of all people, to be snooping around.

"I think I see something." A whispered voice to his right strained to be heard over the rustling leaves. He could hear footsteps on either side of him, but could not see either of the boys.

"What is it?" Wil asked.

"I think it's the river."

One of the stipulation that Cindy gave before allowing Wil to borrow her car, was that the boys had to be taken home before any more investigating. Wil did try. They refused to tell him where they lived and wanted to go back to their bikes. When Wil stopped the car at the spot they claimed to have stashed their bikes, Al turned to him with a sly smile. "You know we are going to follow you right? You might as well just take us with you." Wil hadn't spent much time arguing with them. After his experience earlier today, he preferred having the backup, youthful or not.

He could see light reflecting off water through the trees ahead of them. It had been Bash's suggestion to start at the Riverlawn mobile home park. He thought it was far enough from the ruins near Cry Baby Lane that it would not be patrolled by the King's Men.

Wil didn't know the area well enough to have an opinion, so he hoped the big guy was right. So far his plan was unfolding well. The river had been found easily enough. "Now we just follow the river?"

Though no moon could be seen and the storm clouds kept creeping in from the west, there was a bit of light by the river. The water seemed to gather up and reflect all available light in thousands of ripples and eddies on its surface. Wil could just make out Bash's silhouetted form stretching out to point. "This way."

Though both boys were carrying flashlights, neither had used them. Wil didn't have a flashlight, but he did have a Louisville Slugger. A lightweight aluminum baseball bat that Cindy kept in her car. "A gal can never be too careful." She had said. And a man is about to do something stupid and dangerous, he had thought in response.

The trio had been walking single file for some time when a sudden burst of light startled Wil. "Watch your step guys," the big guy called back softly. He used the beam of the flashlight to highlight a tree that had fallen into the river, across their path. He easily climbed over and continued along the bank.

Wil sat on the trunk, which was only about a six-inch drop from a full stand, then slowly spun his legs to the other side. The rest and water at the library had made him feel much better, but Wil didn't want to push himself too hard. He still felt a little weak from blood loss, or stress, or trauma. All of them.

A cool breeze cut through the humid air right as Wil saw the first flash of lightning. Barely a second passed before the thunder cracked in the sky. This time it was much closer. He thought he saw something in the quick flash of light.

"Bash." He whispered. The footsteps in front of him stopped. "I think I saw something. Let me see a light."

Al caught up from behind and handed over the plastic tube. Wil pointed it at the outline of a tree and flipped the switch. The circle of light landed on the base of an oddly misshaped and moss covered tree trunk. It looked square and angular, with a wide but flatish base. Wil rubbed some of the moss away to reveal rough hewn stone underneath.

"This is a stone wall." Wil said excitedly. "I think we found the distillery."

Al looked around at the forest surrounding him on three sides. "Where?"

Wil whirled the end of the bat in a small circular motion. "Here, or around here. It's been 200 years since the fire. Looks like the Wallwood has taken this place back. His light found another moss covered stone, half buried in the dirt. Rough hewn and broken, its once sharp edges had been dulled by centuries of wind and rain.

Thunder cracked sharply like a gunshot, before settling into the gentle rolling quality it had tonight. All three jumped at the sound. Wil didn't even remember seeing a flash to announce it.

"That sounded close." Bash said quietly, a little worried.

"Yeah." Wil agreed. "Lets look around for a few more minutes then we can head back to Cindy's car before the storm hits." He thought it was already too late for that. Even if they left right now they would only be halfway back before the clouds burst. If they were going to get wet anyway, he thought they should at least make the most of it. He didn't know when he would be able to come out here again, if ever.

There were plenty of stones that had spent the past 200 years being eaten by rain, wind, lichen, moss, and snow. There had definitely been a large building by the river at one time. Nothing Wil saw suggested that the building was a distillery.

He was just about to call out that it was time to leave when his light found something bluish.

"What is that?" Bash called out a little too loudly.

Wil approached the round object, and noticed that there were actually three of these things in a line. Hugged by trees and oxidized to a blueish-green, three copper stills were distilling foliage and earth on the banks of the 'mighty' Elkhorn, in the middle of the Wallwood.

"I think these are exactly what we are looking for, boys." The copper had corroded, but the stills seemed to be in good shape. Wil knocked on the side, producing a short lived hollow clang.

"Is that metal?" Al asked.

"Copper." Wil answered. "These are Bourbon stills. They couldn't move these bad boys to the new location. Too heavy. I bet each one of these holds at least 500 gallons."

"Whoa!" One of the boys cried out. It was a little dramatic in Wil's opinion.

"Oh shit!" The other one called.

Wil saw that they were looking past the large copper stills and into the Wallwood. At first, Wil thought that the glow was from a bon fire, but it was much too big for that. Before he knew what was happening, Wil found himself running toward the flames. His thoughts kept flipping back and forth between the hopes that there would be an article in this for him and the fear that someone might be in serious danger.

36

The Faltering One

"Once we get there, you'll see she is just having an innocent gathering with some friends." Or at least that's what Lloyd hoped they would find. He was more afraid that there would be drugs involved. He didn't want Cheryl to get into trouble, he had been invited as a friend. After all, he did enjoy their conversation, and he was definitely planning on visiting her again. But, on the other hand, if she was breaking the law... The way the Sheriff had been acting, it seemed like he suspected her of being involved in the disappearances.

"I hope you are right Father." The younger officer didn't turn around to look at Lloyd.

"Reverend, uhh, and please call me Lloyd."

Sheriff Hawkins let out a gravelly laugh. "Don't mind him Rev, he's Catholic."

Lloyd laughed a little. He thought it sounded a bit stiff. "Well, Christians of all stripes must stick together in dangerous times." He might have said more. He even had a joke line ready for situations like this; Catholic, huh? Well, we all have our flaws. He always got a chuckle with that line, it was all in good fun. Lloyd didn't really feel like performing right now. He began to pull on his fingers until each knuckle cracked.

He wasn't quite sure why he was unable to conjure the energy needed to play the part tonight. Maybe he was just drained from the day's events. Maybe it had more to do with his current situation. This was the first time Lloyd had ever been in the back of a police car. Even though he knew he was not in trouble, it was an unsettling position to find himself. He didn't know which he found more unnerving; the steel mesh between himself and the officers, or the lack of a door handle on his door. He felt caged.

Lloyd swayed with the curving country road, each bending turn creating more nausea than the last. The headlights of the Sheriff's jeep created moving shadows in the trees as they passed. Lloyd decided that this area was far more inviting during the day, or at least, in his own car. When he had attempted to pop every knuckle on both hands, he started the process over again.

Lloyd listened to the rise and fall of the engine as he watched the passing Wallwood. His thoughts had drifted back to his conversation with Cheryl. She had claimed that she worshipped the same God as Lloyd, just not through Jesus. Instead of following God in human form, she worshiped by showing reverence for the gifts God created for mankind.

"This is it." Sheriff Hawkins' growl pulled Lloyd back into the car from the past. The jeep slid over to the side of the road, Lloyd could see no evidence of the driveway he had used in the daylight. The lights outside the jeep turned off as the lights inside turned on. Both lawmen opened their doors and exited the vehicle, leaving Lloyd alone for a few seconds.

Lloyd almost had a panic attack in the few seconds it took Sheriff Hawkins to open his door. Being alone in his cage was a bit too claustrophobic. Lloyd stepped out onto the pavement and found himself in the middle of the narrow country road. The forrest hugged the asphalt tightly, leaving little room for the parked jeep.

Sheriff Hawkins grabbed the radio off of his belt and produced a loud burst of static. "We are in location, you in position?" He held the bulky walkie against his lips as he spoke.

Lloyd didn't like the sound of what he said. It appeared that there was a plan in place and Lloyd had not been made aware.

The radio crackled to life again almost immediately, "Five-minute ETA."

The big man shook his head. "Get there and wait for the signal."

"Is all that really necessary, Sheriff? For a few old women?" Lloyd struggled to keep his voice even; his show smile was long gone.

"I learned a long time ago, Rev," A large hand clapped Lloyd on the shoulder. "Never go anywhere without backup." Sheriff Hawkins squeezed his shoulder before letting go.

The hatch on the back of the vehicle slammed shut behind Lloyd. He turned around to find the younger officer holding a rifle. He pulled the bolt action, clicking a round into place.

"Now wait a minute!" Lloyd was unable to hide his anger. "The only weapon we will be needing is the Word of God." Lloyd looked to the Sheriff for confirmation.

The big man only shrugged. "You've got your weapons," he patted the service revolver on his hip. "and me and Deputy Mosely have our own."

Lightning flashed and thunder flowed across the sky. A cool wind began blowing through the trees. Leaves rattled, branches rubbed together and a shiver ran down Lloyd's spine. He did not like this at all. It was almost as if the night itself was pushing in on him.

Lloyd followed the sound of the gravel crunching under the officer's feet until the Sheriff turned on a flashlight. He held it high over his left shoulder as if it were a weapon and not a tool. Lloyd could see the lawman's other hand hovering over the butt of his gun.

There were a couple of cars in the driveway, but no lights. It was so dark that Lloyd thought they were in the wrong place entirely. His relief was short lived; it died when the Sheriff's light found the porch. The same mismatched rails and slats that he had been struck by earlier that same day.

The Officers slowly walked up the steps and took position on either side of the door. Lloyd remained on the gravel driveway. How could he have let himself get drawn into this mess. At this point, he didn't know what else to do, but to continue tagging along. At least he would be able to apologize to Cheryl immediately.

THUNK THUNK THUNK

The knocking of the metal flashlight was muted by the heavy wood of the door. After a few seconds of silence, the Sheriff nodded at Mosely. The young man reached over and turned the knob, pushing the door open.

The Sheriff's light revealed an empty entry hall. "You sure she said she was gathering tonight?" The light fell on Lloyd. Before he could even give a nod, the radio let out two short burst. The light fell to the ground as the big man pulled the radio off his belt again.

"What?"

"sskkkk...In the woods...sskkkk around back...sskkkk"

Lloyd found himself jogging behind the officers around the corner of the house. He could see the glow in the woods well before he could see the actual fire through the trees. The Sheriff's light had been turned off, but lightning was striking several times a minute to light their path. The rain wouldn't be far behind.

By the time Lloyd crossed over the little wooden bridge leading into a narrow wooded trail, he could hear voices over the rolling thunder.

"To the South we sow our sorrow, to grow happiness tomorrow,"

The wind gusting through the trees tried to drown out the chanting, but the voices rose higher.

"To the West we wash away our worries, our hates, our fates, our furies."

The cool breeze began to gust heavily, and the chanting grew louder.

"To the East we entertain in bliss, we sit, we watch, we wait, we kiss."

Lightning flashed, lighting up the trail, spiderwebbed with a million shadows from the canopy above. Thunder clapped over top of the now hysterical voices. Lloyd caught up to the two lawmen just in time to see the Sheriff pulling a dark bandana over his head, in the flickering light of the fire. Deputy Mosely was adjusting the same mask so that his eyes were lined up with the holes in the fabric. Then he saw It.

The three naked women standing around a blazing bon-fire did nothing to draw Lloyd's attention away from the beast that stood with them. It danced around the fire with animal legs under a human torso. The head was goat-like and alien. The fear that blossomed inside him at that moment was unfathomable. His limbs stiffened, mouth dried up, and eyes squeezed shut. Then, he heard the shot.

37

Borrowed Time Eventually Runs Out

Lightning flashed and the wind picked up causing the flames to flare. Sparks flew into the air, like so many lighting bugs racing to the sky. Moonbeam briefly thought of the water she had in buckets to put the fire out at the end of the night, but the ecstasy of the moment drove the thought from her head.

This wonderful creature knew the ceremony perfectly. It stepped around the fire and threw its arms up in sync with Moonbeam herself. It alternated between growling and purring to match the chanting of the women. It was almost as if the creature, or should she call him dogman, had been watching her for years. Of course it had. She remembered seeing animal-like faces in the woods during the ceremonies of the past. She always told herself it was a trick of the fire light, but was never able to fully convince herself of that. She also had her suspicions about her recovery from cancer. She didn't remember much about that night, only that she woke up in this meadow and felt a little stronger.

The ceremony was coming to an end. She threw her arms into the air and screamed, "The North will never know!" Thunder exploded across the skies at that exact moment. Nature had acknowledged her ritual. "The North will never know!" As the thunder rumbled off into the night, the chorus of crickets, the crackle of fire, and heavy breathing became the only sounds. It was relatively silent compared to the intensity of the ritual.

Moonbeam felt the shot more than she heard it. A whip cracked inside her sternum and sent a shockwave through her whole body. Her ears only picked up an intense ringing. For an instant she could see a black mist falling in front of the flames. The spray exploded from Dogman's shoulder, which violently jerked forward.

The tone in her ears was still blocking out the crickets and fire crackling when she regained control of her body. She ran to the creature, who had fallen to one knee, left arm hanging limply at its side, right claw clutching at its opposite shoulder. She caught movement on the other side of the meadow.

Two masked men entered the meadow from the shadowed trail that lead back to her cabin. One of them pulled the lever of the rifle they were holding causing an empty cartridge to fly out from the barrel. It winked several times with reflected fire light as it tumbled to the ground. The other man was holding a pistol, he was one of the biggest men Moonbeam had ever seen.

Moonbeam scrambled around the creature to shield it from more gunfire. Donna joined her immediately, Shawn was there a few seconds later. The young woman was almost as worried about covering herself as she was about covering the creature.

"Well I'll be damned." The large man with the handgun spoke. "The stories are true after all." The voice was deep and rough and barely audible over the ringing in her ears. "Come on out here boys, it's time we make things right with the past." He turned toward the northern edge of the clearing, and three more men stepped out of the Wallwood. Each one was wearing the same light colored Zorro mask covering the top half of their head and face. The newcomers were all wearing long grey robes to match their masks.Only one was armed, he held a small pistol in one hand.

As they walked over to join the first two men, who were both wearing tan shirts and dark slacks below the masks, the big man growled again. " You too, Rev."

After a few seconds, a third man crept into the meadow from the shaded lane. At first it was only a shadow, but slowly faded into a man wearing a dark suit with sandy blonde hair and wide eyes. It was the Reverend Lloyd Todd. Though his eyes were opened wide enough to take in the whole scene, he was somehow able to avoid eye contact Moonbeam. He was either ashamed of her nakedness, or something else.

"I had always heard stories about this beast." The big man shook his head. "But, I didn't believe them." He holstered his pistol. But the rifle remained leveled at the creature's head. "Legend is, that a creature that looked just like this, slaughtered a group of King's Men while they were lynchin' some family of criminals." The firelight that rose and fell on the mask never illuminated his eyes, they remained black holes. "After that, the King's Men moved heaven and Earth to keep people away from that place." The big man waved his arms around. "From this place."

The creature was breathing rhythmically, a short, hard snort every few seconds. Moonbeam took a few steps forward, slowly at first. "But you left my family alone? We have been here for generations." She stared into the soulless holes where his eyes should have been. "Almost a century."

He merely laughed, a deep rumble that could have been thunder. "I've often wondered the same thing. I can only guess, maybe they thought the Rutledge clan would get murdered by these things sooner or later."

Moonbeam looked over her shoulder at Dogman. No, that didn't quite fit. These creatures had not so much as approached her family until now, as far as she knew. "I haven't been murdered yet." She smiled at the big man with the metal star on his chest.

"No, you haven't." He nodded to the men behind him, two of them broke off from the group and approached the fire. "But you won't be living out here much longer either." The two unarmed, robed men were each wrapping long strips of cloth around a stick they plucked from the fire, creating a torch.

The Sheriff continued as they worked. "I actually stopped following some of the protocol for protecting against these abominations because I didn't believe in them." He snorted. "But then Reverend Todd came to town. The Rev always preached to do everything in the service of Christ. Isn't that right Rev?"

Reverend Todd looked dazed, like his mind was somewhere else completely. The big man continued even though Lloyd had given no response.

"I found more passion in my work, in my public and private life. You really inspired me Rev. After all, this whole thing is about keeping people away from the influence of Satan." He spat.

Lloyd broke out of his shock and looked at the Sheriff with a mixture of horror and shame. He fell to his knees and began a chant of his own in a low voice. Moonbeam could only make out a little bit before the wind caught it and carried his voice away. "...hallowed be thy name, Thy kingdom..." A shower of sparks shot up from the fire.

The Sheriff proceeded without missing a beat. The newly made torches were now aflame. "Remember Abraham and Isaac? You must be willing to do anything in His name. And everything you do, do it to honor Him."

He bent down to talk to the Reverend directly. "Anything you do with Christ in your heart is good." He reached over and patted the praying man on the back before standing back to his full height. Lloyd cringed at the touch, but never broke his prayer.

He took a step toward Moonbeam. "Even an action that appears evil can be good if it is done in the service of God."

"Do you actually believe that crap?" She looked from the large masked man to Lloyd. The Reverend was in his own world, so she focused on the Sheriff. "You know, you should really get a better disguise. Or at least take off your uniform before you play dress up in the woods Sheriff."

The big man growled. "You associate with demons and you are lecturing me? You deserve every bit of hell that I can provide to you." With a sharp hand gesture, the men holding the flaming torches tossed them into the Wallwood. The fallen foliage lit immediately and grew faster than she would have thought possible.

She instinctively lunged toward the buckets of water, but another whip cracked in her sternum. A spot of dirt a few feet in front of her exploded as her ears began ringing again.

She turned to see the Sheriff's revolver still smoking. He was speaking but she couldn't make out the words over the hum in her head. A fat raindrop landed on her arm, and the breeze that carried it stoked the flames burning the Wallwood, and pushed them toward her home.

38

The One Who Reacts

Al was running as fast as he dared through the trees to keep up with Wil. He could hear Bash's whispered screams coming from behind him, but could not make out the words over his own footfalls. The growing fire provided enough light for Al to keep his feet, but thin twigs were scratching at his face and arms.

Suddenly, Wil stopped running, and Al could see him holding up a hand against the not so distant flames. Al stopped and Bash's heavy footsteps stopped right behind him.

"Whadya think Al?"

Al held one finger up to his lips, and motioned for Bash to follow him. As they approached Wil, Al found out why the reporter had stopped so suddenly. Al could hear voices up ahead over the crackling flames. A deep gravely voice followed a couple of screams, women or children.

Wil made the same "Be quiet" gesture Al had made, and then slowly began to weave through the woods toward the voices. The three of them crept closer until they could see figures standing in a clearing that had been cut into the Wallwood. They were completely silhouetted against the fire. They may have been shadow people for all the detail Al could see.

One of the figures was some sort of scare crow, or at least that is what Al thought until the huge creature reared its head back and roared. The sound was a low rumble overlaid by a high-pitched squeal.

"What the hell is that thing?" Wil whispered. The trio had stopped in a spot that gave them a view into the meadow without exposing themselves to those inside the clearing.

"Dogman." Al and Bash answered in unison, which normally caused a fit of giggles, but tonight it only generated an icy spike of fear in Al's gut.

There was commotion inside the clearing, a deep voice growled. "Hold steady boys! We can't let that thing get away!"

As his eyes adjusted, Al could start to see that five or six figures on one side of the clearing were wearing masks.

"Those are King's Men." Wil whispered excitedly.

The battle in Al's stomach intensified. Swirling butter-flies versus frosty fear, nerves versus terror. Al found himself unable to do anything but let the scene play out in front of him.

A slender silhouetted figure broke away from the hud-dled clump of people around Dogman, taking several slow steps toward the King's Men. "Em, No!" a high pitched voice cried, but the shadow of the naked woman took step after de-liberate step.

"You claim to do good work, to follow Christ." The shadow figure seemed to vibrate a little as the fire danced be-hind her. A soft sizzle could be heard as the rain began to fall a little harder. "But, all you do is pick and choose what you want to follow in an effort to justify your own prejudices..."

Her words were abruptly cut off by a tremendous crack. A single blast, that was sharper than thunder, rolled through the trio in the woods. Wil felt the power of the shot in his chest. A shadow spray sprang out behind the woman. She took one more step before falling to her knees. A flash of lightning revealed the old woman's face had grown a third eye in her forehead. A single red tear rolled down her nose before she fell forward.

The women screamed, but she did not move. The deep voice growled, but she did not move. The winds howled, but she did not move.

"Sorry." A new voice called. It was male and youthful. "I was aiming for the beast."

Al could not pull his eyes away from the dead woman. The scream that filled the air a few seconds later, finally got his attention.

Dogman had crossed the meadow in the blink of an eye. The beast ripped the rifle away from the masked man and swung the butt of the gun into his face. Al heard the impact, a sickening crack, over the screams and crackles of flame. The other masked men seemed frozen in place, the creature had moved so quickly, they could not react.

Dogman was reaching down with one disfigured hand to grab the fallen man when the big man in the police uniform was able to pull his gun free from the holster. He quickly pointed the gun at the creatures midsection, only a few feet away. The two pops that came from the gun were almost muted in Al's head among all the other sounds vying for his attention.

Dogman's head whipped toward the large man holding the gun, his snout opening in a scream of pain and rage. With a single quick motion, Dogman flicked his wrist, sending the prone man flying into the other uniformed man. Both men crumpled to the ground in a heap. One of them lay limply on top of the other, who was scrambling to get back to his feet.

Al didn't notice that Wil was gone until he saw him creeping into the meadow unnoticed by the King's Men or the Beast's women. The reporter dropped the aluminum bat and picked up the rifle. Al could not continue to watch this like a movie, he had to act. But he was frozen in place. What could

L. M. HOSLEY

he do anyway?

The fire was roaring strongly now, despite the downpour. The crackle of flames and the hiss of steaming rain were almost deafening. Visible vapor was rising above the flames and began to creep along the ground into the clearing. The unnatural mist tentacles were slithering toward the huddled mass over the unmoving woman. Two silhouetted figures were sobbing over the body.

"Come on!" Al turned to Bash and yelled to be heard over the fire and rain, to be heard over his own fright.

Rain was running down Bash's bald head and into his face. His normally large eyes were more like dinner plates than saucers. He ran a large squeegee-like hand down his face, before responding. "Where?"

"They need our help!" He pointed to the huddled figures outlined against the fire. Before Bash had a chance to argue, or Al had time to think, he pushed himself forward toward the meadow. The heat increased with every step, but each step melted the paralyzing ball of fear in his stomach a little bit more. The flames were so hot by the time he reached the pair of sobbing women, that Wil was unsure how much of the weight of his clothing was rain and how much was sweat.

Al tried his best not to look at the naked form that was lying on the earth. The other two women didn't seem to notice him in their grief. Their bare skin was shimmering with rain in the firelight. He could hear grunts and cries of pain to his left, but he couldn't really make out what was happening against the spreading fire.

"Come with me!" A woman with a mass of dark hair looked up at him, there were several dark curls plastered to her face. Her eyes were wide and puffy, but she did not seem to see him.

He tried again. "It's not safe here!" He had to scream to

236

be heard over the sound of the roaring surroundings. The heat was nearly unbearable, but she continued to stare blankly.

The other woman had limp blond hair that form fit her head like a helmet. She continued to sob over her friend. Al was still trying not to look down at the body, but he could not help but notice that the hair that should have been white was turning a deep red.

Bash knelt down beside the blond woman, took her hands and began to lift her to her feet. She allowed her self to be led away without protest. Al was not having the same luck.

He reached out his hand to grab hers right as another gunshot cracked. From this close, all sound seemed to stop before and after the concussive blast. His heart jumped into his throat and the pit of his stomach began to freeze again. His ears rang, but not loud enough to block out the sound of the shot rolling away through the woods.

"Please, come with me!" Al shouted over the hum in his ears. It's hard to say whether it was the urgency in Al's voice or the scare of the shot, but she took his hand and stood. Wil surveyed the area before running back into the woods, but all he could make out was a man in a muddy suit, on his knees with his arms raised, screaming into the storm.

Two more gunshots followed them as they fled the meadow. Al led the dark-headed woman past Bash. He was lifting the short-haired woman out of the mud. She had apparently slipped. Al did not stop until he was safely inside the treeline. He led the dark-haired woman to a thick tree that should shield them from any more gunfire.

"Are you ok?" Al asked. He was very aware of her naked body, but she seemed not to notice. She must have been in shock or something. He pulled off his backpack and dug out the sweatshirt. He handed it to her while averting his eyes.

Bash carried his ward the last few meters out of the

clearing. "She's been hit!" He called out to Al before carefully leaning her against a nearby tree. Al could see the red streaks running down her leg. The rain would never wash it clean, only change the path of the already flowing blood.

"What do we do?" Al was out of ideas.

The dark-haired woman had pulled the now soaked sweatshirt over her head. She curled up beneath the tree with her knees pulled inside the shirt and wrapped her arms around them.

"Need ta' put pressure on the wound. Try'en stop the bleedin'." Bash was urgent.

"With what?"

"Will this help?" The small voice was almost missed among the chaos behind them. Al turned to find the young woman holding a roll of duct tape she had found in his backpack.

Al grabbed the tape and ran to Bash. "Here."

Bash took it and turned toward the bleeding woman. "This is going to hurt."

The mostly circular wound was right above the knee. Blood was rushing out, but being diluted with rainwater immediately. It was the discolored flesh that made Al's knees give a little. Bash quickly placed the duct tape and began to wrap. He turned her leg a little to expose a smaller hold on the back of her leg. He adjusted the path of the tape to cover this one as well.

"Good news." Bash tried to sound cheery, but he just sounded strained to Al. "The bullet went straight through." She winced a little as he wrapped her leg.

The small voice was now right behind Al. "Donna? Are you ok?" The dark-haired woman knelt down and took Donna's hand.

The older woman ran her hand through her soaked hair, pushing some away from her face. Her skin was very pale. "I've been better." She turned to Bash and Al. "You boys wouldn't happen to have another shirt would ya?"

Al peeked around a tree while Donna dug in the backpack for something to wear. What he saw filled his heart with terror.

39

Not a Marksman

The sight of the grey masks sparked a fury inside Wil that burned hotter than the woods. He kept seeing the nearly empty bottle of bourbon propped up in his passenger seat. As a reporter he knew it was better not to be a part of the story. As a human, he knew it was safer to stay unseen in the woods. But still, as soon as the rifle was thrown free, Wil found himself running toward it. He wanted to make sure these assholes couldn't hurt anyone else. Now was the best time he could think of to try, when else would he have the help of a seven-foot tall, hulking beast?

Wil watched the monstrosity throw a full-grown man into another with a flick of his wrist. Then started to question his own logic. Would that thing be able to tell the difference between him and the King's Men? He bent down to pick up the rifle, never missing a stride. 'Too late now,' he thought to himself.

He saw two of the King's Men running into the Wallwood, away from the beast. The one who remained was pointing his gun at the creature's back. He was visibly shaking. Before Wil even noticed the stringy grey hair spilling out of the bandana, he swung the rifle with all his strength. The heavy wooden butt of the gun connected with the man's wrist producing a muted crack, and a piercing scream. The pistol flipped into the puddle that the ground had become. The rain continued to fall harder and harder.

Wil turned the rifle around and pointed it at the

masked man who was bent over and clutching his wrist. "Freeze." Drops of water sprayed from his lips when he spoke, Wet grey strands of hair were hanging out from under the masking bandana. The soaked bandana was now more of a charcoal color than smokey.

The masked man slowly looked in Wil's direction, then to the gun at his feet. He continued to be doubled over with his wrist held tightly against his chest.

"Don't even think about..." Before Wil could even finish his sentence, the masked man lunged for the pistol, so Wil pulled his trigger. He only meant to scare the old man into stopping, but nothing happened.

Time seemed to slow down. Water droplets were flung off the old man's hair as he grabbed for the half submerged gun. Wil squeezed the trigger again, and again, but nothing happened. As a last ditch effort, Wil charged forward.

Each step seemed to take forever, his shoes were getting stuck in the now saturated earth. Time continued to dilate around him, he could almost count the drops of water that made up the splash produced when the masked man grabbed the submerged gun. When he connected his shoulder into the man's chest, the pistol went off, and time seemed to regain normal speed.

Sharp pain shot through his ear and all sound on his right side was immediately replaced by an unyielding buzz. The old man fell backward gasping for breath from the impact. The gun had fallen back into the mud, Wil bent to pick it up and tucked it into his belt behind his back. With the masked man still writhing on the ground, Wil took a second to glance at Dogman.

The beast was holding deputy Mosely by his neck again and the Sheriff was scrambling on the ground away from the fight. Suddenly the large muddy man turned around, flinging mud from his extended arm. He fired two wild shots in the direction of the creature. Mosely jerked once and then seemed to go limp.

The Sheriff slipped in the mud, losing the gun. It slid, splashing through the puddled ground, and came to a stop a few inches from where the Reverend continued to scream his prayer into the raging heavens. The creature dropped Mosely's body, it made a sickening thump as mud splashed up around him. The big man dove in the mud for his revolver. Wil wondered it if would still work after falling in the mud several times, but he lunged for it as well. The gun in his belt had been completely forgotten.

The masked man was much closer and reached the gun first, knocking the reverend face first into the mud in the process. Wil slid to a stop and brought his rifle up. He knew it wouldn't shoot, but the Sheriff would not.

"Don't move!" Wil screamed. Now that the reverend had stopped his prayer and all combatants were relatively still, the meadow seemed oddly silent. The roaring flames, screaming wind, and boiling rain were simply background noise. The reverend was laying flat on his chest in the mud right next to the still smoking fire pit. Dogman was looming several yards away from the still-armed masked man. Wil could see that his breathing was labored, but against the bright flames no injuries could be seen in silhouette.

The Sheriff looked at Wil in surprise, eyes wide behind the sopping material of the mask. He looked down at the rifle and smiled. "I thought you'd be dead by now."

"I'm glad that you were wrong." Wil replied. He saw the Reverend begin to pull himself out of the mud. He started his prayer again, but this time it was softer.

"Our Father, who art in Heaven…"

The big man ignored him. "Oh, I bet you are." he growled.

"Hallowed be thy name…"

The deep voice continued. "Unfortunately for you, I know something that you don't."

"Thy Kingdom come…"

"What's that?" Wil had a feeling it had something to do with why the rifle wouldn't shoot. He began to feel around for a safety switch.

The big man raised the muddy pistol. "You have to cock that one after every shot."

"Thy will be done…" The Reverend swung a heavy branch, that was still smoking, into the back of the masked man's head. The big man went stiff upon impact, and fell forward into the mud. "On Earth as it is in Heaven." Lloyd finished.

He dropped the smoking stick and looked down at the unconscious man. "I am sorry Sheriff, but you left me little choice." The reverend shook his head and sighed. "I'm afraid it was you who led men away from the teachings of Jesus."

Dogman fell forward onto his hands, or whatever he had at the end of his arms. The creature seemed to struggle a little bit before getting into a sitting position. Wil could see blood dripping from several gunshot wounds on his torso.

He wanted to help but, had nothing to offer. Throwing the rifle down, Wil saw that Reverend Todd didn't appear to have any ideas either.

"Wil!" He heard the call a split second before he heard the heavy steps approaching from behind. Wil turned just as another beast walked right past him. Brownish black fur from fore-arm to claw. Upper arms and chest nearly hairless and human. Fur started to grow finely on the shoulders and grew thicker up the neck. The head was covered in short thick hair, A long snout decorated with a group of long white whiskers sprouting from its chin. The seven foot giant completely ignored Wil as he walked by.

Suddenly, Al was right beside him with a ball of twine. "We need to tie them up before they wake and run away." The boy smiled and pushed a few strands of wet hair from his forehead. "It's Bash's idea."

"What about them?" Wil pointed at the creatures. The newcomer was mixing something into the mud and wiping it over the wounds of his friend.

"Dogmen are tough." The boy's smile widened so much that Wil worried he might drown in this downpour if his mouth opened any further.

Wil watched as both Dogmen climbed to their feet, and began walking toward the center of the meadow. When they reached the body of the woman who's face he had not seen, they both howled. The sound was primal, pained, and raw. The injured beast knelt down and gently picked up the body of the old woman. They disappeared into the Wallwood carrying a fallen friend. Wil's heart grew heavy as he began to realize who she must have been.

The fire continued to rage on the southern side of the clearing. The rain was slowing the fire down, but didn't seem like it would ever put it out completely. Wil also knew that the rain would eventually stop.

"Hey Reverend?" Wil called. Lloyd was still staring at the spot the creatures had entered the trees. He slowly turned to face Wil. "You got a car here?"

Lloyd shook his head.

"We need to get word to the fire department before this fire gets out of control.

"Oh!" Lloyd dropped down into the mud and began to rummage through the Sheriff's pockets. After a few seconds he produced a set of keys. "The Sheriff's jeep has a radio."

Wil turned to Al. "Take the keys and call for help. The Reverend and I will make sure these clowns don't go any-where."

FRIDAY
September 24th

40

Returning to Work

"After shooting Deputy Mosely, Sheriff Hawkins turned the gun on me." Wil heard Steve's voice from the little hallway that ran between the press room and advertising. 'So, we are back to this..' Wil thought as he walked toward the pressroom, and Steve's reading.

"'I thought you'd be dead by now.' The Sheriff called. And I was thinking that I soon would be. At that moment, Reverend Lloyd Todd appeared and hit the Sheriff with a log."

Wil turned the corner to the press room. They were all huddled around Steve's desk; Sherry, Shannon, Jackie from advertising, Linda, and that freelance guy, Johnny or Jeffrey. Mr. J is the one who noticed Wil first.

"Hey, there he is." The whole group began cheering and clapping.

"What's all this about?" Wil could feel his cheeks flooding with warmth.

"It's a good story man, you really got the scoop on this one." Steve said with a smile on his ruddy face.

"Scoop?" Sherry playfully smacked Steve in the back of the head. "You're a hero, Wil!"

"We are all proud of our local celebrity." Beth had opened the door to her office and was leaning against the door frame with her arms crossed. "But this publication isn't going to proof and print itself."

Wil floated over to his desk, receiving several con-
gratulatory pats on the back and "good jobs" as the crowd
dispersed. He picked up the paper and looked at the headline
print on the first page. My Night in the Wallwood by: Willard
Frye.

"I do have a question about all of this." Steve's chair
creaked as he leaned it back. "I interviewed Sheriff Hawkins
and Charles Waterfield in the jail. They seem to believe that
they were in mortal battle with the Devil himself." Steve
placed his hands behind his head, and leaned back further.
"You didn't see anything like that did you?"

Wil laughed, of course he saw. How could he miss the
seven-foot tall creatures that brutalized the Sheriff and his
deputy. "If I had seen anything like that, don't you think I
would have mentioned it in the article?"

"I do." Steve shook his head. His ruddy cheeks jostling
with the movement. He added, "They were just so damn per-
sistent about it."

"All I know is what I saw." Wil feigned looking through
the paper to avoid making eye contact and telling the lie.
"They turned on each other. I'm not sure why." He flipped to
the last page of the paper. "Did you interview Shawn Parks,
Eric Sebastian, or Albert Taulbee?" They had all agreed not to
talk about the creatures. Al had been afraid that people would
seek them out and drive them away. Or repeat the events they
had witnessed on a much larger scale. It was better that no
one knew the creatures were out there. "Or anyone else who
was there?"

Steve's chair crashed to the ground as he leaned forward. "I have interviewed all of them. Every single person
who was there. Only the Sheriff and his buddy saw anything
fishy." Steve lowered his voice. "It's a strange thing."

"What is?"

"Do you think she put a spell on them?"

"Who Cheryl?" Wil couldn't believe this was coming from Steve.

Steve's cheeks were getting darker. "I mean, no one else saw anything at all." His jowls quivered as he cleared his throat. "I've looked into Hawkins' eyes. He truly believes he has seen the Devil."

Wil laughed again. "I suppose anything is possible. Unfortunately we will never get a chance to ask her." He noticed the time on his computer, 10:48am. Wil shot out of his chair. He had a lunch date with an intelligent woman that had a lovely gap between her teeth. But there was something he had to take care of first.

He knocked on Beth's door. He was resolved but the delay between the knock and her answer was excruciating.

"Come in." She called after several seconds.

Now that he had felt the thrill of taking down some corruption, he had developed a taste for it. He pushed open the door and walked confidently inside.

"What can I do for you Willard?" Her desk was piled as high as ever with loose sheets of newsprint and intact newspaper.

"Beth," He started, "I know that you like stories about Buffalo Crossing, but how would you feel if I told you I had some evidence of some interesting activity between a big-name bank and some Frankfort city officials."

Her eyes narrowed at him for a moment, and her head rotated slightly to a quarter turn before she leaned back from her desk and motioned to the opposite chair. "Corruption in the capital city." Her lips curled slightly into a curious grin. "I would politely ask you to fill me in on what you know."

Wil took a seat and a deep breath.

41

The Ones who Regrouped

"Wait, wait, wait…" This must have been their third or fourth time through the events of the equinox, Al had lost count. Jay was making them stop and explain in further detail every single part of the story. "So, you dress this old woman's gunshot wound with duct tape, and then gave her your shirt?"

"Yup." Bash confirmed. "I got the idea from Captain Barry Allen in that movie we went to see with your dad."

"Shellflash?" Jay was incredulous. "He used a strip that was torn from his shirt in the movie."

"Well," Bash looked at Al, "We had duct tape."

Al had missed this so much. The last week was the longest they had ever gone without getting together since they met in kindergarten. Al was grounded, so the boys had gathered at his house. After riding home in the back of a police car and scaring his parents half to death in the middle of the night, Al was in trouble. It really didn't matter where he was, or what manner of heroics he had partaken, he was still grounded. He didn't really mind though. He had no plans of pursuing any more mysteries anytime soon.

Jay just shook his head in response. "So then," he held his hand up, palm out. "I want to make sure I get this right." He squinted his eyes, and his voice took on that disbelieving tone he kept reverting to for any question involving Dogman.

"A second Dogman creature strode out of the woods, tore off the tape, and slapped some mud on the wound before doing the same thing to the first Dogman?"

Al and Bash had promised that they would not tell anyone about the 'creature', as Wil had called him. Jay, however, didn't count.

"That's right." Al replied.

Jay turned to look at Al. "Then they joined hands and left whistling 'Lions and Tigers and Bears'?"

"No." Bash was laughing at the mental image. "They took away the body of the old woman with them."

Jay turned back to Bash. "The old woman who turned out to be Moonbeam, the pot smoking, Dogman seeing, hippie we interviewed a few years ago?"

"Yeah." Al hung his head forward a bit and looked at the hardwood flooring in his room. He had only talked with her one time, but he would never forget her end.

Jay looked from Al to Bash several times, exaggerating every swing of his head. Eventually he flung his arms out to the side and exclaimed, "You can't make this stuff up, folks."

A pillow slammed into Jay's chest, knocking him off the ottoman. He came up laughing, face so red his freckles had vanished. When he caught his breath, Jay took off a pair of imaginary glasses and began to clean then with his finger tips.

"You know…" Jay stopped his pantomime and grabbed the pillow. He threw it with one swift motion back at Al, who caught it easily. "Everyone in town is talking about what happened. Even my parents." He looked away. "I wish I had stopped being a wuss and been there with y'all."

Al turned to Bash. "Can you even imagine…"

Bash cut him off. "How much trouble he'd be in?"

Jay's face reddened further, it was now darker than his

hair. "I wouldn't be in that much trouble. My parents would have been wowed by my triumphant return on the back of a firetruck."

Al laughed. "You get grounded when you come home with muddy shoes."

"Yeah." Bash agreed with a hearty laugh. "You'd never be able to hang with us again."

Jay leaned over and placed his arm around an imaginary person. "At least I'd still have you, Invisa Boy. At least I'd still ha..." He was promptly hit with two more pillows. He kept his perch on the ottoman this time. "Okay, okay. But seriously, now that we know Dogman exists, shouldn't we be out there gathering evidence or something?"

Al shook his head. "I think they want to be left alone." His voice was flat.

Jay looked as if he had been stabbed. "They were hanging out with those naked hippie chicks."

Bash snorted. "So?"

"So," Jay continued, "why them and not us?"

"For starters," Bash's voice was thick with approaching laughter. "They were a bunch of naked ladies, I'd pick them over you guys every time."

A guffaw burst out of Al's mouth. Jay only scrunched his face up, as if in thought. As understanding dawned on him, he pursed his lips and raised one eyebrow and began to nod. Jay turned back to Invisa Boy. "He's got a point." He turned back to Al and Bash. "Where can we go to find some naked ladies?" Jay threw his hands up in defense against incoming pillow missiles, but none came. They were already safely at his feet.

"No ammo man." Al laughed.

Jay slowly lowered his arms, still half expecting a sneak

attack. "So you are done investigating Dogman? Like, for good?" He actually sounded sad.

Al had absolutely no intention of looking for the Dog-men, or trying to expose them to the world. After all, he had watched several masked representatives of the world try to kill one of them in the name of God. Al just didn't think man-kind could handle the knowledge of something like Dogman, something so different.

"It's not just Dogman." Al said. "I don't know if I want anything to do with the unknown anymore." He was tired, and felt lucky to be alive. He was glad for the experience but, never wanted to go through anything like that again.

Jay gasped excessively. "What? No more bike trips?"

Al shook his head. He felt a large hand come down on his shoulder.

"C'mon man. We can still check into the small stuff." Bash raised one eyebrow.

"I dunno guys."

"Well," Jay started. "I'm not convinced we have com-pletely ruled out 'high strangeness' up on ole Thorny Hill." He gave a sharp look at Bash.

After a few seconds, Bash jerked a bit and his eyes widened. "Oh! Uhh... Yeah we should go check it out again."

Al put his hands behind his head and leaned backwards to lay on his bed. "You guys can do what you want. I'm grounded."

"Oh! Oh!" Jay was getting excited again. "What about the Devil of the Wallwood?"

Bash shook his head. "That one needs snow." When Jay only looked confused, Bash added, "So you can see their hoof prints."

Jay nodded. "Right right right. We can wait until winter

and then…"

"The Wallwood Devil is Dogman." Al cut Jay off but remained staring at the ceiling.

"What!?!" Jay was incredulous.

Bash looked over at Al approvingly. "Oh yeah, they had the hooves. I hadn't put that together yet."

Jay puffed out his lower lip. "Huh." Then his face came to life again as he was struck with an idea. "We could go explore the cave at the bottom of Cry Baby Lane."

Bash shrugged. "If you go, I'll be right there beside you."

Al only rolled his eyes and kept staring at the ceiling. Deep down he knew that wherever the two of them went, he would be there too, most likely leading the way.

E

Lloyd came to the cabin with a bouquet of daisies to place in the meadow. There was no other place he could pay his respects to Cheryl. There had been no obituary, no service, and no funeral. There hadn't even been a body to lay to rest.

Approaching the house he saw the postcard sticking out of the crack between the heavy wooden doors. No one answered when he knocked but the door was unlocked. When he opened the door, Lloyd was hit with the stench of decay. He tossed the card on the long wooden table in the entryway without looking at it. Following the buzzing sound to the kitchen, he found what he assumed had been some kind of fruit on the counter. There were several different kinds but, discolored and covered in flies, they were completely unrecognizable. It took him several trips to the water pump around the back of the cabin, but he was able to clean up the kitchen.

Lloyd solemnly walked to the meadow through the shaded path. Quick flashes of fear struck him, like lightning, as he remembered that night a week earlier. He continued to see and feel these snapshots of memory stirred by his surroundings. He dared not leave before he honored this unique soul. He owed her that much.

He said his prayer and laid the daisies in the remains of the fire pit. The meadow had grown larger, with the help of the fire. However the fire left a blackened wasteland in its wake, stealing most of the meadows prior beauty.

While Lloyd was leaving he began to think about the fruit in the kitchen. No one had been here since it happened. And then his mind drifted to the post card. Who would send a postcard to a dead women? Someone who didn't know she had passed away. The card had a picture of some European Pointy Cathedral.

I'm sorry I stormed out on you like that Em. But as you can see I took your advice! This silly little card says Milan, but I'm actually in a little town called Rho.

I am staying an extra two weeks. I took my camera and have really been getting some good shots. So good that a local vendor art gallery has asked to make prints of some of my pieces to sell to tourists. Isn't that fun!

It's lovely here Em. The buildings, the food, the people, the WINE! The next time I come I am taking you with me. Which may be sooner than you think, if I get my way. And there is nothing you can do to stop it.

Addio Mia Amore

Cathy

Whether out of respect for Cheryl, or guilt about his involvement in her death, Lloyd felt compelled to be the person to inform Cathy of Cheryl's passing.

He returned to the cabin several times a week to wait for her to arrive. While he was there he swept the floors and wiped down the tables. Over the next several weeks, he expanded his chores to the grounds around the cabin. He kept the shaded path and the meadow clear of growth and fallen branches. He even planted a few trees where the forrest had burned.

Lloyd still maintained his church and his small apartment. But his congregation started to shrink as his sermons lost their passion. More and more of his belongings kept making their way out to the cabin. He loved being out in nature, Cheryl was right about that. Something about the fresh air and the bird song was soothing.

He often found himself contemplating his faith while sitting on the porch, breathing the fresh air, seeing the green, and listing to the birds. He was still a Christian, oh yes. But maybe, he had been too judgmental of those who did not share his own specific beliefs. He knew he would find his passion again, he just needed to find his footing first.

He ran into Shawn regularly while he was there. The young woman had moved into an apartment in Woodford County soon after Cheryl's murder. She claimed that she kept seeing it replay over and over again inside her head while she was at the cabin. Despite that, she returned quite often. She even brought Donna by on a pair of crutches a couple of times.

Cathy never showed though. Had she found out about her friend's death in town? Perhaps she had found out while still in Italy. Were her memories of this place too painful for her to visit? Lloyd knew that she may have come by while he was not there.

Lloyd would occasionally find bundles of herbs or flowers on the porch when he arrived. He caught the owner of the green grocer burning what he called 'sage' around the porch of the cabin. Lloyd didn't mind, he knew everyone had their own way to cope with loss.

The afternoon of the winter solstice, a large group of people showed up to the Cabin unexpectedly. At first it was just a few people filing past the house and into the meadow. Lloyd joined them after he saw the third small group of people pass into the shaded trail while he was sitting at the big wooden table. He found about 10 people in the meadow viewing the damage from the fire and sharing memories of Cheryl. Soon ten people became fifteen, and fifteen became thirty.

Lloyd enlisted the help of several young people to gather firewood. A large man with a long scraggly beard and a flannel hat lit the small fire that Lloyd built. As soon as it was lit, Lloyd was transported back to that night. Even though he was wounded and threatened, the beast only attacked after Cheryl was murdered. It also stopped fighting when the threat was gone. It could have ripped everyone there limb from limb, but he did not. Mostly, Lloyd remembered the sadness in its howl as he bent down to take Cheryl's body. It sounded so human in its anguish.

The soft voice of a woman pulled Lloyd's eyes away from the growing flames. "I got a dog when I moved out of my parents house." She was wearing a red parka and her voice was cracking. She cleared her throat before continuing a bit louder. "That dog followed me everywhere, I never even had to buy a leash." She laughed and a few puffs of white were visible for a second before blowing away. "I used to tell my husband that he better be nice to Bruno, because I will choose him over you in a heartbeat." Her teeth retreated back behind her lips as her happy demeanor changed. "Then when we brought my newborn son home from the hospital, he got sick. And he stayed sick." She took a deep breath and laughed out loud, this time there was no humor, only nerves. "I remember walking out of the Dr's office and sitting on a bench, and sobbing. At some point, someone sat down on the bench beside me and began to rub my back but I was crying so hard that I could barely breath, let alone care who it was. I just sat on that bench cradling my son, and continued to let the waterworks fly."

She reached inside her pocket and pulled a white cloth out to wipe her eyes as the smile returned to her face. "I don't know how long that hand rubbed my back before I heard a soft voice asking me what was wrong. I just kept repeating 'He's allergic, he's allergic' in between my sobs.

"Eventually I calmed down enough to see Moonbeam through the tears. She had no idea who I was, just some crazy woman crying in public. But of course I knew her. The Devil Woman." She emphasized the last two words with sarcasm. A small laugh rippled through the crowd. "Anyway, she took Bruno and gave him a wonderful life out here. She even allowed me to come over to see him anytime I wanted."

A young man in a thick grey sweater and blue scarf spoke up. "Was Bruno a black lab?"

"Yes, he was."

He put his arm around a suddenly smiling older woman with short blond hair and tears in her eyes. She looked vaguely familiar to Lloyd. "I loved that dog!" The young man nearly shouted.

He went on to explain that he had lived out here with Moonbeam and his mother for almost an entire year after a domestic dispute. During that time, Bruno and he became inseparable and his mother saved enough money to make a down payment on a small house with a big back yard for Bruno.

The day progressed with more stories about Moonbeam; some were funny, a few were inspirational, most of them were mundane. They painted a picture of a woman Lloyd had never met. He knew of her intelligence and wit. He knew of her strength and bravery. He had not even considered that she harbored any compassion.

Lloyd announced that he would be planting the gardens the weekend after Derby, while there were about fifteen people still in the meadow. He encouraged everyone to bring some kind of seeds and some kind of garden tool.

When spring rolled around, Lloyd was surprised at how many people actually showed up to help. It was slow at first, but around 10 am people started trickling in to help till the plots and plant the crop. Few stayed longer than a couple of hours, but for everyone that left, three came to replace them. By nightfall, eight of the garden plots were seeded. It was much more than Lloyd had expected.

Lloyd did his best to take care of the garden, but found that eight full plots is a bit much with only a hand pump for well water. With the help of some late spring rains, he was able to produce a nice first crop. He took out an ad in the BCJ for the Community Garden out on Rutledge Road. The garden was picked clean and regrown a few times during the next couple of months. The garden was a hit with the town, so Lloyd went ahead and planted some fall crops. He only used two of the garden plots to make it more manageable.

In early September he took out another ad in the paper for the Equinox celebration on Rutledge Road. At least a hundred people showed up, completely filling the now larger meadow. He saw people he knew, and people he didn't, members of his own congregation, current and former. Strangers with curiosity or fear in their eyes. He saw love and pain in the crowd as well. The young man and his mother who kept Bruno were there. They were standing next to the woman who had worn the red parka, but was now in a black t-shirt and jeans. He saw Shawn and Donna standing near the owner of the Green Grocer. He found himself wondering if Cathy was one of the strangers in the crowd.

Though it was the Equinox that brought them to the meadow, these people were here to celebrate the life of one woman. A woman intelligent enough to beat him at his own game. A woman kind enough to open her home to complete strangers in need. A woman strong enough to stand up to a man with a gun while naked. She was safety to those who needed it and a pariah for everyone else. She was truly a good woman.

The crowd had left a circle of space around the fire pit anticipating the heat. Lloyd stepped into the open space, his show smile returned to his lips. It came unbidden, which was not something Lloyd was used to happening. His blood felt hot. He felt like he used to feel right before a big sermon; excited, elated, electric.

"Welcome to Moonbeam Ranch!" Lloyd's eyes flashed in the fading light of day, a storm on the verge of breaking. The crowd erupted in a cheer. Lloyd's passion was back.

www.ingramcontent.com/pod-product-compliance
Lightning Source LLC
Chambersburg PA
CBHW070742180626
46818CB00007B/2956